MIRROR BALL MAN

JOEL BROWN

MARY —
HOPE YOU LIKE IT!
SEE YOU AT THE
BLACK DUCK!
JOEL BROWN
11/11/10

For Rosemary

www.mirrorballman.com

First edition 2010
Printed in the United States of America

ISBN 9781453693919

MIRROR BALL MAN

IF YOU WANT TO TELL PEOPLE THE TRUTH, MAKE
THEM LAUGH, OTHERWISE THEY'LL KILL YOU.
-OSCAR WILDE

ONE

I carried my guitar across the park at dusk and stopped in the shadows under a tree to watch the crowd entering City Hall. Once upon a time, I played for thousands of cheering, lighter-waving fans, but these days I was relieved when anyone showed up to hear me at all. A turnout this big should have been cause for celebration.

This wasn't a concert, though, it was a showdown. I had butterflies for the first time in years, and I was playing this gig for free. What the hell was I thinking?

A statue of a local hero loomed in the center of the park, looking as if he wanted to answer me. Balding and stern-faced, abolitionist William Egremont Otis risked his life speaking out against slavery. A quote was carved on the side of the polished stone pedestal: "I will not retract a single word; and I will be heard!" A nearby streetlight gave him an orange halo as he stood with one arm outstretched, offering me a hand up onto the path of righteousness.

Or maybe he was telling me, *Hey, suck it up.* I had it easy. I wasn't going to be attacked by an angry mob, tarred and feathered and chased through the streets. The way my career was going, I would have been grateful for the attention. No such thing as bad publicity, right?

The sidewalks emptied. The tall windows on the second floor of the old brick building glowed, and I thought I could hear the murmur of the crowd inside. Time to go.

A couple of smokers stood at the top of the granite steps, wizened townies getting a last fix before the meeting. One of them held the door for me and my guitar. "Go get 'em!" he rasped around his cigarette, then started coughing up a lung. I was tempted to bum one any-way, to put off my entrance for a few more minutes.

The buzz of the crowd got louder as I climbed the stairs to the auditorium. Years ago, when my last album came out on an obscure indie label, I played a concert here and sold every seat. Well, almost. Tonight standees packed the back and sides of the bright room and the narrow balcony. Blood sport always draws better than the arts. When the crowd saw me, half of them broke into applause. The other half mostly folded their arms across their chests and stared straight ahead. Oh yeah, *this* was going to be fun.

As I made my way to the stage, a big, angry-looking guy in red suspenders and rockabilly sideburns jumped to his feet in front of me. "Give 'em hell, Baxter!" Wonders never cease: The preeminent bully of my high-school era had joined my cheering section. Red Suspenders and his sidekicks chased me down High Street every afternoon when I was a freshman, howling lurid threats involving fireworks and tender bodily orifices. He looked crestfallen now when I ignored his high-five attempt.

Developer Jules Titward, the mayor and my friend Davey Gil-lis were seated on metal folding chairs lined up in front of the red vel-vet curtain. The empty chair on the end was for me. Davey winked as I climbed the stairs to the stage. He knew I would rather have been doing something fun, like getting waterboarded by the CIA.

The mayor, bald and slight, bounced up to shake my hand. "Thanks for coming!" His blue eyes were soft, moist and eager to please.

"Glad to be here," I lied.

"Me, too! It's going to be exciting!" Behind his back, people called him Echo, because of the amazing coincidence that whatever you said was always exactly what he thought, too.

Jules studied his nails, ignoring us. He had fine blond hair and smooth, arrogant features. Normally a clothes horse, he wore a wrin-kled peach polo shirt under a blue blazer, khaki slacks, and deck shoes with no socks. There was something contemptuous about the outfit, especially the bare ankles. Looked like he'd skipped a shave, too. Let-ting us all know that we weren't worth the effort.

An easel at the side of the stage held an artist's rendering of the hundred-room hotel Jules wanted to build. The City of Libertyport owned the site, a gravel parking lot on the waterfront, and everyone expected the city council to sell him the land. Supposedly it was a done deal. Davey and I were here to change that.

The councilors sat down front, along with Tom Dorsey, the musically bylined reporter from the Daily Town Crier, a clean-cut, earnest kid who chewed on his pen and blinked rapidly. Abigail Marks, editor and sole proprietor of LibertyportGossip.com, sat next to him, glowing with anticipation. Her long, wattled neck, beaky nose and bug eyes gave her a vulturish appearance. The kid avoided looking at her directly, as if eye contact might start her pecking at him.

Abigail's lavender suede blazer and matching newsboy cap were awfully sporty for a retired teacher. When I sat down, she smiled at me and batted her lashes. I hoped she couldn't see me shiver.

The mayor stepped to the microphone. "Thank you all for being here tonight for this public forum on the proposed Harbor Hotel. We hope that what you hear will help you make up your minds on a very important issue for the future of Libertyport."

In the background of the sketch, the Queen Elizabeth II approached the hotel dock, railings lined with passengers, a Chamber of Commerce wet dream. In real life, of course, the cruise ship would have run aground before it got into the river. On shore, faceless tourists trudged toward the hotel entrance from all directions, like zombies. That part was scarily realistic.

"First we'll hear from Jules Titward," the Mayor said, "who'll explain why this project will be good for our city."

One or two boos mixed in with the applause. Jules frowned as he walked to the microphone and unhooked it. Abigail came halfway out of her seat to see who was booing, then smiled to herself and made a note on her little pad. Tom Dorsey didn't dare move.

"Thank you all so much for coming," Jules said, sounding anything but grateful. His voice was a nasal Yankee bray. "I think you can see from the sketch that my partners and I want to build a quality structure that will reflect the historic architecture of our great downtown while providing a top-shelf lodging experience for travelers who come here to work or play."

His wife, Elaine, smiled up at him dutifully from the front row. She was a beautiful woman, with sculpted cheekbones and straight, shoulder-length blond hair. We were briefly an item, a long time ago. When she caught me watching her, her smile widened and her baby blues sparkled. Whose side was she on?

Jules turned to the easel. "Note the classic brick facade and decorative cornices designed to blend with the downtown. This project will be the crown jewel of three decades of revitalization."

It must have been the fiftieth time he'd made this pitch, and his boredom showed. He ran through the features of the building's design – the atrium lobby, the water view for every room – then moved back to center stage.

"I know many of you share our vision of what the Harbor Hotel will mean to our community." He turned to frown at Davey and me, his voice rising. "There are also those who understand the merits of this project but continue to oppose it for their own narrow interests, or simply because opposing things is what they do. I believe they cannot be allowed to stop a project that will benefit every member of this community. Thank you all for your time."

He stabbed the mike back into its stand as if sticking a fork in us, then returned to his seat amid applause and more boos from the back.

The mayor cleared his throat and waited for the noise to subside. "Thank you, Jules, for your heartfelt and, I must say, quite convincing presentation. And now, representing the other side, it's local restaurateur Davey Gillis."

Davey stood up slowly. A former lobsterman, he was powerfully built, with a pot belly and an unruly Santa Claus beard. His old brown suit ran tight across the midsection and short at the wrists and ankles. His eyes were fixed in a permanent squint from sailing into too many gales as a young man, and it made him appear cranky even on those rare occasions when he was in a good mood. He wasn't now.

Davey owned a waterfront restaurant and bar called the Rum House, which sat right next to the parking lot in question. Very convenient for his customers. At the microphone, he settled his dime-store reading glasses on the tip of his nose, then pulled a crumpled piece of yellow lined paper from his pants pocket.

"This thing is a monstrosity," he began. "It's going to block the river view for everybody downtown."

Including a big chunk of the scenic panorama from my bedroom, but I wasn't about to bring that up. I'd bought my house with rock-star money, and there were people in town who still resented me for it, even though the house was all I had left.

"Right now you can walk along the boardwalk and see all our beautiful old brick buildings that Jules was talking about and the steeples and everything," Davey said. "I think that's how a lot of tourists fall in love with this place. Build the hotel, and all that's over."

He usually didn't talk so much. People paid attention. Tom and Abigail both took copious notes.

"Another thing is, unlike what Jules said, this isn't going to be good for local business. Anyone who eats or drinks or stays in the hotel won't be supporting the restaurants and bars and inns we have now. I gotta admit I'm a little biased about that one."

He looked up over his glasses. A few people laughed, and there was scattered applause. Red Suspenders shouted, "Tell it like it is!"

"Then there's parking. I know Jules is going to have a garage, but you're going to have to pay to use it, and that's if it's not full of out-of-towners. And we're losing a hundred and fifty free spaces. I bet half of you people got your cars on the gravel lot right now, and you didn't pay a dime. You really want to lose that?"

Cries of "No! No!" from the back. Jules shook his head, reddening. Davey talked about the tax breaks Jules wanted and how the hotel jobs would go to people from out of town, since nobody could afford to live in Libertyport on a chambermaid's salary, not anymore. Finally he folded up his notes and stuffed them back in his pocket.

"Maybe this would be the perfect project for Portsmouth or Portland or someplace like that, but it just ain't right for us. Thank you." He sat down to cheers and applause.

"Before the question and answer period," the mayor said without enthusiasm, "we'll hear from local protest singer Baxter McLean."

Because I opposed the hotel, suddenly I was a "protest singer." People usually called me a folksinger, but I wasn't the kind of guy who held hands and sang "Kumbaya." I considered myself a singer-songwriter. The press called me a one-hit wonder on the rare occasions when they mentioned me at all.

No one seemed surprised that tonight's agenda included music. Libertyport had been an arty little burg ever since a few painters and sculptors moved downtown in search of cheap rent back in the rough-and-tumble '70s. Even Jules came from a family of artists, but that gene hadn't been passed along to him, and he channeled his energies into business instead. He'd told the mayor he couldn't care less whether I sang or not. Now he picked at a nail as I hung my guitar around my neck. I tuned briefly and stepped to the mike, feeling a tremor in my gut. Small town politics were the worst.

"You all know I don't like to talk much."

"Yeah, right," Davey said, getting a few chuckles.

"So I thought I'd make our case this way."

I fiddled with the guitar mike, and the audience made root-canal faces until it stopped squealing. The powers-that-be didn't mind if I sang, because this whole meeting was arranged to humor us, political cover for a decision they'd already made. But they weren't going to bend over backwards to set up the equipment correctly. I doodled on a couple of chords in lieu of a sound check, then began to strum a simple waltz.

And then I opened my big mouth.

I sang against losing the water view. I sang against selling public land for private profit. And, OK, I sang to save free parking for Davey's customers.

We find his plans are lacking
So let's send the innkeeper packing!

Not exactly "Blowin' in the Wind," but it would have to do. Jules made a great show of not paying attention, crossing his legs, folding his hands around his knee and studying a water stain on the ceiling. His arrogance made me determined to get a reaction out of him. My nerves evaporated, and I found myself drawing out vowels and snapping off consonants, turning the song into a rollicking, sarcastic broadside. The hotel opponents quickly picked up the refrain.

> *He needs the council's backing*
> *So let's send the innkeeper packing!*

By the last verse, the laughter and singing were louder. Jules scowled like a Mississippi sheriff in a civil rights documentary, as if he knew history was turning against him.

> *It would be wrong to give him a whacking*
> *Sooooo let's send the innkeeper packing!*

I strummed a final flourish as the place went wild. It had been a long time since I'd received an ovation like that. Caught up in the moment, even Mayor Echo applauded vigorously.

Jules met my eye and mouthed *Fuck you*. We weren't best buddies before, and we never would be now. I could live with that, but there was something desperate in his eyes, beyond the anger I expected. Before I could react, or even figure out what I was seeing, he turned away. He looked to his wife for support and didn't get it. Instead she made a sad-clown face, her lower lip pushed out in a stage frown. *Poor you*, her face said. She did everything but play the world's tiniest violin. He didn't know where to look then.

Hotel opponents crowded into the Rum House after the meeting to celebrate. A doryman's young widow opened the bar in a fetid wharf shack when the British still ruled the Colonies. I liked to think of her as a sad, romantic figure *a la* "Brandy (You're A Fine Girl)," but newspapers of the day hinted that the widow was peddling more than booze.

The building had been expanded repeatedly in the last two and a half centuries, and the fish stink was mostly gone now, but the Tavern

Room retained the original low, beamed ceiling and creaky, wide-board pine floors. A plaque by the bar claimed Paul Revere had stopped in for a few ales when delivering a bell to a local church, cover for a clandestine rendezvous with his Revolutionary compatriots. Davey was always vague about the source of that information, but with the lantern-shaped lights turned low, it was easy to believe we weren't the first rebels to sink a few pints here. Everyone insisted I had turned the tide against the hotel. I hoped they were right, although I'd begun to feel a little guilty about the song.

I sat at the bar, tracking the baseball game on the flat-screen TV and watching townies mingle with artists and other aging counterculture types. Usually the two groups kept their distance, but Jules had given them a common enemy. Everybody wore jeans, and it was hard to tell them apart without knowing the players. In Libertyport, if you saw a guy in a faded Red Sox cap driving an old pickup with a tangle of driftwood and fishing net in the back, you couldn't be sure if it was a dump run in progress or the beginnings of a gallery installation. Of course, there were clues: A townie guy wouldn't be caught dead wearing Birkenstocks.

Before I'd finished my first beer, two of the swing votes on the city council came in, still in suits and ties, having sensed the shift in momentum to our side. Davey greeted them like long-lost buddies and got them drinks but "forgot" to charge them. Abigail Marks swooped down seeking quotes for her blog, but Tom Dorsey had gone back to the newspaper to make deadline.

When Davey brought me a refill, he was almost smiling. "Your song was the ballgame, amigo."

"Thanks for making me write it."

"You're welcome. What did you think of my speech?"

"You were a regular William Egremont Otis."

"A who?"

"Never mind. You did good." I nodded toward the councilors, who were smiling uncomfortably under Abigail's interrogation. "We might have enough votes now."

"We better."

A gaggle of yuppies in springy pastel sweaters huddled together at a table near the door, tapping on their BlackBerries and looking around warily. They'd moved here in droves lately, driving up real estate prices, demanding better schools and services, pushing property taxes skyward. The last of the old-time corner bars and doughnut shops had been replaced by organic day spas and "polarity therapy" centers designed to alleviate their stress while relieving them of their cash. The townies and the artists both hated them, and the yuppies knew it, so they usually avoided the type of watering holes where alcohol might bring that hostility into the open. They were charged up after the meeting like everyone else, though, and not ready to call it a night. Bending elbows with the locals would provide them with colorful anecdotes for the office tomorrow, if they managed to escape with their lives. The sweaters didn't help their chances.

One of them bellied up to the bar and deposited an armload of empty wineglasses. "No one's bothered to bus our table," he complained to Davey. "Can you at least bring us another round?"

"I'll get right on it."

"Good thing," the yuppie said, walking away.

"Asshole," Davey muttered, not loud enough to be heard over U2 on the jukebox.

"Are you feeling OK?" I asked.

"Why?"

"Normally you would have thrown his ass out of here."

"Ahhh, we need all the help we can get to stop this hotel thing."

"I'm surprised they're not siding with Jules," I said.

"Speak of the devil."

I turned to see the developer marching straight for us, eyes blazing. I put my beer down as the din of conversation died. The councilors slouched and turned their backs, trying to hide. Abigail Marks bared her teeth in a predatory grin. Here was a juicy part of the story that the newspaper wasn't going to have. She didn't take out her pen or notebook, though. She could render a more vivid scene if she didn't get tangled up in the facts.

Bono, unaware of the impending confrontation, kept singing about the power of love. Jules looked possessed by the kind of rage that makes any man dangerous. I slid my guitar behind me, in case he was tempted to put one of his boat shoes through it. But he locked eyes with Davey.

"You are not going to fuck this up for me," he said.

Davey stood feet apart, hands on hips, and regarded him coldly. "Get out."

"I don't care how many stupid songs your buddy here sings." That desperate look flared in Jules' eyes, and he slammed his hand on the bar, hard enough that my beer jumped. "You don't know who you're dealing with."

"I don't care, either." Davey was older by a decade, but he was also six inches taller than Jules and fifty pounds heavier. Despite the belly, he had never lost the muscles gained hauling lobster traps as a young man. "Get out of my bar."

"A lot of people are going to get hurt if this doesn't go through. I'm going to make sure it does."

"I'm telling you one last time."

Davey kept a baseball bat under the sink. I'd last seen him brandish it at three Diablos from Lynn who stopped by on their way home from Bike Week in Laconia and expressed their disappointment that the Rum House was not as they remembered it. They left in a hurry. Waving a Louisville Slugger at Jules in front of half the town wasn't going to help our cause, though. I slid off my stool, ready to stop this before it got out of hand, but after Davey stared him down for a moment, Jules took a step backward, and the strange expression on his face faded.

"Fine, I'm going. But this isn't over. You can't stop me."

He wouldn't have been so mad if we weren't on the verge of doing just that, but this wasn't the moment to point that out. He turned and stalked out. The quiet held until the door slammed shut behind him, then the voices resumed, louder than before.

I took a long drink of my beer. Davey shook his head and moved off to man the taps. The excitement had quickened everyone's thirst.

Abigail appeared at my side.

"That was quite the showdown," she said.

"Just a friendly conversation."

"It didn't look so friendly to me. Care to comment for my blog?"

"I don't see how that would help anything."

"Oh well then. Ta-ta, and thanks for a fantastic evening!" She wiggled her eyebrows as if we'd been naughty together, then bustled off.

When Davey came back, he looked almost calm.

"Don't worry about Jules," he said. "That prick is doomed."

Unfortunately, he was right.

TWO

My morning walk took me through Hewett's Boatyard. A few puffy white clouds scudded eastward across the blue sky. Gulls wheeled and cawed above the docks, and a clean, briny scent like Wellfleets on the half shell filled the air. The sailboats moored in the middle of the river swung their sterns downstream as the tide turned out to sea.

Still recovering from last night's festivities, I wasn't fast enough to jump out of the way when Shimmy Jimmy came flying around the corner of the Rum House on his bicycle, eyes wild with panic.

There are guys like Jimmy Wilmot in every small town, guys who were born "not quite right" or hit their heads diving at the quarry or drank and drugged themselves into a permanent fog. They roamed the streets on bike or on foot, left to their own devices, a part of the scenery that was easy to overlook until they ran you over. The ancient Huffy had been built before space-age technology and weighed a ton. Jimmy, forty-odd years old and fond of pastry, wasn't exactly light either. Since he had no short-term memory, he visited Dunkin' Donuts several times a day, rotating among the three local franchises. For most people it would have been a recipe for morbid obesity, but Jimmy rode that bike hour after hour, day after day, year after year, until all that grease was converted to solid muscle. I swore once before the collision, railing against my doom. Then the handlebars caught me in the gut, Jimmy's helmet struck me on the chin, and I went down hard.

When I came to, I wasn't sure of the time of day or where I was. I tasted blood. Jimmy stood over me, an anguished grimace on his handsome, oddly youthful face. He was about to burst into tears. His

Prince Valiant haircut made him look even more boyish, but his hair was steely grey. He was actually a few years older than me.

"Shimmy Jimmy killed the shimmy man," he moaned, even though my eyes were open. "Jimmy's in trouble."

My vision seemed oddly acute. I could see every pebble molded into the blacktop in front of my face. I heard the mellow buzz of a light plane, or maybe it was just my ears. A car crossed the Route 1 drawbridge, and the sea-monster moan of its tires rolling over the steel grate brought me back to the present. I got to my feet slowly, memory trickling back.

"No, Jimmy, you're not in any trouble. It was an accident. I'm fine." Actually I was pretty dizzy. I must have hit my head on the pavement. A concussion seemed likely, but he didn't need to know that. "How about you? Are you all right?"

"Jimmy's fine and dandy." He didn't look so sure.

"That's good, Jimmy. Looks like your bike is OK, too." My skull wasn't going to do much damage to that frame. I picked it up and handed it to him. He jumped on eagerly, but his forehead was still creased with worry.

"Jimmy gotta shimmy go!" He pedaled off, disappearing quickly among the looming, shrink-wrapped hulls of the boatyard. By the time he reached River Street, he would have forgotten what happened. It was hard to get mad at him. Skinned knees and a bump on the head were trivial compared to what he'd lost.

Nerves still jangling, I brushed myself off and limped onward, glad there were no witnesses. The windows of the Rum House were dark, the only customer a produce delivery truck at the back door. The party-fishing tubs that docked out back had already headed downriver to the Atlantic. Anglers' cars and pickup trucks were lined up on the near side of the parking lot, along with several empty Bud Lite suitcases and a scattering of ice cubes. How could Jules want to take all that away from us?

I crossed through the sculpture park, past the elk made out of rusting rebar and the giant brushed-aluminum tea set. Like I said, we are an arty little burg.

A busload of tourists blocked the boardwalk ahead, decked out in sunhats and fanny packs and Freedom Trail souvenir hoodies, waiting for a whale-watching trip. The Miss Libertyport was shorter than the other tour boats, top-heavy and ungainly looking, and they eyed her dubiously as they listened to the pre-boarding lecture from Captain Bob. Wielding a megaphone at the top of the gangway, he informed them of the function of baleen, the nutritional value of krill and the location of the life rafts.

Bob Norment desperately wanted to appear an old salt. He wore a Greek fisherman's hat tilted just so and gnawed a pipe that he never lit. The only seamen I knew who wore those hats were in Old Spice commercials, though. Bob's little round glasses and neatly trimmed moustache gave him away: Until a year ago, he'd taught Earth Sciences at the high school, his class renowned among students as an easy A. Finally he saved enough money to quit teaching and buy the boat, a move he'd planned for years. His wife never believed he'd actually do it, and when he did, it broke up their marriage.

One night in the Rum House, he had confided to me that his dream was to host a show about marine life on Animal Planet. He thought he was "a good communicator" with "a lot of knowledge to share." TV gave him a new dream to cling to. I could have told him that fame, once you got it, was out of your control. It could love you and leave you and still never quite let you go. But he didn't ask.

I didn't want him to spot me now and point me out to the crowd. I didn't want to have to smile and wave, or worse yet, "sing a few bars for these fine people," like last week. Getting talked into another *a cappella* dockside serenade would ruin my morning in a way that getting run over had not. The tourists would see my scraped knees and dazed expression and think that I was a burnout, the Shimmy Jimmy of one-hit wonders. It wasn't far from the truth, which gave me all the more reason to avoid them.

I slipped between two planters and cut across the parking lot. I could pick up the boardwalk by the embayment. Commercial fishing captains tied up in the man-made inlet all winter, then relocated to channel moorings ahead of the summer influx of beer-emboldened amateur skippers and cigarette-boat showoffs. Now, at the turn of the season, it was empty except for feuding gulls.

I was almost all the way across the parking lot before I saw Jules, lying face down on the gravel next to his BMW in a small pool of his own dried blood.

The Beemer was an expensive new seven-series sports sedan, dark blue. Jules had the annoying habit of parking it at an angle across three spaces so it wouldn't get scratched. Now his body was hidden between the car and a clump of beach roses. You had to walk in just the right spot to see him. My good luck. Already queasy from the collision with Shimmy Jimmy, I fought off a wave of nausea.

Jules still wore last night's clothes: deck shoes with no socks, the peach polo. A reddish-brown stain surrounded what looked like a bullet hole in his back. No need to check for a pulse. His head was turned to one side, his eyes open and still and lifeless. Even in death, he had an arrogant expression, as if he still didn't think his killer was quite up to the job.

The police station was just up the hill, next to City Hall. I could have run there in seconds, but I spent a lot of lonely nights watching "Law & Order" reruns in motel rooms, and I knew you weren't supposed to leave a crime scene unattended. The thing to do was call it in. I had a cell phone for the road but never carried it at home. I hated them. There was one guy in every audience who forgot to turn his phone off, and if I only played one ballad the whole night, that's when it would ring. If I was ever going to kill someone…

I could have borrowed a phone from one of the whale watchers, but they would have trampled the crime scene, swarming with their video cameras. *Honey, get "Hard Copy" on the line!* Their kids didn't need to see this. Capt. Bob had started taking tickets and sending them up the gangplank, and I decided to let them get safely aboard ship.

Pay phones were a dying breed, but Davey kept one outside the front door of the Rum House so last-call drunks could ring Port Taxi. I trotted back to it and dialed 911, keeping one eye on Jules' car.

"Libertyport Police, this call is being recorded. This is Officer Karpinski, what's your emergency?"

"There's been a murder."

"You're kidding!"

His reaction deftly illustrated the town's low crime rate. I told him what I'd found. He must have known he'd squeaked, because when he spoke again, his voice had dropped an octave. "Don't touch anything. We'll be there in thirty seconds," he said and hung up.

I jogged back to the BMW. What would people think? Me and Jules, together again. He lay where the hotel bar was supposed to go, to take advantage of the fishing boats and other local color outside the windows. A creepy coincidence. I hoped no one suspected it was anything more.

Sure.

Sirens approached. I found myself staring at Jules' body, which was just wrong, so I looked for clues instead. The car doors were closed, but drops of blood had sprayed the inside of the driver's window. Weird. His keys were on the front seat and the motor was off. The glove compartment hung open, papers spilling out onto the floor. Jules' blazer lay across the back seat, as if he'd tossed it there.

The first cruiser skidded to a stop, spraying gravel as its siren died. A paunchy older patrolman struggled out of the driver's seat, one hand on his holster. He pointed at me with the other and yelled, "Step away from the body, *now!*"

I could hear the whale-watchers calling to each other to come see. As I backed away from Jules, I instinctively put my hands up, but that made me look guilty, so I put them down again. The cop approached the body, already winded, hand still near his gun.

"Who did this?"

"No idea."

"Right." He scowled at me for a long moment, feigning suspicion while he caught his breath, then grabbed his radio.

In less than five minutes, every cop on the job was there, from the chief on down, plus an ambulance and a fire truck. They all tried to look busy, and the ones who didn't have any reason to be there tried the hardest.

Wide-eyed Tom Dorsey came running from the Town Crier office with an expressionless, seen-it-all photographer in tow. Abigail Marks showed up a few minutes later, resplendent in a robin's egg blue suede bomber jacket and a matching fez topped with an ostrich feather. I wondered if she'd gone home to change for the occasion. For once, though, she looked as shocked as Tom.

I repeated my story a half-dozen times for various combinations of cops: I was out for a walk, enjoying our beautiful waterfront as I did every morning, and cut through the parking lot to avoid the whale watchers. When I found Jules, I called 911 immediately.

All true, except I left out Shimmy Jimmy.

No doubt he had seen the body – it explained the terrified look on his face – but he would have forgotten about it already. There was no reason to drag him into this.

I caught a lot of suspicious looks from the cops. I couldn't blame them. Twelve hours ago, I'd been onstage singing about giving Jules a whacking.

A detective took me into the back of the town's mobile disaster command center, a repurposed short bus obtained with federal funds after the Sept. 11 attacks. He gloved up and swabbed my hands with tiny sponges, which he dropped into a ziplock bag. He sealed the bag with tape, then dated and initialed the tape. "Gunshot residue test," he said and winked. He fingerprinted me and gave me a baby wipe for the ink, then pointed to the door. "Take off."

By the time the Miss Libertyport eased away from the dock, the whale watchers had broken out their video cameras and gathered along the railing on the upper deck for a clear view of the crime scene. Nature in the raw, just in a different form than they'd expected.

"See the man in shorts?" Capt. Bob said over the public address system, his excited voice clear above the plangent throb of the boat's big diesels. "That's folksinger Baxter McLean, the most famous living resident of Libertyport. His song 'Mirror Ball Man' went to Number Two back in the '80s. Let's give him a wave!"

I, of course, waved back.

THREE

I wanted a drink, but the Rum House wasn't open yet. Besides, it would look like I was drowning a guilty conscience. I slipped away before Tom or Abigail could ask me any questions and headed for coffee instead.

Under the circumstances, it seemed strange that Dock Square looked as pretty as ever. The curving rows of brick buildings had all been built at the same time, after a disastrous fire in 1811, and they had a pleasing, vaguely British uniformity, broken only by the colorful signs and awnings over the storefronts. Cascades of spring flowers overflowed window boxes and the baskets that hung from the faux-antique streetlamps. The only ugly note was the piercing whine of the leaf blower used by a city crew clearing trash off the plaza.

The Chamber of Commerce brochure extolled our lifestyle: "Libertyport commands the south bank of the mighty Merrimack River near its confluence with the vast Atlantic. The great mansions of the sea captains and shipping barons who built the city can still be seen along historic High Street. Dock Square offers a lively mix of antiques stores and upscale shops, exciting art galleries and gourmet restaurants. Nearby Plover Island features miles of scenic beaches and the tranquility of a large nature preserve. All this within an hour's drive of downtown Boston!"

True enough, but the brochure omitted the decades after World War II, when the factories moved south and people finally noticed that the river was a toxic sump. By the 1960s, the downtown businesses that survived were mostly notorious bars, and weeds grew waist high in the square. Civic leaders realized they had to do something before the spreading blight infected the whole town. Urban renewal grants were sought and won. Forward-thinking local businessmen bought up vacant buildings for pennies on the dollar and began renovating. They chased out the bikers and the vagrants, and their wives opened relentlessly charming little shops and restaurants. Starving artists moved into the apartments and condos upstairs. After a few years Boston commuters began to arrive, driving up prices and pushing out the artists. Now the downtown rivaled Rockport as a tourist Mecca, and the stench of scented candles hung over Dock Square like a toxic fog.

Still, it was a pretty nice place to live, and hardly anyone ever got murdered.

Caffeine junkies were double-parked in front of Starbucks as usual. I walked on to Foley's, a Civil War-era drugstore that sold newspapers, magazines, tobacco and lottery tickets under a red and green neon sign. The soda fountain had been turned into a coffee bar. The marble counter dated to the turn of the last century, the chrome stools to the Eisenhower administration. The second-hand espresso machine huffed and puffed like a steam engine, the CD player skipped and the old toaster occasionally flipped a bagel to the floor. In short, the place had a charm that the ex-KGB brainwashing experts who ran the Starbucks marketing department would never understand. The coffee was good, too.

"Mr. McLean, you're late," Dreadlocks said in mock alarm when I stepped to the register. "You want your usual?"

The staff was part of Foley's charm, although I hated it when they called me Mister. It made me feel old. My predictability amused them, for they were young, eighteen or twenty, and their lives were changing fast. Most of them didn't stay long enough for me to learn their names, so I secretly assigned nicknames. Dreadlocks had delicate features, a carefree smile and the world's gnarliest wad of tangled brown hair. The Beatnik, who poured my coffee, accentuated her dark, dramatic looks with silver studs through her ears, nose and oddly sexy unibrow. Blondie, tall and pretty and fresh from the Abercrombie & Fitch gene pool, washed dishes in sullen silence. She was new, on the bottom of the totem pole.

"We heard all the sirens," the Beatnik said. "What's happening down by the water?"

"Jules Titward was murdered."

I wasn't so predictable this morning. Blondie dropped a juice glass, and it shattered at her feet.

"No way!" Dreadlocks and the Beatnik gasped in unison.

"I found him."

"What happened?"

"Somebody shot him."

Blondie shrieked, "Oh my god!" and burst into tears. She stood waving her arms for a moment, as if treading water, then ran for the bathroom.

"I think Ashley knew him," Dreadlocks said.

The Beatnik rolled her eyes. "Not necessarily. Everything is, like, a crisis with her."

Their shock quickly turned to curiosity, and I told them a short version of the story I told the police, once again leaving out Shimmy Jimmy. My bagel began to smoke like a burning oil tanker before I finished. The Beatnik yanked it out of the toaster with wooden tongs, dropped it in the sink and put in a new one. Then she went to coax Ashley into coming out and cleaning up the broken glass.

I read the Boston Globe while I ate. I got through the important stuff first – the sports and funnies – then turned to the arts section to see if any of my more successful friends were featured. News of a million-dollar recording contract or a Grammy nomination could inspire a productive envy in me that led to a busy morning of songwriting and booking gigs. More often, it produced nothing except an empty wallet and an especially excruciating hangover. I couldn't stop myself from looking, though. Fortunately, this morning's headline names were all strangers.

Dreadlocks worked the register, sharing the news about Jules with the regulars. Many of them had been at last night's meeting and turned to look at me suspiciously. The line began to grow. It was hard to concentrate on the paper. I kept having dizzy little headrushes that I suspected were a side effect of my collision with Shimmy Jimmy. I was shaking one off when Chief Investigator Ray Wankum of the police department slid into the booth across from me, toting a large go cup and a clipboard.

"You didn't do it, did you?" He sounded hopeful.

"You're kidding."

The detective shrugged. He was tall and thin, with a jarhead crewcut and acne-scarred cheeks. He wore a dark green blazer, a beige polyester shirt and a green knit tie. Uniform colors. "People will think it was because of the hotel."

"I can't help that."

"Still, you finding him. And finding him *there*."

"Why would I kill him? Our side's winning now."

"Maybe." Wankum sipped his coffee. "But Jules dying puts the hotel on ice for sure. And you did get kind of personal last night."

"I didn't do it, I swear."

"What about your friend Davey?"

"Believe me, if he was going to kill Jules, he would have done it before he had to put on a necktie and give a speech."

Wankum took another sip to hide his smile and didn't say anything.

"What makes you think he was killed over the hotel, anyway?"

"You kidding? You get a standing ovation for singing about running him out of town, then somebody shoots him the same night, on the *exact spot* where he was going to build the thing. That sound like coincidence to you?"

He made a convincing case. If he was right, I probably knew the killer. Maybe my snarky little song even inspired the crime. Someone had sent the innkeeper packing for good. *There's* your queasy little rush.

"What have you got so far?"

"I shouldn't tell you anything," Wankum said, but he liked to share the inside dope. It was a way of letting us civilians know just how dark and dangerous a world we lived in, and thus how much we needed his protection. He looked around to see if anyone was listening, then consulted his clipboard. "The M.E. says it happened between midnight and three. He'll have a better fix later. Jules was shot three times in the chest with a small-caliber weapon, maybe a .22. They could always find something else at the autopsy, but it looks pretty straightforward. You don't own a gun, do you?"

"Nope. I'm a folksinger." Any port in a storm. Right now it sounded more innocent than singer-songwriter. "Maybe it was a hold-up?"

He shook his head. "Jules still had his wallet and his Rolex."

"The Chamber will be happy about that." Headlines about street crime could cut into the tourist trade.

"I heard he came in the Rum House earlier."

"True."

"We're told he and Davey got into it right there in front of everybody."

"I wouldn't say that, exactly."

"What would you say?"

"Jules was spoiling for a fight, but Davey just told him to leave. And he did. The whole thing lasted maybe thirty seconds."

"That doesn't mean Davey didn't track him down later. He has a temper, your friend."

"He was happy last night. It was Jules who was looking for trouble."

"You left when?"

"Midnight. Ish."

"You bring anyone home with you?"

"No."

"No?" He looked surprised. My reputation had survived a decade of marriage and two largely celibate years since the divorce.

"No."

"Was anyone else there? Your boy?"

"Zack was with his mom." Amy and I share custody.

"So no one saw you after you left the bar?"

"This is beginning to sound like I should have a lawyer."

"You have the right to one, remember?" He slid a laminated card out of his wallet and held it up so I could see the printed Miranda warning.

The yellowing card dated to his rookie year on the force, when local teenagers nicknamed him Rambo for his single-handed efforts to shut down the party scene in the woods below the water tower and out at Plover Island Point. That summer I battered clams at the Rum House three nights a week to earn gas money. One Friday night I was soloing a joint behind the dumpster on my break when he appeared out of the darkness, stealthy as a ninja, and caught me.

At seventeen, I was already immune to his lecture about the evils of dope, but I went a little weak in the knees when he said that I'd have to spend the weekend in jail until my parents could bail me out on Monday. Still, I wasn't about to narc on the fry cook, who dealt out of his locker and ended every transaction with a pointed reference to boiling oil. When Wankum asked me where I got the weed, I described a mysterious Blacksmith Alley degenerate straight off the cover of "Aqualung," my favorite album at the time. When I finished my stoned babbling, he shook his head and made me swear that I'd never touch the stuff again, a promise we both knew was meaningless. Then he flicked the roach into the river with an exasperated sigh and told me to get back to work.

He had never let me forget this act of mercy, and his recitation of the warning now was sardonic and long-suffering.

"Do you understand these rights as I've read them to you?"

"Sure. But you're joking, right? You really think I killed Jules?"

He tucked away the card and didn't say anything.

"And then I came back this morning and pretended to discover the body? Why would I do that?"

"I don't know. People do crazy shit all the time, way crazier than that."

"They did that test to see if I fired a gun. It will prove I'm innocent."

"Hope so. And you're absolutely sure your buddy Davey couldn't have done it?"

"No way."

"Maybe he got someone to do it for him. He has a lot of interesting friends, not all of them such good citizens."

"Anybody who's run a bar on the waterfront for all these years is going to know some interesting people."

Wankum shrugged. Maybe so. "By the way, what'd you do to your head?"

"What?"

He pointed. I reached up and felt a lump on my forehead. Ow. "I fell, just before I found Jules. Tripped over my own two feet. Hadn't had my coffee yet."

"You should get that looked at." Wankum said it casually, but he continued to stare for a moment. I could see him thinking that maybe Jules and I scuffled in the parking lot when I came out of the Rum House, and then I pulled out a gun and... "Later on, swing by the station and I'll take a formal statement. We'll want the clothes you were wearing last night, too."

"Sure, whatever." I sighed and rubbed my eyes, suddenly dizzy again. "Maybe Jules got in a fight over a parking space. He always parked his Beemer sideways like that, so it didn't get scratched. People got pissed about it." I knew it was lame as soon as I said it.

"I don't think it's that kind of deal. Three in the heart? Sounds like someone knew him pretty well." He stood up to go. "You didn't notice anyone else around this morning, did you? Anything they saw, no matter how small, could be significant."

I became very interested in the last piece of my bagel. "I would have told you."

"I'd be surprised if you were the first one to see the body. It's pretty busy down there in the morning, people walking their dogs or jogging or whatever. If you hear of anybody, I'd sure like to talk to them."

I thought of Shimmy Jimmy and the look on his face just before we collided. Jules had already been dead for hours by then. Jimmy couldn't have had anything to do with it. Not a gun and three in the heart. There was no point in putting him through the terror of a police interrogation. He couldn't tell them anything.

"No," I said, "there was nobody."

"What an exciting morning!"

I'd just turned back to the Globe when Abigail Marks slid into the booth across from me and folded her knotty, age-spotted hands on the table. I caught a whiff of lilac perfume. She sat perfectly upright, member of a generation raised to believe that posture was character. But her face was alight with prurient curiosity.

"I wouldn't put it that way."

"Well, you certainly come out ahead."

"I don't know what you mean."

She thrust her pointy chin to one side. "You were always a smart boy. Don't tell me you don't see the benefit here."

As an English teacher at the high school, she'd given me good marks for my early attempts at lyric writing, but she relentlessly exploited her students' insecurities. Mouth off in class and she'd find a way to remind everyone of your acne problem or your reputation for promiscuity. Once she asked me to read aloud my essay on spelunking, complete with exhibits, and I got my stalactite and my stalagmite confused. "Hold it like it hangs, Mr. McLean," she said, drawing a lewd roar from my classmates, who repeated the line endlessly.

She wrote LibertyportGossip.com pretty much the same way she'd taught, her City Hall scoops salted with sly allusions to long-ago infidelities and other old wounds. Never married, she showed a curious fondness for sexual metaphors. The rumor, familiar even to her students, was that she'd been left at the altar as a young woman and it had warped her.

"I don't know what you're talking about."

She sighed. "The hotel, of course. Jules was the one pulling the financing together. With him out of the picture, the project is kaput."

"I'm not thinking about that now. A man is dead."

"Yes, it's so horrible you're sitting here reading the paper and drinking your coffee just like every other morning."

"I'm not talking to you about this, Abigail." I'd called her Miss Marks till I was thirty.

"You can be an anonymous source. Why don't you just tell me what you saw down there?"

I picked up the front page and looked for something to read.

"I wish you'd been so quiet when I had you in class." She sat back and contemplated me from a distance. Finally she drew out her notebook and pen with a flourish. "For the record, did you kill Jules?"

I interested myself in a Reuters story on military unrest in East Timor.

"I'll put you down for a 'No.' Maybe your friend Davey Gillis did it?"

Members of the Timorese army had gone on strike over working conditions, and there was concern for the safety of Australian tourists in the war-torn country.

"Where did you go last night after you left the Rum House?"

If she hadn't been my teacher, I might have been able to tell her to fuck off, as she so richly deserved.

"Don't you even want to express your condolences to the family?"

When I still didn't answer, Abigail huffed in annoyance and stood up. Her smile had evaporated.

"I'll leave you alone, then. Don't blame me if people think you're guilty."

"As long as you don't encourage them."

"I only write the truth," she said, nose in the air, then turned and marched away.

"What a bitch," the Beatnik said, rushing over to refill my coffee. "I can't believe she had the nerve to come in and ask you questions after what she wrote about you last night."

"What did she write?"

She looked more shocked than when I told her Jules had been killed. "Don't you read her blog? Everybody else does."

"Why?"

"To see what she says about them, of course."

"I might have looked at it the last time I turned on my computer."

"And when was that?"

I liked computers every bit as much as I liked cell phones. "Last week. Maybe."

She gasped and pretended to stagger. "Wait right here."

Ignoring pleading looks from customers with empty mugs, she put the coffeepot down on the table and raced back to the register. She disappeared under the counter for a moment, then came back with her laptop and sat across from me. While she powered up, I read the stickers on the lid, including *Save Tibet* and *I Fucked Your Boyfriend.*

"Here," she said, turning the computer to face me.

At the top of the screen was the familiar view of the town from across the river – the white masts, brick buildings and steeples – with *LibertyportGossip.com* slashed across the sky in a blood-red horror-movie font. She clicked her fingernail against the first item:

Cheap stunt fails to stop developer

By ABIGAIL MARKS

The shameful and doomed attempt to block developer Jules Titward's Harbor Hotel plan took another step into the gutter at City Hall last night. At a "public forum" called to pacify opponents of the sensible fast-track approval process, local has-been Baxter McLean actually had the nerve to sing a song attacking Titward's motives and integrity. And the yahoos and NIMBYs on his side cheered wildly.

Of course, all of us who've been subjected to McLean's tuneless warble at various events over the years know that his 'artistry' is just so much fingernails-on-the-blackboard to those who appreciate real music. Another Mozart he is not. But the effrontery of last night's performance was truly stunning, coming as it did on the heels of a long list of whines from local booze-slinger Davey Gillis.

Gillis, at least, has reasons to oppose this truly spectacular project: He'd actually have to secure the required parking for his business, and he must be terrified at the prospect of a competitor who offers edible food and potable beverages. But McLean's incoherent broadside was probably motivated by no more than a couple of free rounds of the rotgut he swills with enthusiasm every night at Gillis' bar. That's what he was doing, anyway, when Titward bravely entered the waterfront dive later and confronted the duo, who shrank from his words. Titward vowed the hotel will be built in spite of them. We devoutly hope so.

Posted Wednesday at 12:35 a.m. / Permalink / Comments (23)

Reading about yourself is tough. A few years ago I'd been described in print as "tall, lean and almost handsome," and the qualifier haunted me still.

"NIMBYs?"

"Not In My Back Yard."

"Ah."

"It's pretty harsh." The Beatnik closed the computer and stood up, shaking her head. "I don't know why someone would write stuff like that."

"She's an unhappy woman."

"Whatever. But she better not come in here bothering my customers again. If she does, she'll get a little something extra in her hash."

She pretended to hawk and spit, silver tongue stud flashing, then picked up the coffeepot, smiled at me sweetly and bopped along to the next booth.

"You're here to have your head examined?" Dr. Paul said.

I nodded gingerly. "My ex-wife told me I needed it a long time ago." She couldn't believe I wouldn't give up music for a more stable career. To be fair, she sounded sad about it, as if she really thought I was out of my mind. Maybe I was. She divorced me soon after.

"You tripped and fell?" Dr. Paul said, leaning in close to examine my bump.

"Yes."

"Think maybe it's time to lay off the sauce?"

"It happened this morning, on the way to coffee. I was perfectly sober."

He pursed his lips doubtfully. Dr. Paul Belanger was slight and studious, with a smooth, unlined face and a marathoner's lean physique. Under his white coat, he wore a light blue dress shirt and a navy bowtie with white polka dots. The fuddy-duddy touch seemed intended to counteract his boyish appearance.

"How did it happen?" he asked, poking at my head.

"Ow. This is like the confessional, right? Whatever I tell you is confidential?"

The doctors' group operated in a renovated silver factory by the river, just west of downtown. The hot, noisy smithing floors had been replaced by blond wood, white walls and the soft clacking of computer keys. Former factory employees arriving for appointments looked around in wonderment. The second-floor examination room had a tall, narrow window that looked across the water to the marshes and wooded islands of Seabury. A moored sailboat bounced in the wake of a cabin cruiser that had already passed out of sight.

"To be honest, it's hard to know what the rules are these days. If you're about to do harm to yourself or someone else, I have to report you. But beyond that, there's a whole range of conflicting codes. The government, the hospital, the AMA, my insurer. All I know for sure is, whatever I do, someone can sue me."

He was a fan, had all my albums. They aren't easy to find, but he'd tracked them down on the Internet, paying collector prices. He referred to this as his "last remaining vice." I trusted him anyway. Maybe it was the bowtie.

"I had a little collision."

"Car accident?"

"Bicycle versus pedestrian. I was the pedestrian."

"One of the local racing team in their all-too-revealing spandex shorts?"

"Shimmy Jimmy."

Dr. Paul paused to look me in the eye. "It's a wonder you're alive."

"Barely."

"Follow the light with your eyes."

I did as I was told.

"So what happened? He's not the type to sneak up on you."

"We came around the corner of the Rum House at the same time, from opposite directions."

"Was this before or after you found the body?"

"You've heard."

"I read Abigail, same as everyone."

"It was right before."

He looked in my ears with a gadget. "Did you kill Jules?"

"I wish people would stop asking that."

"It's a logical question. You and Davey went after him pretty hard last night."

"You were there?"

"Of course. 'Send the innkeeper packing!' Very funny, really."

"Thanks."

Dr. Paul hmmm-ed. "Maybe it was a robbery."

"Cops don't think so. He still had his wallet and his Rolex. And whoever it was shot him three times in the heart."

"A jilted lover, maybe. Do you have any dizziness?"

"Every time I think about seeing his body."

"What about nausea?"

"Not anymore."

"Did you eat breakfast?"

"Bagel."

"And you kept it down?"

I nodded. He bent down to clean the pebbles out of my bloodied knees with an antiseptic wipe. "I could put a dressing on those, but they'll heal better if I don't. Just try to keep them clean." He discarded his latex gloves, washed and dried his hands, then leaned back against the wall and folded his arms. "So why didn't you want to tell me about Shimmy Jimmy?"

"Because I didn't tell the cops about him. They'd be giving him the third degree now."

"Which is the last thing he needs."

"Exactly. He didn't shoot anybody."

"Almost certainly not. I'm impressed he can ride that bike. A lot of long-term head-injury cases have problems with balance and coordination."

"What about his speech?"

"All kinds of atypical shimmy symptoms crop up." He smiled at his own joke. "The human brain is wondrously complex and strange. As if you didn't already know that."

"What does *that* mean?"

"You being an artist and all."

"Ah. What happened to Jimmy, anyway? A car accident, right?"

"Well, I'm not his doctor. But basically, massive brain trauma due to teenaged stupidity. They ought to invite him to the high school for show-and-tell every year before prom. The way I hear it, spring of senior year, he got smashed on a Saturday night and wrecked his Trans Am. He was in a coma for weeks with a closed head injury. When he finally came out of it, he'd suffered severe brain damage. He's lucky he's not in a permanent vegetative state."

"Lucky?"

"Not as lucky as you." Dr. Paul picked up my chart and clicked his pen. "You're going to be sore all over tomorrow, but if there's any concussion, it's minor. I don't think you did any real damage. I'll give you some painkillers. Take it easy for a couple of days. Let me know if you have any seizures."

"Seizures?"

"And don't kill anybody."

"I'll do my best."

FOUR

I was battling Red Suspenders with Nerf swords in an inflatable boxing ring in Fenway Park when a noise woke me. My first thought was that I'd have to write Dr. Paul a thank-you note for the awesome painkillers.

Someone was knocking. I rose from the couch, glided to the front hall and opened the door. A dozen people in shorts and matching dark-green T-shirts stood on the brick sidewalk looking back at me. Most were middle-aged, with glasses and fanny packs and the kind of dorky sunhat advertised in the back of Yankee Magazine. One teenage boy skulked in back, sullen and bored. The rest smiled blissfully, like some sort of cult. Blinking in the sunshine, I wondered if I was still dreaming.

With an effort I focused on the logo on the shirts. It showed a line drawing of a guitar, harmonica and fiddle, encircled by the words *Cape Ann Folk & Blues Appreciation Society.* Reading all the way around made me dizzy again. A square-jawed sort with wavy grey hair and steel-rimmed glasses stepped forward and stuck out his hand for a shake. He wore sandals with black socks, and his eyes had the twinkle of a fanatic. "Donald Antwine, president of the society. Really appreciate you granting us this audience!"

As he pumped my hand, it came back to me with a horrible clarity. In March, after a benefit concert in an Ipswich church, Antwine waylaid me at the bake-sale table and asked me to be the "honored guest" for one of his group's monthly Meet the Artist events. Whacked out on triple-fudge brownies, I agreed, and apparently today was my lucky day. I'm sure I had it written down somewhere.

"Uh, come on in."

The green T-shirts followed me inside single-file, like a family of ducks. Make Way For Folkies.

My house was a classic three-story Federal on a quiet block off Green Street, with the white paint peeling from the clapboards and black shutters missing the occasional slat. I wasn't much of a handyman. One of the two brick chimneys tilted alarmingly over the narrow driveway toward the house next door. Density wasn't a big concern in the olden days, as my neighbors were reminded whenever I plugged in my Stratocaster and rocked out.

The place was much too big for me now, even when Zack was here. I'd bought it for a song, pun intended, when the downtown was still downtrodden. It was worth a fortune now, but despite my financial straits, I couldn't bring myself to sell. Except for the '63 Strat and the gold record, the house was my last souvenir of my glory days. More importantly, Zack still called it home, even though he lived with his mother more than half the time.

The green T-shirts looked around the front hall with earnest curiosity, as if the recycle bins and stepladder and yellowed cut-glass chandelier had educational value. They missed the gold "Mirror Ball Man" single, which hung on the wall under the stairs. I wasn't the kind of guy to point it out.

"How exactly is this supposed to work, Mr., uh..."

"Antwine. Call me Donald. Generally our guests of honor talk about their careers, answer questions from the members and play a few songs. All very informal of course. But this is your home, so I guess it's up to you!"

Everyone except me tittered as if this qualified as wit. Maybe I should forget the painkillers and have some of what they were having.

I led them into my music room, originally a formal parlor. Two tall windows faced the street. Two more, on either side of the fireplace, looked into the law office on the ground floor of the Calamine-pink Italianate monstrosity next door. The lawyers' working hours seldom overlapped mine, but I'd learned to put on a robe just in case, after disrupting an early-morning divorce mediation by appearing in the altogether to jot down a sunrise lyrical inspiration. Another song I hadn't finished. Newspapers and dirty dishes lay scattered about. An enormous jade plant filled a sunny corner, surrounded by a carpet of dead leaves. The green T-shirts ignored the squalor, eyeing my guitars and amps, the stacks of CDs, the pads with scribbled lyrics.

"This is where the magic happens," I said. They ooohed and aaahed politely, missing the self-mockery.

My ex-wife had decorated the walls with framed posters that documented my rise and fall, from the "Mirror Ball Man" tour to THE 1998 STOP HUNGER NOW BENEFIT STARRING LILY FORD, TAJ MAHAL, PETE SEEGER & ARLO GUTHRIE, JOHN HALL, PERUVIAN PAN FLUTE ENSEMBLE, BAXTER MCLEAN. When you were billed below the guys in serapes, maybe it was time to hang it up, but I wouldn't, or couldn't, and it had cost me. To Amy, being married to an itinerant musician was an adventure, fine and dandy until Zack came along, but a child needed security, financial and otherwise, as well a male role model who was around more often than not. I said I would find a way to send Zack to the college of his choice, even if it was Harvard. She just shook her head, sadly but calmly, and I saw that the marriage was over, although we hung on for years.

Now I threw the windows open to let some fresh air in and collected an armload of empty beer bottles from my last songwriting session, which gave birth to "Send the Innkeeper Packing." The old couch and chairs were already arranged in a rough arc facing the shallow brick fireplace. Zack and his friends had set it up that way a few weeks ago, when the nights were still cold enough for a fire. I'd come downstairs at midnight to find them playing a round of "Burn or melt?" A few blobs of olive-green plastic stuck to the hearth were all that remained of the toy soldiers he'd outgrown.

"Where would you like me to, uh, begin?"

President Donald perched on an ottoman at my feet, beaming. "At the beginning, of course."

So I did.

One grey November Saturday when all the other UMass freshmen were at the football game, the aspiring singer-songwriter sat on his dorm-room bed and taped a satirical talking blues about a disco Casanova who had outlived his era. "Mirror Ball Man" was inspired by an older guy who'd been hitting on my crush in an Amherst bar the night before, a sleazebag with a shiny, synthetic shirt unbuttoned to the navel, a gold chain and a bunch of obvious pickup lines. In the song, the pretty girl shot him down on the dance floor. In real life, I was the one who went home alone. The words were funny, but my vocal was a yelp of hormonal outrage.

On Monday, with no girl and nothing to lose, I mailed the cassette to impresario Sol Greenspan, whose name I'd come across in a book about the Cambridge folk music scene of the early '60s. Sol had fallen on hard times, but he hadn't lost his ear. He passed my tape along to a record-label executive who had gotten his first job in the music business as Sol's unpaid teenaged assistant. The executive later claimed to have recognized the song's potential immediately; I've always thought he just took pity on his old mentor. He signed me with a miniscule advance and hired a seedy producer in a black leather blazer to help me re-record the song professionally.

We entered the studio in Boston's Back Bay on a cold Tuesday in January. The producer sat at the board snorting coke while I sang the song over and over; I came to learn that this was the accepted industry definition of "professionally" at the time. I was nervous, trying too hard, and intimidated by the producer's clenched, skull-like grimace. Nothing we laid down matched the appeal of my low-fi dorm-room demo.

Late that night, I returned to my desolate Combat Zone hotel room exhausted and despairing, believing that I'd blown my big chance. The producer, who was more than wide awake, got to poking around in a studio closet after I left. He found an old beatbox, powered it up and dubbed a simple rhythm track onto my demo, a comic counterpoint of bleeps and bloops, like an early video game. To me it sounded like a cheap joke, but the record company released his version as a single; according to my contract, I had no say in the matter. To everyone's surprise, none more than my own, it turned out to be my ticket to One-Hit Wonderland.

For a few weeks that spring and summer, you couldn't turn on the radio without hearing "Mirror Ball Man." Newsweek said I had "mined the zeitgeist," whatever that meant. Johnny Carson told "Mirror Ball Man" jokes. I played for thousands of people with the beatbox on a stool next to me. I opened for Elvis Costello, Lily Ford and Jackson Browne, then headlined a brief tour of my own. I dropped out of college, or actually a record-company lackey visited the registrar's office and dropped out for me. I received a substantial advance for the hastily recorded "Mirror Ball Man" album and spent it just as fast, assuming it was simply life's first installment on my talent.

Funny about that, though. None of the other songs on the album hit the Top 40. They were all straight singer-songwriter stuff, no beatbox. People wanted "Mirror Ball Man II," and I couldn't, or wouldn't, give it to them. My next album, "Second Time Aground," won praise from the critics, but I never cracked the charts again.

I recorded three more albums for three different independent labels: "Whatever Happened To Me?" (1989); "I'm Not Doing This For My Health, You Know" (1993); and "Please Remain Seated Until My Career Comes To A Complete Stop" (1999). All were well-reviewed, but sales never indicated any resurgence of wide public interest in my music, and each of the labels went broke in turn, a coincidence I could sometimes joke about if I had enough to drink.

The only money I made from "Mirror Ball Man" now came in the form of occasional checks for $43.42, royalties from a collection of '80s novelty songs advertised on low-rent cable channels. On the CD, "Mirror Ball Man" came right before "The Future's So Bright I Gotta Wear Shades." Meanwhile I needed a miner's headlamp to see next Tuesday.

I earned my living on the road. September through May, I toured the college towns from New Haven to Orono, contending with the full gamut of road hazards and laughing, drunken frat boys who called for "Freebird" while I was tuning up. When school let out, I hit every summerfest and small-town concert series I could find. I tried to think of it as paying my dues after the fact.

Along with the occasional Rum House gig, I earned just enough to keep food in the fridge for me and Zack, who was twelve, a hungry age. I focused on my next gig, my next scheduled contribution to his college fund, and tried not to think about the long term.

Maybe that was why I felt protective toward Shimmy Jimmy,

because we had both been left behind, watching our futures go on without us.

I didn't tell the green T-shirts all of it, of course, but my story was downbeat enough that no one met my eye when it was over.

"*Fas*cinating," President Donald said finally, marveling at something three feet above my head. "Any questions, people? Anyone?"

The teenage boy asked, "Do you still have the beatbox?"

"We broke up in '87. Creative differences."

President Donald let out a yelp of a laugh, but the boy nodded as if it was a serious answer, and maybe it was.

"Do you get sick of people requesting 'Mirror Ball Man' at your concerts?" someone asked.

"Usually I feign deafness."

They chuckled appreciatively, but it was true. Every successful singer has to fight hit fatigue, but playing that song was just too complicated. The people who shouted for it didn't know the history. They didn't know what it was like to get applause from five thousand students in a college gym, then hear an even louder ovation when a roadie brought the beatbox onstage. Once in a while, if I was feeling generous, I might go ahead and play the song anyway. It always got the biggest hand of the night, but I could see in the faces of the crowd that there was a piece missing. They wanted to hear the song exactly the way it sounded on the radio, back when they first heard it, back when they were young. They wanted the bleeps and bloops. Which made me even more reluctant to play it the next time.

President Donald said, "Would you play it for us now?"

"Why not."

I took my guitar out of its case: A beautiful 1959 Berwyn D8 six-string acoustic, handcrafted by a mad genius of a Lithuanian luthier and his Mexican apprentice in an industrial suburb of Chicago. My father gave it to me for my sixteenth birthday, a gesture of confidence in my talent that I'd barely appreciated at the time and that brought tears to my eyes whenever I thought about it now. I am pretty much an atheist, but I always hope that wherever Dad is, he knows how I feel. President Donald surrendered the ottoman to me and dug his digital camera out of his fanny pack. The green T-shirts watched with rapt attention as I tuned up.

I nodded to the boy. "Come over here."

He was almost as tall and skinny as I had been at his age, with a wispy beard, bad skin and stringy black hair pulled back in a ponytail. I wondered why he was hanging around with a bunch of old folk-music geeks instead of listening to gangsta rap with his friends and trying to get laid. He shuffled forward with his shoulders hunched and head bowed, as if trying to make himself less visible.

"You know the song?"

"Sure."

"Can you beatbox?"

He nodded and began bleeping and blooping, imitating the cheesy electronic rhythm track that had changed my life when I was not much older than he was now. I let him go on for a few bars, then put my fingers to the strings.

He's a mirror ball man, he's a disco God
Doesn't see time passing, doesn't see that his is gone.

The green T-shirts applauded enthusiastically when I was done. I played three more songs, and they gave me a standing ovation when I finally put the guitar down.

"Thanks for your support."

"No, thank *you!*" President Donald said.

Posing for pictures with my arms around their shoulders, I realized they weren't as insane as I'd first thought. Just pleasant, mildly obsessed fans. It was people like the green T-shirts who kept the music alive and musicians fed. I felt almost tenderly for them, but they brought me closer to my past, too, and I was relieved when they were gone.

FIVE

I gave my name to a young cop sitting behind bulletproof glass, and Wankum came out to fetch me. He shook my hand firmly and looked deep into my eyes, like a Toyota salesman trying to make sure I didn't back out of our deal.

The station buzzed with urgent conversations, ringing phones and radio calls. I felt the other cops' eyes on me as I followed him back. He led me into a small conference room and closed the door.

"Thanks for coming in. When something like this happens in sight of the station, well ... we're grateful for your cooperation."

"Sure. Here are my clothes from last night."

"I appreciate this." He took the paper shopping bag from me and set it on the floor in the corner. "We'll get those back to you as soon as we can."

"No problem. Did you get those test results back? The gunshot residue?"

"Not yet."

"They're going to prove it wasn't me."

He didn't say anything, and I wondered if I was protesting too much. He sat down at the table and motioned me into the chair opposite. There wasn't much space in the little office. Or air. The light came from a fluorescent strip in the ceiling, and the lone window was covered by a vertical blind. When some kids ran by on the sunlit sidewalk below, laughing and shouting, I flashed back to a specific afternoon in seventh grade, the despair of sitting in detention after school while my friends went out to play. This was detention for grownups.

Wankum set a mini-recorder on the desk, turned it on and identified the two of us, the date, time and location. Then he said, "Just tell me what happened this morning, from leaving your house until the first officer got there."

"Well, I was out for my morning walk-"

"You take the same route every day?"

"Most days. If it's raining I might go straight to Foley's. But usually I try to loop around the waterfront. It's pretty. Reminds me why I like living here."

I wanted to drink in the scene as much as I could, fix it in my mind before Jules plunked down a big ugly hotel in the middle and ruined it. But I didn't think I ought to say that.

"And what happened today?"

"I was just past the sculpture park, and I saw that Capt. Bob was giving his nature talk to a bunch of tourists. They were blocking the boardwalk. So I cut through the parking lot."

"This was after you tripped?"

"What?"

"After you tripped and hit your head."

"Right."

"Where did you fall, exactly?"

"In front of the Rum House. Toward the corner of the building."

"What happened?"

I felt a twinge of guilt about leaving out Shimmy Jimmy. But if he knew I hadn't told the truth about that, he might wonder what else I was lying about. It was too late to change my story now. "I hadn't had my coffee yet. I just tripped over my own two feet." I showed him my size-twelve Chuck Taylors and the corners of his mouth lifted for a second.

"Fine, go ahead."

"Well, I was walking across the parking lot and passed Jules' car and, um, there he was."

"Did you recognize him right away?"

"Pretty much. He had the same clothes on as the night before, and I could see his face."

"What did you do then?"

"I went back to the pay phone and called you guys."

"You don't have a cell?"

"Didn't have it on me."

"Most people carry theirs everywhere."

I shrugged. "I don't."

"Did you touch anything at the scene?"

"No."

"Good."

My story was still short and boring. When I finished, Wankum asked me most of the same questions over again, in a slightly different way. Finally he turned off the tape.

"You said your son was with his mother."

"That's right."

"She's married to the headmaster at Governor Willey, right?"

Governor Willey Academy was the prep school just outside town, often referred to by its students as free, wet or chilly.

"You know she is."

"So Zack gets a free ride."

"He does."

"What's tuition down there, anyway?"

His son was a year younger than Zack. Apparently he thought I had some pull at the school. It didn't matter whether I was a murder suspect or not.

"Maybe ten thousand in the junior high. A lot more in the upper grades."

Wankum shook his head. More than a chief investigator could afford.

"They have special scholarships for locals?"

"Probably. I'm not the expert. Amy could tell you."

"I don't think she knows who I am."

"I'll tell her to expect your call." As if that would help.

"Thanks." He sighed and leaned back in his chair, folding his hands across his midsection. Now the quid pro quo. "I think Jules was meeting someone."

"Why's that?"

"He was shot inside the car, probably from the passenger seat."

"Makes sense. There was blood on the inside of the driver's window."

Wankum raised an eyebrow.

"I noticed while I was waiting for you guys to come."

"Huh. Well, there were also three shell casings on the passenger-side floor, .22's."

"So what do you think happened?"

"He's meeting someone he doesn't want to be seen with. So they sit in his car to talk. It goes wrong, the passenger pulls out a piece. Jules freaks and jumps out of the car. The shooter calls him back, and when Jules leans in to listen, he gets shot. The shooter shuts off the car, gets out. Runs around and pushes Jules's door shut, so the dome light goes off, then leaves. Nice, clean job."

"What about fingerprints?"

"I figure you wore gloves."

"Funny."

"Looks like the door handles and stuff were wiped, but we're trying."

"No one heard anything?"

"A couple of yuppies from the condos on the square heard the shots, but they figured it was just kids with firecrackers. That's how we know the time, about one-thirty. They complained about the lack of police presence on the waterfront at night. I explained that it's a budget issue and told them to take it up with Mayor Echo."

"One-thirty, everyone at the Rum House would have gone home by then?"

"Everyone except the cleanup crew, three Dominicans from Somerville who were blasting reggaeton over the sound system while they worked." He said *reggaeton* as if for the first time, rolling the "r" experimentally.

"Did Elaine report him missing?"

He opened a drawer, rearranged some pens. "No."

"Did you talk to her?"

"Her mother met me at the door and said she was with the kids and didn't want to be disturbed. I guess it's understandable. Said she'd talk to me later. I went to see Jules' big brother, the painter, but the asshole didn't feel like helping either. Said he was grieving. Looked to me like he was getting hammered. The artistic temperament, I guess. No offense."

"None taken. Emmitt didn't say anything useful?"

"He only talked to me for a minute. Volunteered that he had an alibi. He was in Boston delivering a painting to some rich couple who collect his stuff. They had a dinner in his honor and he stayed over at their mansion on Beacon Hill. I called them and it checked out. He said he hadn't seen Jules in a few days, didn't know what his plans were after the meeting, didn't know anyone who'd want to kill him. Unless it was you or Davey."

"Nice."

"He's a nice guy. Right after that, he practically pushed me out and shut the door in my face. By the way, how's your head?"

A quick change of subject. "I'm alright. My doctor said no concussion."

"Glad to hear it." Wankum stood and offered his hand. "Well, thanks for coming in."

Despite his soft approach, it dawned on me that he really did suspect me of murder. Probably he wasn't the only one. I decided to drive out and talk to Emmitt myself. We'd known each other for twenty years and shared the, um, creative life. Maybe he would tell me something that he wouldn't tell a cop.

SIX

Plover Island was a barrier beach, a seven-mile-long sand dune that protected Libertyport from the ravages of the Atlantic Ocean. A neglected strip of two-lane blacktop connected the island to the mainland across the Great Salt Marsh. My red Sunbird convertible had two hundred thousand miles on the odometer and enough beach sand on the floor to fill a cabaña. It shook and rattled with every pothole.

One faded bumpersticker: *Support live music, kiss a musician.*

The sun beat down as I drove. The pungent stink of low tide filled the air. Red-winged blackbirds clung to reeds in the ditches. A pair of snowy egrets rose out of a muddy creek and flew low across the road ahead of me, their pure white wings flapping in slow motion. It seemed miraculous that they stayed airborne long enough to land gracefully on the other side.

Halfway across the marsh, an old shack bore the faded slogan *NO EVACUATION POSSIBLE* in red block letters. The sign was a twenty-year-old relic of the controversy over the building of the nuke plant just up the coast. A federal wildlife refuge occupied most of the island, but the northern tip was crowded with summer cottages and an increasing number of year-round homes. If there was a meltdown, the traffic off-island was going to look like "Road Warrior," and most of the summer people would fry in their cars. That wasn't reason enough to stop the nuke plant, and neither were the rallies I had played. Occasionally now a table of greying activists would turn up at one of my shows and, four wheat beers into a nostalgia trip, request my anti-nuke anthem from back in the day. It was called - surprise! - "No Evacuation Possible."

Emmitt spoke at many of the same rallies. He must have been in his late twenties then, a handsome and successful painter with a reputation as a womanizer. From what I heard, he was carrying on a family tradition. I wondered if Jules had, too.

Their father, the painter Alden Titward, moved his wife and young sons to Libertyport from Rockport in the 1960s, looking for unexplored motifs and cheap real estate. He settled the family in a decrepit High Street mansion and bought a Plover Island cottage to paint in, a shingled shack on a small rise just at the edge of the refuge, high enough to have both marsh and ocean views. Supposedly he liked the pure ocean light. His portrait of the weathered cottage, with its crushed-shell driveway and a seagull perched on the peaked roof, hung in the Museum of Fine Arts in Boston.

The cottage also gave him a safe haven in which to conduct his numerous boozy affairs. The island was the traditional place for philandering Libertyport husbands to find cheap off-season rentals while they waited for their divorces to go through; it was zoned for discretion.

Alden Titward drank himself to death when Jules was twelve and Emmitt was fifteen. The cottage sat empty for the next few years, until Emmitt dropped out of college to paint. Pure ocean light, et cetera. After he made his first big sales, in his twenties, he tore it down and built a white modernist cube atop the dune, the largest house on the island at the time and the subject of much conversation. Getting one up on the old man, maybe. I'd been to some memorable parties there. Now the island was shedding its raffish reputation, and there were houses like it under construction all up and down the beach. The parties weren't as much fun, though. Emmitt was twice divorced and as famous as his father had ever been, although the critics preferred the old man's work.

A minivan with a Governor Willey Academy parking sticker sat behind Emmitt's vintage Mercedes convertible in the gravel driveway. I rang the bell. After what seemed like a long time, Blondie opened the door.

Well, well.

"Ashley, right?"

She nodded. She had the puffy eyes and determined expression of someone who had been crying and then pulled herself together.

"What are you doing here?"

She glanced inside, then said, "I model for Emmitt?"

"I thought you'd be at school."

"I'm a freshman at Montserrat? College of Art?" She had the teenaged habit of making statements into questions, as if she couldn't quite believe what she was saying.

"This counts as extra credit?"

"I guess," she said doubtfully.

Apparently I wasn't any better at talking to beautiful teenage girls now than when I was a teenager myself. She wore nothing but an old blue button-down Oxford shirt, several sizes too large. It was hard to ignore those long, shapely, bare legs, or the small but infinitely pert breasts poking at the shirtfront. I tried looking down. Her feet were long and thin and tan, with insect bites and scratches here and there, like the feet of someone who went barefoot a lot, but she'd had a pedicure, and her toenails were coated with clear polish…

Ahem.

"Is he here?"

She nodded and bit her lower lip. "He doesn't want to see anyone."

"That's understandable."

She sniffed. "Yeah. It sucks. Jules was a really nice guy."

"But you're here modeling?"

"Emmitt says painting is all that's getting him through."

"I bet." Emmitt had inherited his father's talent and love of the seacoast, but he had his own style, mostly spooky, hyper-realistic oils of cawing gulls and driftwood and dead crabs in tide pools. Collectors paid a premium for the few that had people in them, especially the ones of young girls at pensive moments, never quite fully dressed.

"The police were here," she said as if she'd just remembered. "He talked to the detective for a few minutes but wouldn't let him in."

"I think he'll see me."

She looked into the house again.

"Oh, what the hell," Emmitt said, stepping out of the shadows.

His voice sounded a lot like Jules', the same snooty honk, only deeper. Emmitt was as tall as I was, comfortably pot-bellied, his face red and lined from a lifetime of sun and wind and booze. He wore faded cranberry shorts, a paint-stained navy polo shirt and battered deck shoes with no socks. His chin was bristly, his grey hair long and tangled, a pair of Ray-Bans tucked atop his head. His still-striking blue eyes were bloodshot, and he held a drink. I wondered if Jules had been trying to look like him last night, like a faded print of their handsome, dissipated father.

"I'm sorry for your loss."

"You of all people," he snapped, but his heart wasn't in it. He had remained conspicuously silent about the hotel, which, combined with his history of fiery anti-nuke speeches, led most of the opponents to believe he was secretly on our side. "You might as well come in."

He turned and walked away, and I had the entertaining if morally perilous experience of following Ashley back through the house. The furnishings were chrome and black leather in a style popular twenty years ago. The east wall, mostly glass, offered a commanding view of the surf rolling in on the beach. Emmitt's canvases leaned here and there, in various states of completion, but the only painting framed and hung was a large Alden Titward landscape over the fireplace. It was a melancholy winter scene of Plover Island Light, at the northern tip of the island. The shuttered cottages and frozen grass around the lighthouse were dusted with snow in the blue shadows of late afternoon, while the white tower itself caught the last orange rays of the sun. I'd seen the painting before, and still it was striking. Worth tens of thousands, at least. The hearth gave off a faint whiff of old smoke.

Emmitt's easel stood in the northeast corner of the cathedral-ceilinged great room, where someone else might have put a piano. A small table held his palette, tubes of paint and a couple of jars of brushes. Under a skylight was a stool where Ashley must have been sitting. The easel held a nearly finished picture of her from waist up, bare-shouldered, holding the shirt bunched against her chest. She had her head turned to the side, looking off. The picture gave off a strong feeling of sadness. To the artist, the girl's mind was elsewhere. She was already gone, to a younger man perhaps.

Or maybe *Mister* McLean was projecting.

Emmitt tugged his Ray-Bans down over his eyes, then opened the sliding door to the deck. A breeze lifted the tails of Ashley's shirt, and I didn't have the willpower to look away.

"For Chrissake, put some clothes on," Emmitt said. Maybe he wanted to keep that lovely view all to himself.

"Sorry." She padded toward an orange bikini draped over the railing, the kind that was just a few small triangles of fabric strung together. She slipped out of the shirt, and I stared off toward France while she put on the bikini and a Governor Willey hoodie. She seemed awkward and out of place washing dishes at Foley's, but here she was in her element, not at all self-conscious changing clothes in front of two older men. Maybe it was the natural confidence of the young and beautiful. Or maybe she was used to being looked at, because of the modeling.

"I guess I'm going," she said. She kissed Emmitt on the cheek with a degree of affection that was hard to gauge and trotted out, saying "bye" to me on the way past as if this was just another morning at the coffee shop.

"See you tomorrow?" Emmitt called after her.

"I'll call you."

"I'll be here." He looked into his drink for a moment, as if trying to see whether she would return. "So you're making a condolence call, are you?"

"Something like that."

He waved at a couple of Adirondack chairs. We sat with our knees almost touching. He smelled of sweat and gin and paint thinner. The view stretched from the rock jetty at the mouth of the Merrimack, a mile north, all the way down the curve of deserted refuge beach to the Ipswich River, six miles south. In front of us, two women and their babies sat on a blanket surrounded by beach toys. Nearby, an elderly man threw a tennis ball for his overweight Black Lab. There was no one else in sight.

"So," I said, "I hear you think I did it."

He smiled into his drink. "Officer Wankum wanted to grill me this morning. I think I'm on his list of suspects, too."

"I doubt it."

He looked offended. "I didn't like Jules any more than anyone else did."

"You were his big brother."

"He was a prick. When we were growing up, I could hardly sneeze without him informing on me to my father. Luckily I could always beat the crap out of him afterward. Then, after the old man died, Jules became my mother's favorite." He smiled harshly. "Look at me feeling sorry for myself."

"Losing someone is hard."

Emmitt sighed and seemed to shrink as he exhaled. I wondered how much he'd had to drink. "He *was* a prick, but I can't believe someone shot him. Three in the heart means something."

"Wankum thought you'd have some idea what."

"He asked me flat out if Jules was fooling around on Elaine. It was the first thing the sonofabitch said. Then he wondered why I didn't want to talk to him." He put down his drink and clasped his hands on his bare knees, trying hard to look like he was telling the truth. The sunglasses worked against him. "As far as I know, he was always faithful to her and the kids."

"Maybe it had to do with business?"

A shrug. "Jules never talked to me about business anymore. I tried to talk him out of going forward with the hotel months ago, and he got pissed off." He stared out at the whitecaps. "From what I heard about your performance last night, I can understand why people think you shot him."

"I didn't."

He rattled the ice cubes in his empty glass. "Of course not. You wanna drink?"

We sipped Tanqueray and tonics while Emmitt told a couple of funny stories about the brothers growing up during Libertyport's bad old days. Apparently their father had found less and less time for painting between his drinking and womanizing. After his death, surprisingly few finished canvases turned up, and the boys and their mother lived in genteel poverty. She was at home there, having been born into one of the few unprofitable tributaries of Boston's Forbes clan, but the boys were day students at Governor Willey, and with no money to continue, they suddenly found themselves enrolled in the public schools.

Back then, Emmitt said, the townies lived to pick on outsiders; I said I remembered. He had been good at sports and fought his way to respect, but Jules' only aptitude was for charming the girls, which just made him more enemies. Despite their differences, Emmitt had defended his little brother with his fists more than once. I thought of Red Suspenders. I'd been in seventh grade when my parents moved us here, and I'd often wished I had a big brother to protect me. I wondered if Zack wished for a brother or sister now. It was too late to do anything about that, though.

I turned down a second drink and got up to leave. At the door I decided I had to ask. "How old's the girl?"

He lowered his chin and glared at me over his shades for a moment, long enough for me to realize "How Old's The Girl?" would be a great song title.

"Old enough to know better than to fool around with me, I hope," he said finally. "And screw you for asking."

"What about her and Jules, then? She seemed awfully upset when I told her what happened."

Emmitt looked confused. "You told her?"

"She works at Foley's. I went in there after I found him. She cried and locked herself in the bathroom."

He thought about this. "She's been coming out here to pose since the winter. She and Jules ran into each other a couple of times, but I was always around. I would have known."

"Her reaction seemed funny to me, that's all."

"You're imagining things."

"What about Jules and Shimmy Jimmy?"

He startled. "You mean that kid with the bicycle?"

"Was there some connection between them?"

"Between Jules and that poor bastard? Why do you ask me that?"

"Jimmy looked pretty broken up about what happened, that's all."

He shrugged elaborately. "Maybe Jules bought him a doughnut once, I don't know. I don't see what else it could be. Do you have any more stupid questions?"

"That's it."

"Thank Christ."

He stood on the steps with his hands in his pockets, watching as I got into my car. I waved as I pulled away, and he gave me the finger, smiling sadly.

SEVEN

Back in town, who did I see but Shimmy Jimmy, pedaling by the old brick tower of the Inner Range Light on River Street, chin up, enjoying the bright afternoon. He smiled like a guy who'd just gotten laid or maybe hit a $50 scratch ticket, although neither seemed likely. I almost envied him. Funny how normal he looked, until you noticed he was a grown man riding a kid's bike.

I left the car at home and walked down to the waterfront. Yellow crime scene tape still corralled a corner of the parking lot, rippling in the breeze. The BMW must have been towed away. Three TV satellite trucks idled nearby. Their tall, white antennae poked up like the sailboat masts above the river. Three reporters stood facing cameras, with the harbor as their backdrop. It was just before five, and they rehearsed expressions of deep concern at what they would inevitably describe as a "brutal murder." None of them recognized me as I walked past. Finally, a benefit to having outlived my celebrity.

In the Rum House, Davey leaned his belly against the bar in the Tavern Room, reading glasses at the tip of his nose, perusing the Daily Town Crier. They'd rushed out an eight-page EXTRA edition this afternoon, with murder coverage replacing the page-one spread on the hotel meeting.

"You're kind of underdressed here," he said, pointing to the photo.

"What do you mean?"

"Guy's dead, and you're wearing shorts."

"Just be glad I was wearing one of your T-shirts. Free advertising."

Davey scoffed, but the Rum House was everything to him. A picture on the wall showed Senator John F. Kennedy raising a pint at the bar during a campaign stop in the 1950s, at the tail end of Liberty-port's golden age. Davey liked to point out his father in the boisterous crowd around the future president. The old man was a lobsterman and a steady customer of the local bars. Davey dropped out of high school as soon as he could and worked the traps alongside him; some said his father needed Davey to keep him from falling overboard drunk. Then Davey got drafted. While he was in Vietnam, his father died of a heart attack. As the sole support of his mother and three sisters, Davey got a hardship discharge and took over his father's boat and trap lines. Everyone said they'd never seen a young guy work so hard; few knew that some of those double shifts were spent hauling bales of weed from mother ships offshore to secluded docks upriver.

After a few years of saving, Davey abruptly sold the lobster boat and bought the Rum House, by then a notorious biker hangout. He drove out the bikers and turned the place into a family-oriented seafood restaurant. Libertyport was remaking itself into a popular tourist destination, and he worked eighteen-hour days to claim a piece of the new prosperity. Three decades later, the Rum House was big enough to host a wedding banquet, serve fried clams to a hundred tourists and entertain the Corona-chugging marina crowd with a reggae band on the deck, all at the same time.

Daylight streamed in through the sliding-glass doors from the deck. I went behind the bar and tapped myself an Ipswich IPA, then settled on a stool and watched one of the party-fishing boats return from the sea. A cluster of disappointed anglers slouched along the rail, focusing glumly on their cigarettes and cans of beer. A small flock of seagulls trailed astern, cawing in annoyance. No fish to clean meant no heads and guts flung in their direction. The captain eased the boat up against the dock, and his passengers spilled down the gangplank and race-walked grimly to their cars, like assembly line workers leaving the factory at the end of a shift.

My knees started to throb. I took out the prescription bottle.

"Mixing pills and booze?"

"I'm only taking one."

"You'll be going home in a wheelbarrow."

"I'm a professional musician. We have special expertise in these matters."

He snorted and slid the paper over to me as he moved behind the bar. LOCAL DEVELOPER SLAIN. I skimmed Tom Dorsey's story until I saw my name. I didn't have to look far.

"So what the hell is a 'person of interest?'"

"It means you're a suspect."

"And the difference is what?"

"Saying person of interest just means they think maybe you did it." Davey picked up a large knife and began hacking a pile of limes into wedges with brutal efficiency. "If they come right out and *call* you a suspect, it means they're getting your cell ready."

"The story says it's 'potentially significant' that I found Jules' body."

"You did pretty much croak him at the meeting."

"That was your idea!"

"Looks suspicious, though." He handed me a printout from LibertyportGossip.com. "Read this? She posted it an hour ago."

Breaking News: Investigation Focuses on Hotel Opponents

By ABIGAIL MARKS

Libertyport's police department has abandoned its usual Keystone Cops approach and is moving rapidly to apprehend the individual or individuals responsible for last night's cold-blooded murder of developer Jules Titward. And - no surprise here - the gumshoes are paying special attention to those who so artlessly attacked Titward and his Harbor Hotel plan at a City Hall meeting just hours earlier.

The lead sleuth on the case, Det. Raymond Wankum, declined to speak with LibertyportGossip.com, citing the need to protect investigative details. But one police source said the spotlight is on failed folksinger Baxter McLean and saloonkeeper Davey Gillis, who bashed Titward at the meeting, then retreated to Gillis' waterfront establishment for a liquid celebration that included - as you learned here first - a second confrontation with the prominent businessman.

"Neither of them have a good alibi for the time of the murder," said the source, "and it's not stretching things very far to say they had a motive."

McLean has been questioned repeatedly by police. Libertyportgossip.com will follow developments closely throughout the day.

Posted Wednesday at 1:42 p.m. / Permalink / Comments (11)

"Twice."

"What?"

"She says I was questioned 'repeatedly.' It was twice, once over coffee at Foley's. Not exactly the Spanish Inquisition."

"She's a vicious old bat." Davey put extra vigor into his knife work just thinking about her. "I thought about suing after her 'rotgut' line this morning. When you schmooze me for free drinks, it's always top-shelf stuff."

"What I don't understand is why Abigail's so nasty to you and me, but acts like Jules was a saint."

"I heard he made her a lot of money in stocks." He shook his head. "So who killed him?"

"I don't know. But we better find out quick, before they decide it was one of us."

"When we find out who did it, we should give them an award for their civic contribution."

"You should probably avoid that kind of talk right now."

"Bah. What's with the pills, anyway?"

I told him about my encounter with Shimmy Jimmy.

"That how you got the bump on your head?"

"Yep. The thing is, I didn't tell the cops about him."

"Why bother? He didn't shoot anybody. Unless they got between him and his cruller."

"Right, and maybe he was just panicked, but he had this look on his face. I can't shake the feeling he knew something."

"Shimmy Jimmy? He can't remember your name ten seconds after you're introduced."

"I know. It was just a feeling."

Davey picked my prescription bottle off the bar and tipped his head back to study the label. "We'll see if you feel the same way when these wear off."

"There was something else, too. Emmitt jumped when I mentioned Jimmy. I didn't go into any details about when or where I saw him. Just his name was enough. There's got to be a connection."

"If you say so." He swept the lime wedges into a bowl with the back of his knife, then started on lemons. "So what's up tonight?"

"Nothing special. Couple of beers, maybe a burger, watch the Sox."

That was my ritual on too many nights since the divorce. If Davey was here, we'd talk, play cribbage. If not, I'd be that guy you always see down at the end of the bar, drinking slow beers by himself and staring glumly at the television as the Red Sox snatched defeat from the jaws of victory. I felt a kinship with them in failure. Then last fall they'd won the World Series at last. It was silly, but like so many diehard fans, I'd found my worldview altered, as if some unscalable mountain peak that had been in sight all my life had suddenly been conquered. I was happy they'd won, but I was still here at the bar. They'd gone to the mountaintop without me. When would I reverse my curse?

Davey set down his knife, wiped his hands on a rag. "You're going to be all over the news, you know."

As if on cue, one of the TV reporters standing outside popped up on the flat screen above the bar, brow furrowed. The Miss Liberty-port chugged toward the dock in the background. I could see the boat out the window, too, with a skimpy crowd of whale-watchers gathered near the gangplank. The sound was muted, but the on-screen headline asked, MIRROR BALL MURDER?

"Terrific."

"Think of it as an opportunity. You're going to get more attention than you've had in years. You should make the most of it. Have you got a gig this weekend?"

"No."

"You should play here Saturday night. I can cancel this shitty rock band that I only booked because my wife's sister's rotten kid is in it."

"You really think being a murder suspect is a draw?"

"People love musicians they think are badasses. Johnny Cash. Keith fucking Richards."

"People also love Barry Manilow and Clay Aiken."

"Who's Clay Aiken?"

I sighed heavily and sipped my IPA. It wouldn't be the most cynical music-industry gambit I'd ever been party to, not by a long shot. I grabbed a bar calendar from a stack by the register and looked at Saturday. The band was called Trouser Weasel, and they played Nu Metal, whatever that was. Bumping them would be a service to humanity. "You really want me up there?"

"Most of their fans are under twenty-one. You'll sell more beer, and I won't have to go through all the hassle with wristbands."

"OK, let's do it."

"Great. You'll be huge. Maybe I'll even buy an ad in the Crier. It'll be just like old times."

I slid my empty glass across the bar.

"What time's the game on?"

The Sox came from behind to win. I forgot my problems sometime during their eighth inning rally. Walking home afterward, mildly toasted, I turned the corner onto my block to find two TV trucks idling in front of my house, antenna raised, cameras on tripods, ready to go live. The two reporters, competitors, stood at the curb sharing a cigarette while they waited for the Mirror Ball Murderer.

I slipped down the driveway of the lawyer's office next door before they saw me and hopped the fence into my backyard as fluidly as a teenager. Wouldn't have tried that sober. I stuck the landing and raised my arms to acknowledge the cheers of an imaginary crowd, then went in my back door. I tiptoed upstairs, brushed my teeth in the dark and lay down on my bed.

Church bells struck eleven. The cameramen turned on their equipment, lighting up my house like a movie set. The neighbors were going to love me. The stereo murmur of the reporters' authoritative on-air voices drifted in through the open windows, then the lights went out again. The crews laughed and bantered as they packed up. Someone said something about a "one-day story," and that was relief enough to send me off to sleep.

EIGHT

I left the house the next morning just past seven. It used to be that the only people on the downtown sidewalks at that hour were drunks stepping out bleary-eyed for the first cigarette of the day. Now they'd been replaced by sexy young moms in sports bras pushing jogging strollers with the same relentless drive they'd use later at the office. At the Fitness Fortress, venture capitalists and software entrepreneurs zoomed into the parking lot in their BMWs and Range Rovers, hell-bent for the power spots closest to the door.

The derelict storefront that screamed DIE YUPPIE SCUM in silver spray paint for years had just gone condo itself. Maybe I should sell my house before the real estate bubble burst. But where would I go and what would I do?

Down by the water it was another sunny, pleasant morning. A few more sailboats and cabin cruisers had appeared in the river, but I was surprised by the number still up on jacks in Hewett's yard because their owners couldn't find the time or money to put them in the water. The joke told most often in local bars concerned the two best days in a man's life: The day he bought his boat, and the day he sold it. A flotilla of skiffs drifted near the mouth of the river, so the stripers were running. I made a mental note to call Davey about going fishing.

The cool breeze had blown the last tendrils of yellow crime-scene tape into a tree-shaded corner of the parking lot, where the McNultys were unpacking Xenon from their ancient Volvo. Arnie and Sarah were in their seventies, and Xenon, a golden retriever, was the same in dog years. Arnie and Sarah, working together, opened the tailgate. Arnie took out a plastic milk crate and set it on the ground. Sarah spoke softly, and Xenon limped down onto the milk crate and then to the ground. The three of them headed off to stroll the boardwalk. They weren't hard to catch.

"Good morning all."

Xenon barked once before he recognized me and started wagging. Sarah smiled. Arnie, as usual, showed no reaction. A retired engineer, he lived at a slight remove from other people. Sarah claimed it was his hearing, but I suspected he'd always been that way.

"Oh, Baxter, you startled us," Sarah said.

"I didn't mean to."

"I guess we're just a little jumpy, that's all." Having married a man of few words, she had gotten into the habit of speaking for both of them. "What with the murder, you know."

"I didn't do it."

"Of course you didn't. I don't believe a word of what Abigail writes."

"So you read it."

"It's nonsense, of course, but I like to know what people are talking about. She accused me of being a communist once, and I had to set her straight."

When the McNultys lost their only son in Vietnam, Sarah became the town's most dedicated peace activist. Every Sunday afternoon since our troops invaded Iraq, she stood in Dock Square holding a homemade banner that said, WAR IS NOT THE ANSWER. She stayed out there in searing heat and freezing cold, undeterred by rain or snow or the frequent crafts fairs. This being Libertyport, a lot of passing drivers honked their support. A knothead contingent still gave her the finger or shouted moronic insults. None of it came close to fazing her.

We started walking again. I was comfortable in shorts and a faded NRBQ T-shirt. Sarah wore jeans and a cardigan, Arnie chinos and a tweed jacket, all good quality but a little worn, with a thread coming loose here and there. When the breeze freshened, Sarah tugged the collar of her sweater tight to her neck. Xenon rousted the seagulls scattered along the railing, never coming close to catching one.

"So, you're the prime suspect, then?" Arnie said.

"Oh hush," Sarah said. "Don't mind him, Baxter. We were down here ourselves yesterday morning. We were just leaving when we saw the police arrive. To think we could have walked right by that poor man and not noticed. It's terrible. I suppose we could have found the body, too. Then my husband would think *I'd* killed Jules."

"You said once that you wanted to kill him," Arnie noted. "When he announced that he was going to build that hotel."

She gave him an irritated look that he met absolutely deadpan.

"*Hush*," she said finally, and this time she wasn't kidding. "That's not funny, and you know it."

"She insisted on divesting our investment with Jules," Arnie said. "We've got a chunk of our retirement money with him, in a commercial real estate trust. Back Bay office space, I believe. And it was doing quite well, but because of the hotel, Sarah insisted we pull it out."

"I just couldn't stand to be in business with that man if he was going to ruin our beautiful waterfront," she said.

"She's been pestering him for weeks to close out our account," Arnie said cheerfully.

She heaved a sigh. "And we still don't have our money, and now it will be tied up for weeks with the investigation."

"I haven't seen her so passionate about an investment since we divested our South African portfolio."

"And bought it right back as soon as Mr. Mandela was elected," she reminded him. To me she said, "I did pester Jules, and I feel terrible about it now. Of course, I feel terrible for that other poor soul, too."

"Who's that?"

"Jimmy Wilmot. He looked so distraught."

"You saw him too?"

"Oh, yes. Shortly before we heard the sirens, he came careening past us on his bicycle."

"Right down the middle of the path as if there was no one else," Arnie complained. "Almost ran us down. We barely got out of his way."

I was too embarrassed to tell them that I hadn't.

"Where was this?"

"We parked over at the other end of the boardwalk," Sarah said. "We were walking this way, and he almost hit us."

Arnie harrumphed. "If he can't take proper care around pedestrians, someone ought to take his bicycle away from him."

"That bike is all he has, dear." Sarah put her hand on Arnie's arm. Xenon stopped and looked back, checking on them, before padding on.

"He looked awful, too, poor soul," Sarah said.

"Maybe he'd seen the body," I suggested.

"No," Sarah said, "he was definitely on his way *into* the park. In fact, if I didn't know any better, I would say he was heading right for the body. He can't have had anything to do with the murder, of course. We made the same decision you did, to keep him out of it."

Uh oh. "How did you know?"

"You asked if we had seen Jimmy 'too.' So you must have seen him. And from what I read in the paper yesterday, you failed to mention it to the police. No matter. Your secret is safe with us. There's no reason for that poor man to be dragged into this. He's simply not capable of the deed."

"I certainly hope not," said Arnie. "Otherwise all three of us are protecting a murderer."

One measure of our contentment in Libertyport was the Life Is Great T-shirt store on Main Street. Each shirt showed a little cartoon guy enjoying the active lifestyle: swimming, surfing, kayaking or bike-riding. Many of my neighbors seemed to think it was the law that you had to wear one on weekends. The only one I had, a Christmas present from my son, showed the little guy drinking coffee. I was in front of the store, headed for Foley's, when my cell phone rang. I'd been trying to remember to carry it now.

I checked the caller ID: Mom. Great.

"How did you get this number?"

"Ha ha very funny," she said, in an anything-but tone.

Mom still lived in the house in the South End where we'd moved when I was in the seventh grade, leaving behind our apartment in safe, leafy Arlington and all my friends. Libertyport had seemed like the end of the earth, with its boarded-up buildings and sand dunes, at the edge of the deep blue sea.

"Don't you think you might have warned me?" she said.

"About what?"

"About the murder! I had one of my trips this week, and I missed everything. I got home last night and turned on the news, and I almost had a stroke when I saw your picture." But she sounded calm, not alarmed.

"Sorry about that, Ma. I figured you would have heard about it already."

"I feel so bad for his wife and two little children."

"Me too."

"I think he always had an inferiority complex because his older brother was a successful artist."

"That shouldn't be an excuse for how you live the rest of your life."

"Like hiding your light under a rock because you only had one hit song?"

"I think it's bushel, Ma. Hide your light under a bushel."

"Whatever. So, you're under a bit of suspicion."

"I didn't kill him, Ma, I just found the body."

"Of course you didn't kill him. Your father and I raised you right. Next time, though, you could dress a little better if you're going to be on camera."

"I didn't know ahead of time that I was going to be on TV, otherwise I would have put on a suit."

"Like you own one, smarty pants. You should see how people dress to go on trips these days," she said, neatly changing the subject to her bus tour with the local seniors to the mansions of Newport. "Some of the people got dolled up like they were invited by the Vanderbilts themselves, and then by noontime they were moaning and groaning about how their heels were killing them and their girdle's too tight and can't we leave early. As if the rest of us should have to sacrifice because they haven't got the common sense of a newborn." Mom favored sensible walking shoes, L.L. Bean outerwear, a purse with a sturdy shoulder strap.

"I don't know why you'd want to go to Newport."

"The houses are beautiful."

"But you're always telling me what's wrong with rich people."

"Do you need money?" she asked, as if I was hinting.

"No, I'm fine-"

"I have money if you need it, for bail or a lawyer or to bribe the police. I don't want you to go to prison."

She said it so matter-of-factly, as if this were just another tee-naged escapade, like the times she wrote me excuse notes so I wouldn't get suspended for skipping high school. She didn't approve, but she wasn't going to take it very seriously, either.

"I'm not going to prison, ma, don't worry. Things are a little confused now, but I'm sure it will all be cleared up soon."

"Alright, well, you ask me if you need it, I can't take it with me. Say, have any of the record companies asked you to make another album?"

This was how our conversations always ended.

"Not lately, but you'll be the first to know, I promise."

"They're going to ask you, just wait and see. Being in the news will be just the thing to get them to call you."

Which was not that far-fetched, when I thought about it.

After breakfast, I resolved to talk to Shimmy Jimmy. Normally I passed him on the streets several times a day. He stuck to the main drags, where more people would toot and wave to him. Lately I often saw him pedaling by the ballfields on River Street near the Chain Bridge. Maybe he was hoping for a game to watch. Of course, now that I was looking for him, I drove around for half an hour and couldn't find him anywhere. Some sleuth I was.

I gave up and drove to the supermarket out by the interstate, planning to do some overdue grocery shopping, only to see him in the alley beside the store. He stood with his back to a dumpster, holding his bike in front of him like a shield, surrounded by three members of our local dropout-American community. One of them grabbed for the bike, Jimmy pulled it close to his chest, and they all laughed.

I didn't have much patience with bullies. It went back to my adrenalin-fueled sprints down High Street with Red Suspenders and his lackeys howling at my heels. Jimmy's tormentors were no different, but I knew how to deal with them now. I drove straight at them, and they skittered out of the way. I stomped the brakes, slammed the car into park and jumped out. They regrouped around me at the rear bumper. They appeared to be eighteen or so, old enough to know better.

"Fuck, dude, you almost ran us over!"

"I've got to work on my aim."

They were speechless for a moment, but it might not have been my dazzling wit. Their eyes glowed red and rheumy, and I could smell weed on them even though they were smoking straight cigarettes now. The ringleader had shaggy, dirty-blond hair and the beginnings of a goatee. With his faded black leather jacket, he would have been good-looking in a grungy sort of way, except for the sullen stupidity in his eyes. His sidekicks were a zitty little redhead in a faded jean jacket and a slack-jawed pudge with a grease-stained hoodie pulled tight around his moon face. Moonface had a forty-ouncer going in a wet paper bag. Malt liquor and a couple of tokes no doubt made bullying feel like bravery.

"Are you all right, Jimmy?"

"Boys want to take my shimmy bike."

"Don't worry, Jimmy, that's not going to happen."

"What's it to you?" the leader said.

"Yeah," said the redhead. "What the fuck is it to you?"

They tossed their cigs, preparing to do battle.

"We shall be judged by how we treat the least among us." Since when did I quote the Bible? The three morons looked understandably confused.

"What are you, some kind of professor?" the leader said.

"No, and I don't want to have to teach you a lesson. So why don't you just scatter and leave my friend Jimmy alone?"

My wordplay failed to rout them. The leader met my eye, and I gave him my most furious expression. I had a few inches on him, not to mention age and experience.

"Hey, we were just having some fun," he said, shaking his head. "Sorry, man."

He stuck out his hand for a shake. I didn't believe in his remorse for a second, but I was willing to let him save face in hopes they would go away peacefully.

Nope. As soon as we clasped hands, his work boot came up toward my groin. He was stoned and slow, though, and I jerked him sideways so he kicked the trunk of the Sunbird instead. I grabbed the collar of his leather jacket with my other hand and slammed him face-down onto the trunk lid. He slid to the ground. Unfortunately, Moon-face still had the forty, and he swung it at me, connecting with the knot on my forehead. There was a jolt of pain, and then I felt a weird phase-shift, a warm, queasy little timeout, the same as when Jimmy ran me over. At this rate, I was going to end up punch drunk like a third-rate boxer, dumb as a can o' corn. At least the bottle didn't break.

Jimmy could have rescued me. He was big enough and strong enough to take on all three of them easily, but he was also frozen in a strange, artificial childhood, still afraid of the big kids. He whimpered against the dumpster as I drifted.

The redhead shuffled forward to throw a punch, baggy jeans rustling on the ground. The jeans tripped him and he landed on his ass. I laughed and that snapped me out of my little coma. Two down. It's better to be lucky than good.

I turned toward Moonface and smacked the bottle away. He didn't have a Plan B. He backed away and gave the redhead a hand up. The leader crabwalked away from me and got to his feet too. Before they could regroup, I faked a charge. They ran, scrambling up an embankment. The redhead had the names of his favorite bands block-lettered on the back of his denim jacket with a black Sharpie. Trouser Weasel topped the list. Figured.

At the top, they turned and screamed insults. "Retard mother-fuckers" was about the nicest. I was too busy trying not to throw up to deliver any more snappy retorts. They hopped on crappy-looking bicycles and pedaled away. Moonface rode a banana-seat Stingray just like the one I had when I was twelve. His knees came up almost even with his chin as he pedaled. It had to be humiliating to be their age and still getting around on bikes. Maybe that explained why they wanted to pound on Jimmy. They saw the resemblance and didn't like it.

I leaned against the trunk of the Sunbird, panting and feeling my age. Sparkly little phantoms wandered across my field of vision. It had been a rough couple of days.

"You OK, Jimmy?"

"Jimmy's glad those shimmy boys are gone." He looked less terrified, if not exactly relaxed. "They were bad boys."

"Yes they were. Do you remember me?"

He looked at my face for a long moment, then looked down. "No."

To my surprise, I was certain that he was lying. I hadn't thought he was capable.

"My name is Baxter. Yesterday morning you crashed into me with your bicycle."

"I've got to go now." He got on his bike, but the rear tire sank to the rim. "Oh, no."

"Flat tire, huh?"

"Those boys did it."

"I could give you a ride home."

"No taking rides from strangers, mom says."

I noticed that the longer we talked, the less he said "shimmy."

"I'm not a stranger Jimmy, we've met lots of times. And I know your mother, too."

"You do?" He lit up.

"Did you ever ride in a convertible before?" I asked when we were underway.

Jimmy, smiling delightedly, aimed his face into the wind like a dog. I felt rotten for making the comparison, but also a little relieved that he didn't let his tongue hang out. I drove down High Street, between rows of big old trees fledged with new green leaves. I only had a few minutes.

"Jimmy, do you remember what happened yesterday?"

The happiness drained from his face, and I felt a rush of guilt. His cowering before the three bullies proved to me that he couldn't have had anything to do with Jules' murder. Why was I doing this to him?

"Do you remember running into me on your bike?"

"Jimmy doesn't remember things." But his eyes darted, as if he was looking for a way out of the moving car.

"You don't remember coming around the corner and plowing into me?"

"Shimmy man said it's an accident. Jimmy's not in trouble."

"You're not in trouble, Jimmy, everything's just fine."

"OK." He sounded dubious.

"Do you remember what happened before we bumped into each other?"

"Jimmy's riding his bicycle."

"What did you see before you ran into me? While you were riding your bike?"

He looked away, terrified.

"Are you sure you didn't see a man in the parking lot? A man who was hurt?"

"No."

"Do you know a man named Jules?"

"No! No! No!" He shook his head from side to side violently.

I was afraid he would hurt himself. He knew something, but I wasn't going to destroy him to find out what.

"OK, Jimmy, never mind. If you didn't see anything, that's fine."

"Jimmy doesn't remember things," he repeated like a prayer.

"You like the convertible, huh?"

He nodded and relaxed, and I let him enjoy the rest of the ride. He stuck his head out the side again, but without the same joyful look.

The Wilmot house was a weary Cape with faded vinyl siding, rusty downspouts, and yellowed venetian blinds covering the windows. A ten-year-old Civic sat in the driveway. Several other houses on the block had already been yuppified, and the Federal next door was halfway done. A couple of twentysomething carpenters in hard hats stood on scaffolding outside the second floor, replacing rotting clapboards and listening to Dave Matthews on a boom box. Jimmy lit up when he saw them.

"Hi Don! Hi Rich! I got a flat tire! My friend – " His smile faded for a second as he struggled to remember.

"Baxter."

" – Baxter brought me home!"

"That's real nice, Jimmy," the one called Rich said.

Both workmen gave me the once-over before offering a companionable "hey." It made me happy that these guys, who were just on a job site after all, were looking out for Jimmy. Jimmy lifted his bike out of my car as easily as a doughnut out of the box.

"Come on, Jimmy, let's go inside and say hello to your mom, and tell her what happened."

He stopped, looking horrified.

"Not tell mom!"

"Why not? She wants to know what happens to you."

"She gets mad. If shimmy boys do bad things, she says I wasn't being careful."

My first reaction was to get angry at Grace Wilmot. What was she thinking, blaming Jimmy for what other people did? But I suppose she didn't have much leverage with her son. She had to do what she could to protect him.

"I won't tell her unless she asks."

Just then the door opened and a woman stepped out onto the little porch. She was short and stooped, with grey hair pulled back in a bun and wary eyes behind rimless glasses.

"Hello, Jimmy. Who's this with you, now?"

He glanced at me to make sure I would stick to my promise. "That's my friend B- Baxter. He gave me a ride."

"What have I told you about taking favors from strangers?" She was talking to him but looking at me, assessing my threat potential.

"I had a flat tire."

"You should have called me."

"Yes, Mom."

"Mrs. Wilmot, don't blame Jimmy. I told him that you and I know each other."

She squinted at my face. I tried a smile.

"You used to clean my teeth at Dr. Poland's."

The late Dr. Poland had been the most popular dentist in town, operating out of a ground-floor suite in a down-at-the-heels Victorian on High Street. I'd gone to him ever since we moved to town. In memory, my appointments were always on grey winter afternoons: Curling linoleum and that dentist's office smell, shades down over the bay windows, the buzz of the fluorescent lights, the hiss of traffic on the wet pavement outside.

"I remember you. You're the singer."

"That's right. Baxter McLean, ma'am."

"Still not flossing enough?"

"Probably not."

"And how are your wife and little boy?"

This didn't seem like the moment to mention the divorce. "They're doing fine. Zack is twelve now."

"They grow up fast." Said the woman who was still giving her son bowl haircuts at home as he closed in on fifty.

"Yes they do."

"Jimmy, take your bicycle around to the shed, and then go wash up."

"Yes, Mom."

"And what do you say to Mr. McLean for giving you a ride?"

"Thanks, Baxter!"

"You're welcome, Jimmy."

When he was gone, she said, "I appreciate you taking care of my boy."

"It was no problem. I remembered where you live because I've been here once before. When Zack was little, he left his jacket at Dr. Poland's office, and we couldn't get back before closing time. You brought it home with you so we could come here to pick it up. It was very nice of you."

"I remember now." Her smile came and went quickly. "I'm afraid Jimmy depends a great deal on the kindness of strangers."

"Everybody likes him."

"I feel lucky at the way he's treated in this town. If we lived somewhere else, somewhere that I couldn't let him out of my sight, I don't know what I'd do."

"It must be hard for you, being alone."

"He's a good son, and he does what he can to help me. It would be nice to have a rest once in a while, though."

"There's not some kind of adult day care?"

"There are several, Mr. McLean, but they all have rules and regulations. He's not a senior citizen, he doesn't have Alzheimer's, and he's not mentally retarded or in rehab. Either they won't take him because he doesn't fit their criteria, or he's not eligible for funding so I can't afford to send him. You'd think with all the taxes I paid over the years there'd be something they could do for us. All I could do would be to give him up to become a ward of the state, but I am not going to let them put him in an institution." She closed her eyes and sighed. When she opened them again, she willed a change in mood, not quite successfully. "So he rides his bike, and he has a few friends around town that he can stop in and see. Maybe someday he can stop in and see you."

"That would be fine," I said, feeling this had been coming since she saw me drive up. I couldn't blame her for asking. She had to be in her seventies. She deserved a rest, and she wasn't going to get it.

"I worry about what's going to happen when I'm gone," she said, as if she'd read my mind. "I have a little pension from Dr. Poland, and we both have social security. I suppose there will be enough left to get him into one of those private places, but they're so expensive. It won't last very long. And then where will he be? Who will take care of him then?" Her eyes welled with tears. "I'm sorry. Goodbye." She went back into the house and closed the door.

Don and Rich watched me walk to my car. To judge by the expressions on their faces, they had seen her crying, and I was leaving just in time.

NINE

Some musicians will do anything to avoid playing, just as writers will go to great lengths to avoid writing and painters will procrastinate for months before picking up a brush. We pretend that we're waiting for inspiration to strike. The truth is we're just chicken, suffering from chronic performance anxiety, the terror of the blank page, the empty canvas, the silent strings.

I needed to practice for Saturday night, but first I cleaned the downstairs, loaded and ran the dishwasher and started the laundry. I read three days' mail, then emptied my checking account by paying a couple of the more-urgent bills. Finally I sat down with my guitar, which I decided to restring. A knock at the front door interrupted me while I was tuning up. Phew.

"Baxter McLean? Jane Bassett, Dormer Records."

Maybe it was the head injuries, but I stared at her outstretched hand for a moment before it occurred to me to shake it. "Hello," I said, but it came out as more of a question.

"You're expecting me, right?"

She wore an odd grey suit with black trim that reminded me of the early Beatles. Chestnut hair flowing down over her shoulders, high cheekbones, direct brown eyes. I guess she was a George.

"I am?"

"I'm sorry," she said, "I thought someone was going to call you."

"Sol, my agent, isn't very organized."

She wore black nerd glasses like movie stars wore when they played librarians. A few crinkles around the eyes suggested she was older than I first thought, early thirties maybe. "Can I come in anyway?"

"Of course, I'm sorry."

"No worries. What a great house," she said, looking up the central staircase. "It's beautiful. The whole town is, really."

"You drove up from the city?"

"Took the train. Called a cab from the station."

"You could have called me."

"I'm a modern, self-reliant gal."

"So, um, why is it you're here?"

"You know Dormer?"

"Of course." The famous Cambridge folk label went out of business years ago. I'd read in the Globe that a couple of dotcom millionaires were starting it up again as a sort of hobby. Nice to have that kind of money. "You work for the new guys?"

She nodded. "Sony owned the assets. I worked for them as a brand manager, handling a bunch of small or inactive labels. Dormer was one of them. When Rick and Steve bought the label and took it independent, I asked them to hire me. A chance to really make an impact, instead of being part of some giant conglomerate. They're going to get a web site going, totally reinvigorate the brand."

"So what does that have to do with me?"

"Well, Rick and Steve and I decided that, in addition to reissues, we need some new releases to reestablish the label's profile. We've been listening to demos and going to showcases all over, looking for acts."

"Rough duty."

"In my business, you have to make sacrifices," she said and smiled. "Actually, you wouldn't believe how much awful 'new folk' crap is out there."

"And this leads you to me?"

She laughed. "Well, Rick and Steve and I are looking for some established names for our roster. And the first chance I got, I tracked you down."

"I haven't talked to a record company in six years."

"I guess we've broken your streak, then. Is this your music room?"

"Go ahead."

Now I was glad I'd cleaned up. Record Company Jane looked at the guitars and the posters and the legal pads. She raised an eyebrow at my bulletin board. The headlines I'd tacked up were all zingers like MAN DROWNS IN BAPTISM and BULLETPROOF VEST DEMONSTRATION FATAL.

"Song fodder," I explained. "My ex-wife says cheap irony is my greatest talent. She might be right."

"I *love* your stuff," she said. "I'm so excited to have this chance to talk to you."

"I'm surprised you're comfortable being here. Me being a person of interest and all."

"I'm sorry, what?"

"A person of interest, suspect, whatever you want to call it."

She blinked. "I'm sorry, I don't know what you're talking about."

So glad I opened *this* can of worms.

"Well, we had a murder here in town the other night."

"Oh my gosh!" The veneer slipped for a second, and I got a glimpse of the bright, earnest girl she had been before the music business got hold of her. "Someone you knew?"

I nodded. "I found the body. Some people think I might have, uh, done it."

Not awkward at all.

"Really." Her eyes cut to the door, then back to me. Planning an escape route. I couldn't blame her. "Maybe I should come back another time. I'm sorry to put you out."

"No, I'm the one who's sorry. I understand completely if you want to go."

"I just don't want to get in the way. You must be very busy." She was thinking fast. She hadn't moved an inch, but her body language put her halfway out the door.

I should have told her not to worry about it, come back anytime, nice to meet you. But she would never come back, and I would have lost the best chance at a future I'd had in years. Not just an opportunity to make some money, but to get my music out there again, to be *heard*. When it was out of reach, I'd told myself I didn't care about that anymore, but now that there was a chance, however small, I found I couldn't bear to let it slip from my grasp.

She was also the best-looking woman who'd been in this house since my wife left.

"I didn't kill anybody."

"Okay." At least she wasn't running.

"I'm really sorry to drop it on you like that. I just figured you'd want to know."

"I appreciate that."

I was reeling her back in little by little.

"I would have told you sooner, but I thought you would have seen the papers."

"I read the arts section. The rest just depresses me."

"Well, the victim was a developer in town. A group of us are trying to stop him from building a hotel on the waterfront. Someone shot him the other night."

"But not you."

"The police questioned me because I sang a song about him that was a little rough."

"That's outrageous." Her cheeks reddened. Her job was supporting artists. "That violates your free speech."

"It's alright," I said. "They're just trying to catch whoever killed him. I'm cooperating every way I can."

"Well, you don't scare me." She relaxed and smiled again. "I used to work in hip-hop at Sony. I've been around some pretty heavy types, guys who carried guns. You know, keepin' it real."

"And now you're with me."

"You've been on my list from the beginning. 'Mirror Ball Man' was the first single I ever bought, when I was ten years old." She saw me doing the math. "I'm thirty-three. My older sisters loved their disco, and when that song came out, they just hated it. It immediately became my favorite. I wish I still had the single now, but it disappeared one day when I was at school. I always assumed one of them trashed it."

"That's a shame."

"Can you believe there ever was such a thing as a vinyl forty-five? I don't know what happened to all of mine. And albums! It's like a dream that they even existed."

I opened a closet with a flourish, revealing four hundred LPs, alphabetized. She gave a yelp of delight and went straight to the M's.

"Where are yours?"

"Stored away. I don't keep them out." Generally the last thing I wanted to hear was my own music.

"Too bad." She flipped through my collection, sliding out albums at random and moaning happily. "Where's your turntable?"

I opened the armoire with a flourish. Two minutes later we were sitting in the threadbare but comfy chairs, enjoying the warm sound of Al Green on vinyl, the closest thing to an actual love potion that I knew.

She bobbed her head to the opening of "Let's Stay Together." "Willie Mitchell was just an incredible producer, wasn't he?"

"It's a great record."

"So, do you have a lot of new material?"

"A few things. I'm always writing," I lied.

"We're looking to ramp up pretty quickly. If we make a deal, would you be ready to go into the studio this summer?"

"I don't see why not."

"We used most of our cash buying out Sony, so we don't have a lot to offer you in terms of an advance. But I hope we can work something out."

"I guess we'll see." Smiles on both sides.

"I'd also try to license your music for TV or the movies. That's a big revenue source for a lot of catalog artists these days, and a great way to attract new ears. Unless you're one of those guys who's squeamish about 'selling out.'"

"Not me." Not anymore.

"Great. You're not right for the teen soaps, which is the biggest market of course, but if I can cut one of your songs down to forty-five seconds and get it on one of the forensics shows, then the sky's the limit."

"You can do that?"

"That's one of the reasons Dormer took me on, because I've got those kinds of connections. Have you made demos of your new material?"

"No. But hey, I'm playing here in town Saturday night. Why don't you come? You could hear some new songs then." If I hurry up and finish writing them.

"I just might. Are you going to write one about this murder?"

"I don't think so. Jules and I weren't buddies, but it's a small town. I know his wife pretty well."

She looked thoughtful. "There's a rich tradition of murder ballads in American music. Did you ever listen to the 'Anthology of American Folk Music?' Some great, weird old stuff."

"That's me," I said. "Great, weird old stuff."

She actually blushed.

I drove her to the train station. My cell was ringing when I walked back in the door. Caller ID: My ex. Timing was everything.

"Domino's! May I take your order?"

"Hello, Bax."

"What can I do for you? I could swear I'm all paid up."

She sighed. "Oh, Bax."

"Don't 'Oh, Bax' me."

Amy was known as a fair and reasonable human being. When she called up about a college-fund check that was a couple of days late or a few dollars short, she took a sad, tolerant tone that drove me up the wall.

"I'm sorry. Let's start over." I heard her draw a deep Zen breath. She sounded just as calm and rational as when she told me that she didn't want to be married to an unreliable musician anymore. "Hello, Bax."

"Hello, Amy. How are you on this fine afternoon?" I hated the way I turned into a sarcastic asshole when we talked, but it seemed to be the only way I had of combating all that good common sense.

"I'm as good as any of us can be, I guess, after what happened to Jules."

"It's awful," I agreed.

"Elaine asked me to call you."

"Really? Why?" Amy and the widow were friends. I could see a few possibilities, none good.

"She wants you to come to the wake at their house tonight."

"Say what?"

"I was kind of surprised too."

"You think I did it?"

"No, of course not. Still, I was surprised. I heard about the meeting. Your song sounds like it was quite, um, forceful. But she called me specifically to ask me to ask you. It's a nice gesture. I think it's a way of telling the whole town that she thinks you're innocent."

"Did she say that?"

"Not exactly."

I thought of the strange look Elaine gave Jules when I finished the song.

"I'll be there. What's the dress code?"

"I'd tell you to wear a suit if you owned one. Wear your black jeans and sport coat." She didn't have to say which one. "And hang them up when you get home. They don't have his body yet, but there's a memorial service tomorrow morning, and you'll be expected at the church, too."

"Thanks for the tip."

Another sigh. "I'll see you there." Click.

I sat and tried to think what Elaine's invitation really meant, but I couldn't come up with any possibilities I liked, so I turned to other avenues of procrastination and switched on the computer. I often went days without logging on, so a hundred and sixty-two new emails wasn't unusual. I deleted a ton of spam, marked a couple of fan letters to read later and replied to a booking inquiry from a coffeehouse in Brattleboro. Yes, I was free that night, whatever night it was. I'd drive a hundred miles through a blizzard, sure. Anything for a little applause and a few hundred bucks. Hard to say which meant more to me now.

After email, I looked to see what Abigail Marks had written about me today on LibertyportGossip.com. Expecting the worst, I wasn't disappointed.

Shameless attempt to profit from brutal crime
By ABIGAIL MARKS
Dear reader, most of us are still processing Tuesday night's unspeakable tragedy, the murder of beloved developer Jules Titward by person or persons unknown. We've hardly begun to consider what the loss of this vibrant man and his spectacular hotel project could mean to our community. But two local residents - I can't bring myself to call them citizens - have decided to profit from this horror.

A source tells me that saloonkeeper Davey Gillis just purchased an ad from the local daily rag touting a Saturday night performance at his waterfront dive by none other than saloon screecher Baxter McLean. Obviously they're trying to profit from their notoriety as prime suspects in the Titward slaying.

Maybe we'll drop by the show on Saturday night and request the "Dragnet" theme.

Posted Thursday at 1:17 p.m. / Permalink / Comments (24)

The comments section was an outhouse pit of bilious threats and calls to lynch-mob action, unsettling enough to make guitar practice seem appealing at last.

"There's no such thing as bad publicity," Davey assured me when I called him later. "I've already had three calls from people looking for tickets."

"That's swell. Hey, guess who visited me today."

"Who?"

"Dormer Records."

"That was fast. Those record company guys are total sleazeballs."

"You're the one who wants me to play a show."

"Yeah, but-"

"Actually, she said it had nothing to do with Jules."

"She?"

"Oh, did I mention she's beautiful *and* a huge fan?"

"I'm gonna pretend I believe all that and say great for you, man."

"Thanks. She called Sol the other day about making a deal with me."

"I'd love to hear all about it, but the old biddies from the Red Hat Society just came in, so I've got to make seventeen Cosmos and slip on my thong. Later."

TEN

A stroll along High Street at dusk offered a glimpse of the grandeur of Libertyport's past. Mansions built by sea captains and shipping barons had been lovingly restored by doctors and lawyers and software executives, who kept their hedges trimmed and their door knockers polished. Peeling paint or browning shrubbery denoted cash-poor descendants hanging on to their heritage despite the temptation to sell. Some had subdivided into apartments or condominiums so they could afford the taxes, a faintly shameful concession revealed by extra doorbells and mailboxes. One clan even opened a genteel old-age home. The recent boom had drawn speculators who snapped up vacant lots to build Federal-style replicas that in daylight stood out like new, flawlessly white false teeth in the neighborhood's imperfect smile. The soft spring twilight smoothed over the differences, though, and the houses cast a collective spell, inspiring visions of waistcoats and top hats and graceful carriages. Walking along the hilly brick sidewalk, surrounded by the dignified phantoms of a bygone era, I could almost forget the cars zooming past and the flat-screen TVs flashing behind parlor curtains.

The Titward manse stood just east of Main Street, in the presti-gious section known as The Ridge, at the top of a sloping lawn with a perimeter of ancient rhododendrons inside a black wrought-iron fence. I walked up the steep, paved drive, past the parked Volvos and Saabs and SUVs of mourners. The house was white with black shutters, like mine, but larger – a four-chimney model – and much better kept. I wondered whose cash Jules had been sinking into it. The boxlike Fed-eral design had been embellished during the Victorian era. The main entrance was on the side, shielded by a wisteria-wrapped portico. Light splashed from the tall windows onto the grounds, and even the cupola was lit up.

Two smokers stood under the blooming wisteria. One was the grizzled townie who'd held the door for me at City Hall on Tuesday night, still coughing up that lung. The other was the District Attorney. He was a double minority in Libertyport, a black man and a Republican, which created a dilemma in the voting booth for us good Massachusetts liberals. Townies supported him, though, because he was a Catholic and a death-penalty backer and, most important, a native. He'd gone to BC Law on the money his father earned as head of facilities and grounds at Governor Willey Academy. The coffee-shop consensus was that he would run for statewide office before long. We exchanged an awkward nod, both of us wondering if he'd soon be referring to me as "the defendant." Then I bounded up the steps two at a time, arranging my face into what I hoped was an appropriate expression of sympathy while saying a silent prayer that there would be alcohol.

I got my answer quick enough. Standing in the entrance hall by a table with a huge floral arrangement, clutching empty wineglasses, were the widow Elaine Titward and her good friends Amy James and Marcy Davis. Amy was my ex-wife, Marcy her best friend. If there were three women I didn't want to see together, especially tonight...

"Thank you so much for coming," Elaine said, clasping my hand and offering her cheek for a peck. She wore a modest black dress with a single string of pearls, but her long-ago wild streak was still etched in the tiny lines around her eyes. Though she looked perfectly put together, her face was pale with exhaustion, her eyes red-rimmed and darting.

"I'm glad to have a chance to tell you in person how sorry I am." I'd been rehearsing the line in my head all afternoon.

"Thank you. I'm trying to keep it together for the kids."

A quorum of the town's power brokers was visible through the open doorway to the living room, nibbling finger food and sipping drinks, trying not always successfully to keep their voices and expressions solemn. They blinked in surprise when they saw me, then quickly looked away. Jules and Elaine's two kids stood respectfully among them, making conversation with their elders.

"We had our differences, but Jules was a good guy," I said. That was what you did at a wake, lie about the deceased.

"Thank you. Everyone's kind words are helping me hold on. But I know that someday soon I'm just going to fall apart entirely. Thank God Amy and Marcy are here to help."

She looked at them gratefully, and they smiled back like loyal attendants. Elaine had always been the natural center of attention in any room.

"Is there anything I can do?"

"I bet you'd like a drink, and we seem to have run out of red. Go and open another bottle of merlot, will you?"

She slid away to greet the next arrival, which left me facing my petite, lovely, fair-minded ex-wife and tall, horsey, sardonic Marcy. Amy and I tried to remain on good terms, for Zack's sake. Marcy and I never had been.

"Your presence ought to create some conversation," Marcy said.

"So I'm the floor show?"

"If you like."

We smiled at each other with the old familiar loathing. Marcy was married to a member of the Governor Willey faculty, and she introduced Amy to Headmaster Lawrence James about five minutes after our divorce became official. Won over by his money and stodginess – someone else might call it stability – Amy ended up marrying the jerk. Now the two couples lived next door to each other in a woodsy faculty enclave on the campus outside town. Marcy always waved gaily whenever she saw me dropping off Zack. Rubbing it in. She was smart enough never to step in front of my car.

Amy knew how Marcy and I felt about each other. As far as she was concerned, we were being juvenile. She tucked a strand of her chocolate-brown hair behind her ear, and the familiar gesture broke my heart in a way that a hundred angry conversations about support checks or parent-teacher conferences could not.

"What *am* I doing here?" I asked her.

"I told you. Elaine doesn't believe you had anything to do with what happened to Jules, and she thought this was a good way to show it."

"Elaine's a goddamn saint," Marcy said, apparently a couple of glasses of wine into her evening. "Why does she like you, anyway?"

"My natural charm," I said, eliciting an eye roll in return.

It was the truth, however. Elaine did find me charming, or at least she did once. We'd been lovers for a few months, just after "Mirror Ball Man" fell off the charts, when it still seemed reasonable to expect there were more hit records in my future.

Elaine's late father had founded Gordon Electrical Components, one of the first firms in the industrial park, and helped lead the revitalization of the downtown. Elaine grew up on High Street, in a mansion not unlike this one. She was a Libertyport High cheerleader and Yankee Old Home Days Queen. By the time we met, she was in her mid-twenties, underachieving by working in her mother's dress shop downtown. Dating a musician must have seemed a great new way to antagonize Dad. We were young, it was good fun and it ended without fanfare after a few weeks, when she dropped me for an even more scandalous beau, the amiable North Shore Mafia scion Guido Argento, who dealt pot to our crowd. Times were different then, more casual. We'd lived in the same town ever since, running into each other in Foley's and the Organic Grocer without awkwardness.

It happened more than two decades ago, years before either one of us married, but I wondered what Wankum would make of it. Would it be enough for him to arrest me? I certainly wasn't about to bring it up. I doubted Elaine would mention it to him, either. Maybe that was the real message of tonight's invitation. *Our secret's safe with me.*

I wondered how many other people remembered us together. I wasn't sure if I'd ever told Amy about it, and I couldn't ask her now, not with Marcy standing right there. Marcy would drop a dime on me in a heartbeat.

"At least we won't have to read about this on LibertyportGossip.com," Amy said.

"Abigail's not coming?" I tried not to sound too relieved.

"Elaine called her this afternoon and told her to stay away. I think it was very gutsy."

"I'm surprised the old witch didn't show up anyway," Marcy said.

"Elaine told her that if she did, she'd kick her out."

Marcy shook her head. "I wouldn't want that job."

Amy met my glance and we each suppressed a smile, thinking: Marcy would have been perfect for the task. The leftover telepathy of a ten-year marriage. I decided this was an opening.

"What are you and Zack doing Saturday?" I asked.

She groaned softly, the moment evaporating. "It's not your weekend, Bax."

"I know, it's just that the stripers are running."

"You want to take him out on a boat?" she said as if this were a dangerous and possibly lunatic idea.

"No, just surf-casting. Davey and I are going out to the island Saturday morning. It would just be for a couple of hours, and then I'd bring him right home."

"I don't know, Bax..."

"Zack would really enjoy it, and you can have everything we catch." I knew that the headmaster loved to eat fish – for the Omega 3's, not the sheer pleasure of it – but would never dirty his hands to actually bait a hook.

"Get that wine and I'll think about it," she said.

Dreadlocks passed me in the dining room, dressed in black pants and a white shirt and carrying a tray of mini Thai spring rolls. The kitchen had been modernized recently, with acres of marble countertops, restaurant-quality stainless steel appliances, and a hanging rack full of shiny new pans. Track lighting gave it the affect of a decorator showroom. An island held chafing dishes of the caterer's spring rolls, chicken satay and other trendy nibbles, blue flames flickering in cans of Sterno. A row of foil-covered casseroles, delivered by friends and neighbors who followed the old ways, sat forgotten to one side.

A bright red tea kettle heated on the stove, and a small, dark-haired woman was poking around in the gadget drawer.

"I hope you've found the corkscrew."

She turned in alarm. Her eyes were huge and dark behind over-sized glasses with round, black frames. Her dark hair was gathered in a tight chignon.

"I'm looking for a tea strainer," she said, relaxing, "but I haven't seen either one."

"That drawer looks like screwdrivers and keys. Maybe there's another one for kitchen stuff." I pulled a few handles till I located what we both needed.

"You're the folksinger." She scooped some Earl Grey into the strainer and set it in a white china cup with a red stripe that matched the kettle.

"Baxter McLean, at your service."

"Ora Buffem."

She presented her small, cold hand for a limp shake, looking over my shoulder as if hoping for rescue. Maybe she didn't want to be left alone with a murder suspect. Or maybe she just knew the conventional wisdom among the local women. My popularity had plummeted since the divorce.

"You're the poet," I said as I worked on the cork.

I had seen her name and picture in the Town Crier over the winter, a feature on her signing at the Book Shelf on Main Street. I didn't read it, but I did read the two poems that ran alongside it. They spoke of everyday experiences in rhyme, and on a quick skim they might have seemed old-fashioned, but they were full of hidden meanings. I hadn't spent the time, though, to figure out what they were hiding.

"The truth is, I make my living teaching," she said, naming a small but prestigious university on the outskirts of Boston. She was barely five feet tall, with pale skin and a large mole on her right cheek. Her nose was short and sharp, and her small mouth turned downward at the corners. Call me shallow, but her picture was the reason I hadn't read the newspaper story. "I heard you sing at the town meeting on Tuesday."

"Terrible thing about Jules."

"I understand you're a 'person of interest' in the case," she said. I was surprised to see a faint smile on her face. She didn't look like she had much of a sense of humor. "I take it by the fact that you're here that you didn't do it."

"No, I didn't, although I don't think they'd have much trouble finding a jury to convict me at the moment." I popped the cork and filled a glass from a platoon of them on the island. Being a person of interest was thirsty work.

"Perhaps you can write a song about it. From what little I know of folk music, injustice is a popular theme. When I teach Poetry 101, I use a Bob Dylan song about a race murder that's quite forceful."

"'The Lonesome Death of Hattie Carroll.' Great song. My stuff tends to be a little more humorous."

"I'm afraid I'm not familiar with your music. I only listen to classical."

"I bet you only watch PBS, too."

"Actually I don't own a television."

"Game, set, match." I raised my glass to her, then took a long drink.

She looked surprised, realizing I was offended. "I do have a computer and an iPod. Is any of your music available for download-ing?"

"Some of it." "Mirror Ball Man" had just been uploaded from the record company vaults. The label owned my publishing, but I had retained the pittance that was the performer's royalty for each download. My musician friends kept telling me it would add up. What they didn't say was that it would take centuries. "Most of my stuff was on small, independent labels that aren't around anymore."

"I'll have to check some of the sites I use," she said. "The classical selection online was initially disappointing, so I've become adept at using the so-called peer-to-peer networks. It's not all teenagers out there."

The water rattled the kettle; she made her tea. I sipped my wine, in no hurry to join the crowd. It wasn't that I found her attractive. I couldn't imagine the guy whose type she would be. But we had some sort of connection that I couldn't put my finger on. Maybe because we were both writers. She was one of the few women in the house tonight I didn't have a history with.

"How do you know the family?" I asked.

"My father was in charge of payroll for Gordon Electrical, Elaine's father's company."

"You go to school here?"

"I transferred to Governor Willey for my last year of high school, thanks to a generous aunt. Then on to Smith in her footsteps. Since then I've been teaching."

"Do you live around here?"

She smiled without showing any teeth. "I rented in Medford for a while, and then I inherited my aunt's home. You probably know it, it's the little one on Osprey Island."

The tiny, wooded island sat prettily in the middle of the Merrimack. There were just two houses on it, a large Colonial with a barn and a tiny, well-kept Cape. Historic bridges connected the island to the riverbanks on either side. The idyllic scene tantalized commuters crossing the much larger and rustier Interstate 95 span just upriver.

"I looked at the big house when I had my first hit," I said. "I bought a place downtown instead."

"Have you had a lot of hits?"

"Actually, there was just the one."

"Fame is an interesting thing," she said. "As a poet you don't get much of it. I read at the Kennedy Center once, and I've had my share of awards and so forth. No matter what, once you've had that, you hunger for more."

"I guess so." I wondered how we'd gotten onto this track.

"It doesn't change how you feel about yourself, though."

"I've known a few people in the music business who started believing their own hype."

"I'm sure their problems didn't go away."

"If anything, they got worse." I moved to the window and looked out, trying to escape the topic. In the glow from a light above the back door, I saw Ashley standing on the walk, wearing the same black pants and white shirt as the other servers. She was arguing with a shaggy-haired, unshaven kid in a tattered leather jacket.

The leader of the little pricks from the supermarket parking lot.

They passed a cigarette back and forth. I could hear their angry voices but not what they were saying. After a moment he raised his arm as if to hit her. I had my hand on the doorknob when he lowered his arm, spat a parting line, and stalked away. He'd probably stashed his bike in the bushes down the hill, so no one would see him riding it, especially Ashley.

She turned her back to the house, and her shoulders heaved as if she was sobbing.

"Excuse me," I said to the poet, and stepped outside.

ELEVEN

"He's such an asshole," Ashley said, wiping her eyes. She took my wineglass without asking and drained it.

"Your boyfriend?"

"He thinks."

He'd walked off with the cigarette they were sharing. She took out a pack and lit another one, dropping the match into the grass.

"Does your mother know you smoke?"

She snorted. "She bums off me, like, three times a day." She took a drag and exhaled through her nose, and suddenly she looked familiar. I knew someone else who smoked like that, though she only lit up around me when she'd had a few drinks.

Marcy.

I couldn't believe I hadn't made the connection. Ashley was Marcy's daughter, the squeaky-voiced and curveless tomboy who babysat for Zack four or five years ago. Now she was a beauty who dated a dim and vicious moron, no doubt mainly to piss off her mother. Suddenly the kid in the leather jacket didn't seem such a bad choice. I almost felt guilty for ogling her at the beach. Especially since she knew who I was all along.

"I heard you're a suspect," she said between drags. "Should I even be out here with you?"

"Probably not."

"Shit." She shook her head, but she didn't go anywhere. It amazed me how many people wanted to stand around and chat with me even though they thought I might be a murderer.

"If it makes you feel any better," I said, "Jules' wife invited me tonight, and I don't think she would have done that if she thought I was guilty."

"Unless she tricked you," Ashley said and giggled. "Maybe it's one of those things like when they send letters to all the crooks telling them they've won Super Bowl tickets. And then when they come to get their prize: Busted!"

I whipped my head around, looking for cops, and we shared a laugh.

"So how well did you really know Jules?" I asked her.

She looked at her feet, smoking to play for time. "You already know, huh?"

"I've got an idea."

"It was supposed to be a secret. He said his wife would kill him." She was young enough to say it, but grown-up enough to realize immediately how it sounded. She winced. "I didn't mean-"

"I don't think it matters now."

She nodded and crossed her arms under her breasts, blinking back tears. "It was only a few times. He gave me a ride home from Emmitt's once when I didn't have the minivan. We were getting along pretty good, and all of a sudden he asked me if I could get him some E. Like, totally out of the blue."

"Ecstasy? Jules didn't seem like the type."

"I didn't think so either, but he was going through, like, a mid-life crisis? He just wanted to change it up, he said."

"So you got him some E."

She nodded toward the driveway. "Asshole Gareth can get it anytime. I told him it was for a friend. When I got it, Jules had me meet him at Emmitt's house. Emmitt was away in New York for some gallery show, and Jules said hey, did I want to do some too? So we partied. He was pretty good looking, for an old guy." She shrugged. "No big deal, right? You're not going to tell my mom?"

"Was that the only time you saw him?"

"A few more. One time I took the train into Boston and met him at this big hotel. And the last time was at Emmitt's house again."

"When was that?"

"Like, a couple of weeks ago?"

"That was the last time because he was killed?"

She shook her head no. "I decided I wasn't going to see him anymore. He was weirding me out. At first it was exciting, sneaking around with this older guy. Plus he treated me better than Gareth or anyone. Like he opened doors for me and stuff? Stuff Gareth would never do in a million years. But after a while, I don't know. Really it wasn't all that great. You know." She toed the ground. "And then, at the end? He was like, drinking a lot, and taking pills, and saying 'Yo' and 'bro' and stuff, which sounded kind of stupid coming out of him."

"I can imagine." Forget that rap remix of "Mirror Ball Man."

"Then Gareth figured out I was seeing someone else, which is why he's being such an asshole." She flicked away her cigarette as if it was him.

"Did he know Jules was the one you were seeing?"

"No way. At least I didn't tell him. I was going to break up with Jules, but I didn't want him to get hurt or anything. Gareth would have messed him up." She shivered. "You don't think Gareth killed him?"

"Not if he didn't know about you two." I wasn't so sure, but Gareth didn't seem like the three-in-the-heart type of killer. More of a rusty knife or a tire iron. "Did Jules know you were going to stop seeing him?"

She shook her head again. "I hadn't worked up the courage to tell him yet. I was kind of worried about what he'd do."

"Understandable."

She put her hand on my arm. "You're not going to tell anyone else about this, are you?"

"Not if I can help it." I was afraid of what she'd be willing to do to keep me quiet.

"Thanks. My mom would totally freak if she found out. And if Mrs. Titward found out, I'd feel like shit."

I wanted to tell her: Don't sleep with a man until you're old enough to call his wife by her first name. But I wasn't sure what she called Amy.

"I was supposed to get some wine," I said. "I'm going back in before they come looking for me."

"I'm going to stay out here for a few minutes." She let go of my arm and lit another smoke, staring off down the driveway, in the direction Asshole Gareth had gone. She looked like she wanted to run after him.

The kitchen was empty now. I refilled my glass and stood in the shadows, mulling over what Ashley had told me. Jules was already coming apart when someone killed him. "Yo" and "bro" were bad signs. So was buying E from teenagers. And screwing them.

As I crossed the main hall, Elaine's mother led the children up the stairs toward bed. They both yawned, and then she did too, the grief on all their faces fading into simple exhaustion.

In the living room, Louis Armstrong's trumpet blatted cheerfully from the stereo. The crowd had thinned, but those who remained appeared to be in for the long haul. Emmitt had stretched out on an antique chaise like an emperor, cupping his drink on his belly with two hands, eyelids at half mast. Tammy Dukes, a painter of local reputation, sat by his feet, delivering an animated monologue about her new work. When she saw me, she held up one finger to pause Emmitt. He focused on it with an amused expression, like a drunk driver enjoying the challenge of a field sobriety test. With her other hand, she slipped me a folded paper as if it were contraband.

"It's an invitation," she whispered. "Look at it later."

"Will do."

Mayor Echo sat nearby in an upright chair dragged in from the dining room, sipping from a can of light beer and looking hopeful, as if he thought we might all like to honor Jules' memory by buying life insurance. When he drank, his bald dome turned bright red, like a dashboard warning light. He would require a ride home from the district attorney, who knelt at the hearth with his tie flung over his shoulder, trying to start a fire.

Above the mantel hung a framed poster for the "Painting New England Shores" exhibit at the Portland Museum of Art a few years ago. Amy and I had driven up to see it while Zack was at summer camp. Our last romantic weekend together. The poster image was an Alden Titward oil of a lone clammer raking in the marsh at sunset. It was nice, but I remembered now that "Plover Island Light In Winter" used to hang there. I wondered why the painting had moved to Emmitt's, to be replaced by a mere poster.

Elaine sat between Marcy and Amy on the couch, not talking, just taking in the scene. She looked more tired than sad.

"We thought you'd gotten lost," Marcy said, sitting forward and holding out her empty glass.

"Could I talk to Elaine for a minute?" I said while I poured.

"I'm not sure that's a good idea."

But Amy stood up. "I could use a trip to the powder room."

Marcy gave her a look, then sighed and said, "Alright, whatever you say, sweetie." She stood too, then looked down at Elaine. "Call us if you need us."

"I'll be fine."

Marcy looked at me. "Don't say anything stupid."

"I'll do my best."

When they were gone, Elaine said, "Marcy's just protecting me."

"No, she's always hated me."

Elaine shook her head and smiled. "She finds you attractive, that's why she's like that."

"If you say so."

I sat on a hassock across the coffee table and filled the glass she held out. She was still a beautiful woman, but these last two days had aged her. Her dark blue eyes seemed more deeply set, her cheeks hollowed.

"Don't worry," she said, "I'm not going to tell anyone about us."

I looked around to see if anyone had overheard, but Satchmo made it impossible. "That wasn't what I was going to say."

"I know. I just wanted to tell you. I'm not sure who remembers about us, but I'm not going to remind them." She drank some wine.

"What happened to 'Plover Island Light in Winter'?"

"What happened to what?"

"Your father-in-law's painting. You used to have it over the mantel. It's at Emmitt's now."

"What an odd thing to ask. Who knows. You'll have to ask Jules or Emmitt. That's between them. They still squabble about things like that. All these years later and they spend so much time being screwed up about their father." She talked as if Jules was still alive.

"Is that what was wrong with Jules? He was fighting with Emmitt?"

"What do you mean?"

"I keep hearing that he was acting strange."

She looked away and her gaze settled on Emmitt. "In what way?"

"I'm not sure." I couldn't tell her that her murdered husband had been getting high and sleeping with a teenager. "He looked sloppy on Tuesday night, which wasn't like him. Did he have some kind of substance abuse problem?"

"Substance abuse problem? Do you really talk like that?"

"He liked to drink."

"That isn't exactly unusual in our crowd." She surveyed the room with an arch expression.

"I'm serious."

She sighed. "You're not wrong about his mood. He was under pressure. It was work, mostly. His business has had some reverses over the last year. He was counting on the hotel to get him out of the hole. You and your friends were making it difficult for him."

"Until the other night, I didn't think we had a chance of stopping it."

"Because it was on the waterfront, there were a bunch of extra steps he had to get done, environmental studies and so forth. It wasn't just a matter of getting it through the council. And he figured you were going to fight him all the way. He was confident that the hotel would get built eventually, but he was worried about the short term. It made him edgy."

"You say he was having some business trouble. How bad was it?"

"He told me it was nothing to worry about." She shook her head and frowned, as if she should have known better.

Ashley came through the room, collecting empty glasses. I couldn't help looking at her, and when I turned back, Elaine was crying softly.

"I wish I'd treated him better," she whispered.

I wanted to ask her what she meant, but at that moment Marcy and Amy returned and stood on either side of her. Marcy held out her hand for Elaine's empty glass. Elaine handed it to her, then stood and stepped into Amy's arms, sobbing.

"I think you'd better go now," Marcy told me, with just a hint of triumph.

TWELVE

High Street was quiet as I walked home. The party-hearty summer crowd of weekend sailors and sorority cocktail waitresses wouldn't check in for a few more weeks, and the town still rolled up the sidewalks early. The stoplight at High and Main cycled twice as I approached, but only a single car passed through the intersection. I began to see blue and white flickers in the windows of the house on the far corner. Reflections from down the hill on Main. I walked faster till I turned the corner.

A pack of police cruisers with their light bars on had stopped across from Foley's, in front of the building where Jules had his office. Radio chatter carried on the still air. I trotted down the hill, passing the Irish bar, where an acoustic guitarist entertained a sparse midweek crowd. Our beloved little storefront movie theater was already locked up and dark; only one show on weeknights. Farther down, the CD jukebox was quiet in the bar & grill, and I noticed the tables by the open windows were empty, drinks abandoned. Everyone had come out to rubberneck.

The small crowd parted to allow paramedics to wheel a stretcher out of the office to a waiting ambulance. There were too many people in the way for me to identify the patient. One of the paramedics jumped in back, and the other slammed the doors shut and ran around to the driver's seat. The ambulance zoomed up Main Street, its red and white flashers reflecting on store windows and parked cars. A gust of diesel fumes spread in its wake. There was no other traffic, so the driver didn't bother with the siren until after he'd made the turn at the light.

Jules shared a ground-floor office suite with a couple of lawyers and an accountant in a restored brick building, between a teen dress shop and a mortgage broker. The blinds were drawn. A patrolman guarded the open front door, which spilled yellow light onto the sidewalk. The idling cruisers made a restless undertone.

I saw Capt. Bob at the edge of the little crowd in front of the Life Is Great store.

"What happened?"

"Someone tried to kill Abigail. Hit her in the head."

"How is she?"

"It didn't look good."

"She was in Jules' office?"

"I guess."

"What was she doing in there?"

He shrugged and swayed, and I realized he was drunk. "I hope she's OK."

"Where were you?"

"When?"

"Just now."

"Rum House. I was walking home, and just as I was crossing the square, the police came."

"Where are you living these days?"

"Got a studio on Middle Street. It gets crowded when my kid comes for his weekends, but it's all I can afford."

I nodded in single-dad solidarity. I felt guilty because I had so much space. I was about to say something encouraging when cops poured out of the doorway. Two detectives went to the trunk of an unmarked car, got out their evidence kits and went back inside. The uniforms who came out with them got rolls of yellow crime-scene tape from their cruiser and began pushing back onlookers. Wankum came out with his cellphone pressed to his ear. He did a double take when he saw me and pointed at my chest: *Don't go anywhere.* He wore blue latex gloves, the same as the detectives.

"Two people in one week. I can't believe this is happening," Capt. Bob said.

I couldn't think of anything to say to that, so I waited silently until Wankum finished his call and waved me inside the tape.

"What are you doing here?"

"I was walking home from the wake and I saw the lights."

"You were invited to the wake?"

"Yeah."

"That's fucking odd."

"Elaine doesn't think I had anything to do with what happened."

"How long were you there?"

"Until about ten minutes ago."

"And you've got witnesses?"

"Plenty of them, including the D.A. What happened here?"

He ignored my question and waved over one of the older uniforms, a small, grey-haired man with a calm, serious expression. "Take one of the units and go up to the Titward place. Mr. McLean here says he just left there ten minutes ago. Find out if he's telling the truth. Then go down to the Rum House and see if Davey Gillis is there and how long he's been there. And if either one of them could have done this, call me on the two-way."

The patrolman nodded smartly and trotted away.

"I want you to see something," Wankum said to me. He took two steps toward the doorway, then stopped and pulled a fresh pair of gloves from a back pocket. "Put these on. I don't want you contaminating evidence."

He watched intently while I snapped on the gloves, then turned and marched through the door, leaving me to follow. The gloves made my hands feel strange, as if they belonged to someone else.

The office suite blended eras elegantly. The waiting area boasted a grandfather clock, leather-upholstered wing chairs and gilt-framed paintings of clipper ships that had been built here. The receptionist's antique desk was accessorized with a sleek black mesh chair and a black computer with a flat-screen monitor.

Past the copier, a short hallway ran straight back to an emergency exit, with three doorways along one wall. The middle door was open. The two detectives stood over a large pool of blood on the carpet.

One took pictures with a digital camera, while the other dusted the doorjamb with fingerprint powder. When they saw me, they gave Wankum questioning looks that he ignored. He stepped aside so I could see. Next to the blood on the carpet was a large metal stapler covered with blood. More blood spattered the wall. A pink paisley beanie lay crumpled in a corner. That was bloody too.

"Somebody clobbered Abigail Marks. Hit her two or three times. Split her fucking head open." Wankum shook his head in disgust. "If you did it, you have one chance to tell me, right now."

One of the detectives looked up at me and quickly looked away.

"I didn't do it."

"I saw what she wrote about you and your friend Davey."

"I don't care, and neither does he."

"I find that hard to believe."

I was sick of people I had known for half my life accusing me of murder. "I don't really care what you believe. I didn't do it. And I didn't kill Jules, either."

He frowned and turned to watch the detectives work.

"That's Jules' office?" I asked.

He nodded. "It would be just like her to see the light on and stick her fucking nose in." He emphasized the f-word, an escape valve for his anger, but it wasn't her he was mad at.

"Somebody was in his office? They broke in during the wake?"

He nodded. "Most times it's just asshole kids. They figure it's easy pickings. One year we had half a dozen cases, and I got this one family to cooperate. We put a couple of us in their house early in the morning. We waited when the family went to the funeral and surprised the assholes when they came in. Put an end to that crime wave pretty quick."

"This wasn't kids, though?"

He rolled his neck like a ballplayer loosening up, trying to ease the tension. "There was no vandalism, nobody pissed on the floor or anything, and they didn't take his CD player or his digital camera."

"So nothing's missing?"

"It looks like somebody went through his files. The secretary's on her way down."

"You don't think Abigail was the one who broke in?"

He shook his head, annoyed. "Just because you don't like her..." He let the thought trail away with a sigh. "She was at Town Hall for a zoning board hearing. I was there myself. My neighbor's trying to subdivide. Broke up an hour ago. She was probably walking home and saw somebody inside."

"How do you know when it happened?"

"Downtown foot patrol. At nine the door was locked. At ten it was hanging open."

"No break-in alarm?"

He looked away, and I guessed.

"Jules' keys."

Wankum sighed. "We hadn't gotten around to checking the key ring in his pocket. The one to the front door says 'Main Street' right on it, on a little piece of tape. The other one says 'Office.'"

"How do you know?"

"We found them here, on the floor."

"So the same person who broke into the office and hit Abigail is the one who killed him?"

Wankum didn't answer. He ran a hand over his face, then squared his shoulders like a man with a long night ahead. He made a choked little sound that might have started out as a laugh but turned into something like a sob.

"I had her for freshman English," he said. "I mean, what the fuck?"

"I know."

He coughed to clear the lump from his throat. "I've got to get to the hospital," he growled, retrieving his anger for fuel. He shooed me out the door and stopped by the trashcan at the curb to peel off his gloves.

"Did Elaine say why she never reported him missing?"

He tossed the gloves, then met my eye.

"Just that it wasn't the first time he hadn't come home lately."

"She wasn't worried?"

"Didn't seem like it, no. What's it to you, anyway?"

I shrugged. He stalked away without a word, jumped behind the wheel of an unmarked cruiser idling at the curb and gunned it away up Main Street, lights flashing in the front grill.

I looked around for Capt. Bob, but he was gone. The crowd had thinned out, and in the quiet of the late-night street, I could hear the jukebox back on in the bar & grill. "Yellow Submarine." I walked back up Main Street humming the chorus and got some strange looks until I noticed I was still wearing the gloves.

THIRTEEN

In the morning, getting dressed, I found the piece of paper Tammy Dukes had slipped me, a flier for her art opening at Foley's that night. Maybe she wanted me there because having a murder suspect in the house would up the hipness quotient. Or maybe I was being paranoid. I needed coffee.

The walls at Foley's were bare, waiting for Tammy to hang her work. Dreadlocks handled the register. I got my usual and stuffed my change into the tip cup. A hand-written sign on it said, *You're beautiful and talented!*

"You must be beat after last night," I said.

"By the time it was over and we cleaned up, I was too tired to party. At least I made it in this morning."

"Somebody didn't?"

"Ashley called in sick." Air quotes around "sick."

"How did Ashley meet Gareth?"

She snickered. "You know him?"

"He was there last night. They were arguing outside."

"She keeps saying she's going to break up with him, but some girls like bad boys. Even if they don't, like, bathe enough."

"How did she meet him? It doesn't seem like he belongs at Governor Willey or Montserrat."

"She met him at a dance at Willey last year. He was in the band or something. Ashley said he got her and her friends high." She backed away toward the smoking toaster, smiling naughtily. "I wonder why you're so interested in who Ashley's dating."

The booths were all filled, so I took my coffee and bagel to the counter. The Sox had won big last night, but I found it hard to concentrate on the newspaper. I had to worry whether the palsied old gent in the bucket hat to my right could maneuver his oversized cappuccino mug to his lips without emptying it in my lap. The real problem, though, was that I couldn't stop thinking about Jules and Abigail, and the ambulance rolling away up Main Street, the blood on the office carpet. Even "Zippy the Pinhead" couldn't hold my attention.

Outside, a cool breeze and the sun on the red brick buildings made the day seem bright and clean and new. I stepped off the curb in the middle of the block, and a yuppie mom in a Lexus SUV stopped short so I could cross. She gave me a smile anyway, a blonde with her baby in a car seat and a Labradoodle bouncing around in back. This close to Dock Square, Libertyporters were unyieldingly polite to strangers, even jaywalkers. It fit our self-image of an old-fashioned New England small town where everyone knew everyone else, an idyllic vision straight out of Norman Rockwell, but gay-friendly, with hybrid cars and flat-screen TVs and maybe a couple of joints in an Altoids tin tucked away in dad's workshop where the kids wouldn't find it. No wonder everyone wore Life Is Great T-shirts, because it was.

Of course, the farther we steered from the picturesque square and its flowerboxes, the more we tended to backslide. Among the supermarkets and gas stations out by the highway, we drove with the same short-tempered self-interest as any other harried suburbanites. Downtown, though, we were our best selves. If you got run over here, while you waited for the ambulance you could at least take comfort in the certainty that the driver was an out-of-towner.

I walked through the dank passage near Jules' office, an arched brick walkway where the skateboarders hung out at night when rain drove them off the benches on the Blacksmith Alley pedestrian mall. They'd left behind an empty schnapps bottle, a scattering of cigarette butts and the smell of urine. They loved to poke holes in that Norman Rockwell image. Merchants treated them as if they were the Manson Family, deluging the police with complaints and writing alarmist screeds to the Town Crier on The State Of Our Youth. As a former teen miscreant myself, I didn't find them particularly menacing. But I saw the worshipful way Zack looked at them, and I was bracing for the day he stopped wearing his skateboard helmet and started hanging out on the benches.

Asshole Gareth must have been a regular on the benches at some point. He could have known where Jules' office was and come straight here after he and Ashley argued at the wake. Maybe she was wrong, and he knew about her and Jules. Maybe he shot Jules and hit Abigail over the head. But why didn't he take Jules' wallet on Tuesday night? Why break into the office after Jules was dead? And was he smart enough to have grabbed *those two keys* off Jules' ring? It didn't add up.

Even if he was innocent, though, I could throw him under the bus, let him enjoy a night in jail and a professional interrogation by Wankum. He deserved that much for hassling Jimmy and Ashley and generally being a little scumbag.

The passage opened to the pedestrian mall with its playground and fountain. In tourist season, a rotating roster of street performers would fill the air with harp glissandos, sea chanteys and juggler's clubs. I hadn't been desperate enough to bring my guitar there yet, but supposedly you could make good money on a sunny summer weekend.

At the moment, though, I was after information.

"Look who's here," Velma, my barber, said when I walked into her shop. "Better hide your scissors. He's dangerous."

"Oooh," her co-worker said, "I'm scared."

"Very funny, ladies."

I took one of the chairs along the opposite wall and watched the kids from the Montessori school next door racing to the playground for morning recess. The jungle gym stood on a square of a strange, spongy material made from recycled plastic. When the kids fell on it, they bounced right back up, without pain or tears. Song fodder for the children's album I'd mulled when Zack was younger. Probably would have been a big hit with the yuppie moms, but I'd never get around to it now.

Velma was a tiny blonde wearing stylish red-framed eyeglasses and a blue barber's smock. She sang along with the radio under her breath as she made invisible adjustments to the crewcut of a pixie-ish, white-haired farmer in a plaid shirt and jeans. He was one of Davey's many uncles, one of the last guys around who still cut marsh hay. He giggled like a kid as she gave him an oddly maternal whisk-brooming with a final chuck under the chin. He looked me up and down suspiciously before he left. Me staring back didn't bother him one bit.

"You're next, killer." Velma waved me into the chair and draped me with a cloth. She grabbed at my locks with a grimace. "It's been too long."

"I've been neglecting you," I admitted.

"You've been neglecting *yourself*," she said sternly, running a comb through my hair perhaps more vigorously than strictly necessary. "You should have come in here before the big meeting the other night. You looked like crap up there."

"Can you forgive me?"

"Depends. Did you do it?"

Her sidekick snickered.

"If I had a dollar for everyone who asked that, I could afford a shave too."

"OK, it's not funny," Velma said as she picked up her scissors. "What happened to Jules shouldn't happen to anybody. You got a problem with somebody, you work it out, you take 'em to court, whatever. You don't shoot 'em."

"Have you heard about Abigail?"

"I know! What the hell is going on in this town?"

Of course she'd heard. Everyone came to Velma's. She heard every joke the day it arrived in town, got the inside scoop on every real estate deal and criminal case. She could find you votes, sell your raffle tickets, tell you who to call at City Hall. Each person that she helped passed along their own nuggets of information in turn. She was Switzerland on Blacksmith Alley, although faster with the patter than the Swiss.

"What's the latest from the hospital?" I asked.

"She's still unconscious. Critical but stable." She switched the scissors for the clippers. "Maybe she'll wake up and tell the police who hit her. It's got to be the same person who shot Jules, don't you think?"

"Probably so."

"Are you going to the memorial service?"

"If you finish in time." I snuck a hand out from under the sheet to scratch my chin. "You know anybody who wanted to shoot Jules?"

"The only ones I can think of are you and your friend Davey."

"Thanks a bunch. It wasn't us. I think it had something to do with his business."

She met my eye in the mirror. "I thought you were a singer, not a detective."

"I am playing the Rum House Saturday night. I hope you'll come."

"If you're lucky." Back to the scissors. Snip, snip. "Where'd you get this booboo on your forehead?"

"Shimmy Jimmy ran me over with his bike a couple of days ago." I said it before I remembered that it was supposed to be a secret.

"You're lucky to be alive. He's a big boy."

"Kind of old for a boy. Exactly what happened to him, anyway? I was just a kid."

"He hit a pole on the causeway coming back from the island, hammered, going about a hundred in his Trans Am." She frowned and shook her head. "The car was torn clear in two. I remember the picture on the front page of the paper. The engine was sitting in the middle of the road."

"Amazing he wasn't killed."

"I'm just glad he didn't kill somebody else. The drunks always live, have you noticed? Some boozed-up idiot plows into a family of five and they all die and all he gets is a scratch. It's not fair."

"Jimmy got more than a scratch."

"He wasn't wearing his seat belt, and he had the T-top open. He was thrown right out of the car. You or I would have been in pieces. But he landed in the nice soft marsh." She wrinkled her nose as if she'd smelled something disagreeable. Snip, snip. "It's terrible to say, but he might have been better off the other way. His father died a few weeks later, coronary. Everyone said it was a broken heart over what happened to his son. Jimmy was still in a coma. He didn't wake up for weeks. Think about his poor mother. So many people got hurt by that one accident. It's so stupid. Why'd he have to drink like that and then get behind the wheel?"

"Kids do stupid things."

Velma nodded. "For sure. He wasn't the first one to go out to the island and get shitfaced, then crack up his car coming home. People have been doing that since the Model T."

"Did they ever find out where he was drinking?"

"Not as far as I ever heard. What happens on the island, stays on the island. Always been that way."

The bells tied to the door handle jingled. The two guys who were working on the house next to Jimmy's came in, both of them in boots and dirty jeans, sprinkled with sawdust and carrying coffees in go cups. We exchanged wary nods via the mirror and they sat down to wait. While she finished my haircut, Velma asked Don about his little girl's school play and Rich about his mother's chemotherapy.

I was opening the door to leave when she came up next to me and reached for the knob. "Let me get that for you, hon. There's a trick to it." She stepped outside with me, closing the door behind her. "What you said, about Jules' business? You might be right. I heard he made a big scene about money down at the Schooner in Ipswich last week."

"So?"

She looked at me over her glasses. "You don't know who owns the Schooner, do you?"

"Who?"

"Greg Argent."

Formerly known as Guido Argento, North Shore Mafia scion and my successor in Elaine's bed.

"Yikes."

"You got that right."

The Paul Revere bell in the steeple of the Unitarian Church on Parker Street tolled in a funeral cadence as I approached. Davey waited for me on the sidewalk, fidgeting in his ill-fitting brown suit. Neither one of us wanted to go in, but we let the crowd sweep us up the steps.

Emmitt and others who had been at the wake looked more wounded than grief-stricken.

Even Amy had a pale sheen as she walked arm-in-arm with the headmaster. He held his chin in the air, as if his very presence increased the solemnity of the occasion. I wondered how he'd gotten out of attending the wake: Taking care of Zack, maybe? They both pretended not to see me.

The sanctuary was a white-on-white marvel of architectural simplicity and harmony that has not been equaled in the two centuries since it was built. Tall windows filled the space with glorious soft light. Still, Davey and I chose a pew near the back, a schoolboy reflex.

"Nice haircut," he said.

"Nice suit."

The organist in the balcony started up, and Davey put a finger to his lips. "No bullshit during church."

To my surprise, he seemed to mean it, studying the program through his reading glasses and opening the hymnal to the appropriate page ahead of time. He sang loudly in a lovely baritone that I'd never heard in all the time I'd known him.

Rev. Molly's Subaru wagon always had a pair of mountain bikes or kayaks on top. I usually saw her in spandex and a bike helmet, or a dry suit and life vest. It was strange to find her in a black robe, delicate oval eyeglasses and simple pearl earrings. She took the lectern with a calm, certain expression. She had signed the petition against the hotel, but that didn't stop her from delivering a fine homily about Jules' commitment to our community and his tireless involvement in civic enterprise.

Mayor Echo followed her to the microphone, ashen from some unquantifiable combination of sorrow and hangover. I took his weepy emphasis on the loss of Jules' "vision for our community" as mourning for his shiny new hotel.

Jules' son walked purposefully up onto the altar, dapper in blue blazer and grey slacks. Brow furrowed, he recited from memory a Robert Frost poem that he said was his father's favorite, one they had often read together. I had not thought of Jules as a guy who took the road less traveled, but now the image of him sitting on the edge of the bed, reading to his son just before lights out, brought a lump to my throat. The boy's solemn performance left Velma, Amy, Marcy and most of the other women in tears. I couldn't see Elaine then, but when she went up the aisle at the end, holding her daughter's hand, she dabbed her eyes with a handkerchief. Ora Buffem walked just behind, carrying both their purses. Her eyes were dry but she glanced up from the floor only once, to meet mine, as if she'd sensed me watching. Her look said she was still making up her mind about me.

Davey and I stood and waited for the rest of the procession to pass, feeling the relief that always accompanies the recessional.

"Nice service," he said outside, blinking in the sun. "But where was Jules?"

"The cops haven't released the body. Amy says Elaine is going to spread his ashes on the island later."

"You're sure in the know. How's the person-of-interest racket going?"

"People still look at me like I did it."

"Wankum sent one of his boys to the bar last night to see if I could have been the one who whacked Abigail over the head. It was the first time emceeing a drunk-chick karaoke contest ever seemed like a good use of my time."

"It's kind of depressing. I wish it was over."

"Just think of your share of the door on Saturday night," he said. "After that, you can be as innocent as you want."

"I suppose."

"You'll be off the hook anyway if they catch the guy who did it."

"Don't you mean when? *When* they catch the guy?"

"There are no guarantees in this world. Just ask Jules' kid."

If Davey was getting deep on me, I was really in trouble.

There was one call I'd been putting off. When I got home, I dialed from memory. The phone number hadn't changed in the twenty-odd years I'd been calling it, and probably a lot longer.

"Folktime Productions."

"Sol, it's Bax."

"Hey kid, how are you? I hear you've had some excitement up there."

"Everything's OK, Sol. How are you?"

This led to a predictable litany of ailments from a lifelong smoker who could still be found enjoying a martini at Charlie's most days around five. "But enough of my bullshit, what are we doing about getting you some gigs?"

"I hear Dormer Records is interested in me."

Sol Greenspan, my agent, was a union organizer's son from Gary, Indiana, who somehow ended up running a coffeehouse in Harvard Square in the late '50s and early '60s. He knew Baez and Dylan and the rest, yet managed to avoid getting rich. He was eighty-one now and still operating out of the same office, a warren of tiny, insanely cluttered rooms three flights up in one of the last un-gentrified buildings in Harvard Square. Though we maintained the face-saving fiction that he was still hard at work, I did most of my own booking.

"If you sign with Dormer, my friend, it's all bouquets and blowjobs from here on out. From what I hear, these interniks who bought the place are spending like drunken sailors." I guess interniks were like Bolsheviks to him. "Lord knows anyone on that label deserves a payday after what they've been through."

He told me about Dormer's founder, a Harvard philosophy major who dropped out under the influence of Beat literature and started the label in his attic apartment off Mt. Auburn Street, hence the name. "A few of my artists signed with him and went right from hoot night at Club 47 to Newport. It was a sweet ride back then, kid, and Benedict was a good guy. Paid his artists before he paid himself." Sol chuckled as if that was a mistake he'd never made.

"He was an alkie, though, and he ended up owing money to a lot of people. Then Dylan hit and suddenly the big labels were paying his artists top dollar to leave him in the lurch. And of course the lawyers got into it." I heard Sol hawk and spit, probably into his trashcan. "He died of cirrhosis in the Seventies, a bunch of shit still pending. Eventually one of the major labels came in and snapped up the assets at fire-sale prices. Cocksuckers. From the mid-Eighties on, they bled Dormer for profits from CD reissues and stiffed the artists. I don't know what these Interniks got when they bought it. But I know they've got money.

"Sonofabitch, Bax, if we sign on with them it would be the greatest goddamn thing for both of us. I ain't getting any younger, I don't need to tell you. I'm supposed to give my papers to BU, and maybe I could hire someone to come in and clean out this dump, get everything organized in time for my funeral. I wouldn't mind going out on a high note."

"I'm all for that, Sol, because I'm not cleaning up after you," I said, drawing a raspy laugh. "So what have you heard from them, anyway?"

"From who?"

"Dormer. Their rep was here Wednesday."

Silence on the other end, then an appreciative cackle. "Well, that's a rotten goddamn maneuver. Making an end run around the old man. Trying to cut me out of my share."

"They didn't talk to you?"

"Not a word. I don't wanna sound discouraging, but nobody's asked me shit about you in months. I was surprised, I did get a call last week from ASCAP or maybe it was BMI, checking on your signing status."

"Was it a woman who called?"

"Young thing, yeah. I have her name written down around here somewhere." I heard papers shifting, a stack falling to the floor, curses and coughing. "I can't lay hands on it right now, but I'll call you as soon as it jumps out of this goddamn pile. You think that was Dormer, pulling a fast one?"

"Maybe, Sol, but it's fine, don't worry about it."

"You want me to call those motherfuckers and straighten 'em out on who they're supposed to be dealing with?"

"Why don't you let me work them for a few days, see what they're up to. Then when it comes time to actually negotiate, I'll bring in the hammer."

"That's my boy! I'll do some research, be loaded for bear when they walk in! By August you'll be back at Newport, main stage!"

"Your lips to God's ears, Sol."

"There is no God, you know that," Sol said, coughing again. "Opiate of the masses and whatnot."

I was disappointed that Jane had lied to me. I'd suspected as much, and that was why I'd put off calling Sol. She must have heard about the murder on the news, recognized my name, and called him under a pretext to see if I was signed anywhere. Hearing I was free and clear, she headed for Libertyport. Pretty craven, although not the worst music-business gambit I'd ever heard about, not by a long shot.

"Hey, Sol, I'm playing the Rum House on Saturday night."

"Ah, jeez, kid, you can't keep making these deals on your own, those club owners will screw you blind."

"Davey's my friend, Sol, he wouldn't do that. And if I was talking to anybody else, I'd call you in, Sol, you know that."

"All right, Bax, whatever you say. Just make sure I get my cut, will ya?"

Guido Argento and I both went to the University of Massachusetts – Amherst. When I was an anonymous freshman, he was a senior hockey star, and I knew about him mostly from the school paper. Everyone knew that his father was the frequently indicted, never-convicted Danvers crime figure Carmine Argento, but no one mentioned it. I always wondered, how hard would you check a guy in the corner if you knew his dad was in the mob?

I dropped out after hitting the Top Ten that spring, while he graduated with a degree in business administration. Both North Shore boys, we met when Elaine took me to a party at someone's beach house. It turned out we ran in the same circles. No great shock the former jock was dealing weed, given his family. After I told him I went to UMass, he treated me like an old friend. Then Elaine told me she was breaking up with me to be with him. He came up to me in the Rum House a week later, looking concerned, and said, "Are we cool?" I told him I guessed we were, and in the manner of the young and stupid, we did shots to prove it. Elaine broke up with him, too, before long, and that was the last I saw of him until he turned up in Ipswich with a new name and a new career.

I searched the Internet and found a dozen articles about him in area newspapers, all under the name Greg Argent. Most recounted his exploits in a local amateur hockey league for guys in their thirties and forties. Turned out he was a Governor Willey Academy alum who had led his team to the regionals his senior year. In photos, he still looked handsome and fit, although his hair was now short and steely grey. A couple of articles focused on the restaurant. I didn't find any that mentioned his father, or the name change.

Next I searched for the old man and got three thousand results. According to the Globe and the Herald, Carmine had run a crew that specialized in gambling and loan-sharking on the North Shore. I wondered if he'd paid his son's UMass tuition with a shopping bag full of small bills. He hadn't been directly connected to a murder since the '60s, but a few competitors had "dropped out of sight." He'd apparently controlled two dozen sports bars as well as most of the trash-hauling business on the North Shore, but three years ago he'd died in his sleep at the federal prison at Danbury, Conn., where he was serving seven to twelve for bid-rigging. The shrunken old man in the most recent photos bore little resemblance to his son, but one mug shot from the Seventies showed Carmine with a sharp jaw line, cold eyes and a Bruins jacket. Apparently he had passed on his love for hockey. The question was, what else?

I got out the phone book and called The Schooner. I asked the cheery reservationist to tell Greg that his old friend Baxter would be dropping by.

"I'm sure he'll be excited to see you again!" She sounded like she actually believed it.

FOURTEEN

The Schooner anchored one end of a small strip mall in Ipswich. Its neighbors were a gourmet deli, a dress shop and a garden or-
naments boutique. The restaurant décor was masculine leather and dark
wood, but the Friday lunch crowd was mostly older women. Their expensive, conservative clothes marked them as residents of the horsey
precincts of neighboring Hamilton and Wenham. Most dined with
girlfriends, and shopping bags clogged the aisles. One elderly matron
giggled at the bons mots flowing from the mouth of an aging game-
show-host type wearing a blazer and an ascot, along with a spray-on
tan and one of the worst toupees I'd ever seen. He looked like the em-
cee in hell.

I ordered a pint of Ipswich in the windowless bar off the entry
and watched the midday news with the hulking, silent bartender. I was
his only customer, although the waitresses came in frequently with or-
ders for white wine and Cosmos for the dining room. He wore a black
vest with a white shirt that barely contained his enormous neck. With
his hook nose and five o'clock shadow, he looked like mob muscle
right off the front page of the Herald, but he showed a delicate touch
washing and drying the stemware. A metal nametag identified him,
predictably, as Lou.

"It's a beautiful day," Greg Argent said, coming up behind me.
"Why are you sitting in this cave?"

"It's where the beer is."

"I hear that." He signaled Lou for two more. He wore grey
dress slacks and a black cashmere pullover. His black tasseled loafers
shone, as did his watch and wedding ring.

"So it's Greg now?" I figured, get it out of the way at the beginning.

"Yeah, the name change seemed like a way to make a break with the whole family thing. My dad wasn't happy about it, but..." Greg shrugged.

He didn't say *God rest his soul* or anything, so I didn't feel I had to offer condolences.

"So hey, how the hell are you?" he said. "I keep seeing in the paper that you're playing somewhere around, and I always mean to go, but I never get out of here in time. How's the music biz?"

"I do all right."

"Between the downloading and the record companies, it must be hard to make a buck."

"I make most of my money playing live now. No more gold records."

"But you're not starving."

"Ask me a week from now."

"I book some music in here, Friday and Saturday nights. Usually just a piano player, playing 'Feelings' and crap like that. It's not really your audience. But maybe we could try it sometime. Put up a few fliers, offer a beer special, I bet we'd get a crowd."

"Sounds great." And it would never happen.

A table was already set for us outside under a patio heater. We were the only diners braving the light breeze. Greg insisted that I take the seat with the view out over lawns and gardens to salt marsh. It was almost low tide, and a great blue heron fished in a shallow channel that snaked through the marsh. It stalked its prey from atop its long, sticklike legs, then struck.

"Pretty," I said.

"Thanks. We've had a few weddings under the arbor. Maybe one of my girls, someday."

We both took out our wallets and showed off pictures of our kids. Hey, he started it.

"They're getting big," he said. "It's been a long time, you and me."

Lou appeared, and we ordered burgers. Blue cheese, bacon and caramelized onions on mine. I figured a murder suspect had to eat like every meal could be his last.

"How'd you end up in the restaurant business?" I asked.

"I went up to Canada and played minor league hockey for a couple of years, hoping for my big break. That's why I left town." I thought getting dumped by Elaine had driven him away, but never mind. "What I didn't know was that I was already way too old. The kids going to the pros were straight out of high school. I had some fun, but it was a dead end. I came back here with no plans and got into coke. I was supposed to be dealing but...you know how that goes. It took me about a year to completely fuck it up. My old man had to settle some debts for me."

I was surprised he'd say it right out like that. It made me remember why I'd liked him.

"After I cleaned up, I changed my name, got my real estate license. And after I flipped a few restaurants, I figured out this is what I really like. Hospitality. It's nice, you know? Feeding people. Tough sometimes, but good tough."

"I saw a picture in the paper, you still play hockey."

"Yeah, but the funny thing is, my youngest, Susie, she's the star in the family." He lit up at her name. "She's only a sophomore at Governor Willey, but she was all-state last year."

"No kidding. Congratulations." I wondered how hard you'd check a girl in the corner if ...

"How's Zack?"

"Twelve going on thirty. He's at Willey too, in the junior high. No jock, but he's a good kid."

"I notice neither one of us has mentioned our lovely brides. At least yours got remarried, so no alimony. Here's to divorce."

I wondered how he knew so much about me and Amy. Did he make some calls after the girl at the front desk told him I was coming? What else did he know?

"So, I don't figure you dropped by after all this time just for a social call."

"Not exactly."

"I hope you're not looking for weed, because I've been out of that business for a very long time." His amusement seemed genuine.

"I'm pretty well behaved myself."

"Listen to us. Couple old fucks. Before long it's the early-bird special and *let me tell you about my grandkids*."

"Maybe that's not so bad. You heard what happened to Jules?"

"Yeah. It's terrible." He seemed sincere, though not especially moved.

"I was just at the memorial service. He's got kids, too."

"They figure out who did it?"

I shook my head. Took a deep breath. "I heard he was down here to see you a few days ago."

Greg had picked up his glass but now he set it down and looked me in the eye. "You think I had something to do with what happened to him? Just because of my dad?"

"Not at all. But he was in some sort of fix. I thought maybe you might know what was going on with him."

He shook his head disgustedly, stared off into the distance. "Did Elaine send you?"

"Why would she?"

"I don't know," he admitted. He drained his beer and banged the glass down on the table, looking around for service. "I never said sorry for stealing her from you."

"I got over her."

"I barely did. She was something. I hardly knew Jules, except as the lucky prick who ended up married to her. Didn't see them for years. Then I ran into them maybe six months ago at the country club down here, some charity deal. She still looked great. I had a couple of drinks with them. Not too awkward. So then like, a week and a half ago, out of the blue, he calls me, asks if we can meet. I figured he wanted to sell me a table for the next benefit, or maybe he wanted to have it here. I could use the business, so I said sure."

He paused while Lou served our burgers, then held out his empty glass. Lou took it without a word, put it on his empty tray and walked away brusquely. There was something subtly off in their relationship. Lou wasn't as deferential as you would expect.

"Jules got here around seven. Reeking of gin. Squirrelly as all hell, looking around like someone's spying on him. Asks if we can go back in my office. And we get in there, he closes the door behind us, starts hitting me up to invest with him. Talks about his track record and how he's got nine million under management, real estate trusts, blah blah blah. I'm thinking this is messed up, guy comes by my place at night, half in the bag, and wants me to hand my kids' college fund to him? That's pretty much not gonna happen. So after about five minutes I stop him and say, hey, my money's all invested and I don't really know you from Adam anyway."

"How'd he take it?"

"He acted all disappointed, but I could see he was kind of expecting it, too. And then he gets down to the real reason he came." He paused, shook his head. "Says he's in trouble and he thought I might know someone who could help him out. He needs to borrow fifty grand ASAP, and he can't go to a bank."

Greg had been warming up to his tale, but now that it had veered back to his family business, he looked uncomfortable and picked up his burger. Lou brought more beers and left without a word.

"So you told him no."

"Of course I told him no. Like I said, I'm totally legit. Always have been, except for dope when we were kids, and even then, that was mostly just the friends-and-family plan. I had my little coke adventure, but since I got kids, I'm Mr. Clean."

"What did he say?"

"Asshole argued with me. Said I didn't have to pretend with him. Said he knew I was connected, I must be able to put him in touch with a shark. Made some crack about how since we'd both been screwed by Elaine, we ought to help each other out. It was *not* cool."

"Why'd he need the money?"

"Claimed that he was having a temporary cash flow problem, but we all know what that means. His business was going down the tubes, which surprised me since I been reading in the paper about that hotel he was trying to build. I didn't exactly ask him for details. I just wanted to get him out of there. I had to leave him for a couple of minutes to settle some jihad between the cooks, and I come back, he's out in the bar, hitting up a couple of my best customers. Said he could tell they were rich, and could they lend him fifty grand, since I wouldn't."

"What did you do?"

"I comped their dinner. Say, how's your burger?"

"It's great. I meant, what did you do about Jules."

"I know what you meant. I dragged his ass out of there as quietly as I could, got his keys from the valet and drove him home, had the kid follow us in my car. What's it take, twenty minutes? By the time we got there, he'd been through The Five Stages of Being Fucked Up. He was laughing, then we were best buddies, and then he was yelling at me for being a bastard. Then he got weepy and apologized, and then he passed out."

"Fun ride."

"I felt like I was back at ZooMass after some kegger. He was one pathetic mess. Said he was going to lose his business, his home, even his wife. Said he was sorry for thinking I was bent, then asked me if I had the money to lend him myself. A personal loan. He was begging, basically. But I told him I don't have it, which is true. Between my divorce and the economy, I'm just hanging on myself." Greg took an especially deep drink of his beer.

"How did Elaine act when you got him home?"

"You know her, cool as a cucumber. Said hello like she was expecting me. Helped me get him up to bed."

"Did you tell her what happened?"

He nodded. "She sort of guessed, but she looked appalled when I told her how it went. Apologized up and down. Offered me a nightcap, but I figured that was the last thing any of us needed, me hanging around there. So we talked for a few minutes, and I split, rode back here with the kid."

Lou returned then, walking fast, and bent over to whisper in Greg's ear. Greg swore softly.

"Jesus. Tell him I said Monday, and I meant Monday. Just tell him that. Tell him I need the weekend. And tell him not to call me again."

Lou nodded once and walked back inside.

"Fucking restaurant business," Greg said, reaching for his glass.

FIFTEEN

When I got home, I left the car running in the driveway and sprinted up to the third floor. Well, actually I sprinted to the second floor and trudged panting up the stairs to the third, sparklies whirling ominously in the corners of my vision. Maybe that was the three beers at lunch or the bottle I'd taken to the side of the head yesterday, or a combination of all the injuries of the past week, self-inflicted and otherwise. Or maybe I was more out of shape than I wanted to admit.

The low-ceilinged rooms originally intended for servants or children now served as a sort of career graveyard, the ruins of a lost civilization that might provide dissertation fodder for some pop-culture archaeologist of the future. Amid peeling paint and dust bunnies rested boxes of unanswered fan club letters from 1985, two blown amplifiers that I couldn't afford to have rebuilt, a filing cabinet of increasingly vitriolic correspondence with record companies, and a complimentary case of vanity guitar picks with my name misspelled in the usual fashion (*Mac*Lean).

Footsteps in the dust showed slightly more traffic to the room where I warehoused the remaining copies of my three indie albums. I grabbed a CD from each stack and bounded back down the stairs, slightly dizzy from lack of oxygen, trying not to wonder why I was so eager to please.

I saw Jimmy again, riding toward town near the ballfields, and he pretended not to see me. Fine. I was doing everything I could for him, but there was no point in expecting gratitude.

The old Chain Bridge carried traffic from Libertyport to Osprey Island; a second, newer span passed it on to the town of Seabury on the far bank. The road cut the island in half. On the downriver side was a wooded park, a popular spot for bird watching. A handful of cars occupied the small dirt parking lot. Across the road, on the upriver side, the vacant mansion I'd once considered buying awaited renovation into condos. The fenced property dropped off steeply to the water. Ora Buffem's house was outside the fence, shoehorned onto a tiny patch of land by the Seabury bridge. The tiny blue-grey Cape was very old, its frame sagging at an unsettling angle. But then, there were lots of houses in town that sagged like that and were still standing after two centuries. Some things survived a long time here, even when they shouldn't. There were lilac bushes at the corners and pots of flowers around the front step. I parked behind an old Camry in the gravel driveway and sat for a moment, the sun in my face, wondering what the hell I was doing.

I'd had nowhere near enough beers to find the poet attractive. She was shapeless and dour, her mouth set in a perpetual frown. Analyzing my feelings as well as I could, given the sun and my blood-alcohol level, I concluded that I wanted her professional approval. She was a real artist, university-sanctioned and publisher-approved. She'd read at the Kennedy Center. I'd sold out the Troubadour and the Bottom Line, but that was half a lifetime ago. Validation was hard to come by these days. I just wanted her to say that I was good. That "I only listen to classical music" stuff just made this desire more ardent.

So I was a pathetic, needy asshole. But that didn't stop me from knocking on the front door with the three CDs clasped behind my back, the way another guy might have brought a surprise bouquet. She was going to be surprised, all right.

When she opened the door, she was blotting sweat from her forehead with a balled-up handkerchief, and one or two locks of hair were loose from her bun.

"Oh, hello," she said distractedly, as if still thinking about whatever project I'd interrupted. She blinked a couple of times, then focused on my face with a polite but rather suspicious expression.

"How are you?"

"As well as I could be on a day that began with a funeral."

"It was a nice service, don't you think? The reading, Jules' son."

"It was." For a second it looked as if she might cry behind those big, round glasses. Then she looked around at the sunny summer day and took a deep breath and got it under control. "So what brings you here? Is there something I can do for you?"

"Actually, I brought you these."

I pushed the CDs at her like a love-struck sixth-grader. She hesitated for just a second before taking them.

"Oh, thank you! These are your albums."

"Yes they are. This is a lot easier than finding my stuff online, trust me." Suddenly I regretted this entire embarrassing errand. What a schmuck. At least I hadn't brought my guitar.

"What a nice gesture."

"Well, listen to them before you say that."

"Don't be silly. I'll put one on right now. Would you like a cup of tea?"

"Why not?"

I followed her inside. The floors were original wide-board pine, the ceilings low. We went through the living room, which was decorated in a mix of furniture from various decades, none recent. The walls were covered with family photos and pen-and-ink sketches of local landmarks. Shelves and tabletops held a disturbing amount of bric-a-brac devoted to black Labrador retrievers. A particularly large member of that species was featured in many of the photos, usually standing by the side of an older woman who carried Ora Buffem's dour features on the chassis of an NBA power forward.

"Is this your aunt?" The woman and dog posed formally on the lawn out back, the woman hunch-shouldered in a cape and beret, the dog sitting at her knee.

"Yes. Her name was Devorah, after an Old Testament judge."

"Your name is derived from hers?"

"Yes, although everyone called her Dee."

"A handsome woman."

"That's usually the word people use," Ora said, walking on so I couldn't see her expression. The kitchen was the sunniest room in the house. "The dog's name was Max."

"Your aunt liked him a lot."

"I did too. I spent many happy weekends here as a girl. Whenever my parents were going to stay out late, or go out of town, I would spend the night with Aunt Dee and Max."

"She sent you to Smith?"

"My father didn't make that much even as the head of payroll. He would have sent me to college, certainly, but probably a state school. Aunt Dee sent me to Governor Willey for my senior year and then on to her alma mater."

"I would have hated to miss graduating with my class."

"Yes, many people would. Please, have a seat. Would you like Earl Grey, or perhaps an Oolong?"

"Earl Grey is fine." I hate tea.

I sat at a table that held a bunch of lilacs in a canning jar of water. The scent reminded me of Abigail. On the table was a stack of poems in typescript, with a ballpoint pen on top.

"You're writing? I didn't mean to interrupt."

"I'm grading," she said from the stove, "so I'm glad for any interruption."

Which wasn't quite the same as being glad to see me. "I feel the same way about practicing my guitar," I said. "I'd rather vacuum."

"Yes, it's amazing how much of an artist's life seems to be sheer drudgery."

"I'd always thought I was just lazy."

There was a Bose radio/CD player on the counter next to the old metal breadbox, which was patterned with black Labs romping and playing. She turned it on and unwrapped one of my CDs. "If we had no flaws, there'd be no reason for art."

"What is writing like for you?"

"It tends to dredge things up," she said.

My voice came out of the speakers then, the mock flight-attendant announcement that began the title track of "Please Remain Seated Until My Career Comes To A Complete Stop." She sat opposite me and cocked her head as I welcomed my listeners aboard, promising them headphones and a pillow, a choice of cocktails and a packet of peanuts. I was suddenly mortified by the moronic obviousness of the bit. We'll be taking off in a few seconds, but until then, please keep your seatbelts fastened and your tray tables in the upright position...

The smile on Ora Buffem's face was like the one I forced out when Davey told an ethnic joke. But when my vocal started, she slid the paper insert out of the jewel case so she could read along.

> *It's been a long December*
> *And America loves the Counting Crows*
> *I like their melodies, sometimes*
> *But their words are too much on-the-nose*

"I once caught a freshman composition student handing in a Counting Crows lyric as his own work," she said. "I gave him a C, and that was before I found out he'd plagiarized it."

"When I wrote this, my last record hadn't sold very well, and they were on top of the charts. Of course, this album did worse than the one before."

"It sold more than my last book, I expect."

"I wouldn't be so sure."

> *I've been rock and pop and folk*
> *And everything in between*
> *I've even tried to sing real high*
> *Like Freddie Mercury of Queen*

She tipped her head back, listening closely. Which was what I wanted, right? But hearing my songs in this setting seemed to highlight their flaws. I crammed too many syllables into some lines and not enough into others, singing in a rushed yelp that was either my signature sound or the ultimate expression of just how much I sucked.

I made conversation to distract her from my vocal shortcomings.

"You were friends with Elaine in high school?"

"Sort of. Remember, my father worked for her father," Ora said. "Everyone knew everyone else here then. Not like now. Gordon Electrical was one of the first plants in the industrial park, when it was still all farms out that way. The road wasn't even paved until I was in junior high." Now a steady stream of commuters used it as a shortcut to the interstate on the way to Boston.

"What was she like back then?"

"Elaine?" Her eyelashes fluttered behind the big round glasses. "She was the most popular of the popular girls. We didn't exactly run in the same social circles. She was nicer to me than she had to be. She said hi to me in the halls and so forth. But her clique wouldn't have me. Mostly I saw her when there was some sort of function involving the company."

I bet she was downplaying the viciousness of the snobbery involved. It was easy to imagine why she'd been happy to transfer to Governor Willey.

"Did you know Jules back then?"

She shrugged her narrow shoulders. "I knew who he was. I knew all the popular kids, but I was a year behind them, and I wasn't exactly popular myself. We artistic types don't always fit in well in high school."

"Or anywhere else."

I still love a standing ovation
But I'll never make it to the top
So thank you very much,
But please remain seated
Until my career comes to a complete stop.

SIXTEEN

The typical Libertyport School painting was a soft-focus rendering of what always seemed to be the exact same stretch of salt marsh, where a gently curving tidal creek mirrored the sunset. Often there was a heron posing with one leg cocked, maybe the same one I'd seen at lunch. Dude got around.

Despite the bucolic images, locals approached gallery events with the same objectives as your big-city hipsters: Gossip and free drinks. Plates of cheese and crackers sat on the marble counter at Foley's, next to a box of Chardonnay and a two-liter Diet Coke. The night-shift kid at the newsstand gazed over at this abundance wistfully, unable to abandon his cash register.

"So glad you could make it," Tammy Dukes said, air-kissing my cheek. "I get so nervous. It's nice to have familiar faces."

She fought her nerves with quick sips from a plastic cup of wine. In truth, the handful of people wandering around the back of the restaurant were all familiar – artists and neighbors, Mayor Echo and Mrs. Echo – but I knew what she meant. Making art of any kind meant putting yourself out there, whether it was exhibiting your paintings in a coffee shop or dropping off CDs to a poet who probably couldn't have cared less. You had to believe in yourself, or else drink a lot. I poured myself a generous portion of box wine.

Despite her surf-bunny name, Tammy was a formidable woman, tall with large dark eyes, her black hair woven into a waist-length braid down her back. She wore faded jeans and a grey rag-wool serape from one of the boutiques on the square, and she came heavily armored with silver and turquoise jewelry. She moved to town with her first husband right after college, and those of us who knew her then still called her "Tammy" when we ran into her at the supermarket. But at some point in the last twenty years she'd started signing her paintings with her given name, and that was how she introduced herself these days, with the emphasis on the middle syllable, Ta-*mar*-a, so much more exotic and arty.

"I hope you like the new stuff," she said. "It's something different for me. I projected photos right onto the canvas and painted without sketching or anything. It made me feel like I was tapping directly into the past."

She shivered, all goosebumpy at the memory, and drank more wine.

"Where did you get the images?"

"The Town Crier, the historical society, the library. I must have looked at five hundred pictures. This town has more goddamn history than you can shake a stick at."

This was the Tammy I remembered from our twenties, a bawdy sort who always wanted to dance after her first husband, an alcoholic sculptor-carpenter, passed out. Her second husband was a humorless engineer who didn't socialize with us artsy types. They had one child, a sweet, artistic boy who I'd last seen melting toy soldiers on the hearth with Zack.

"Where's Neil?"

"Waiting for a plane home from Cleveland. He called my cell from the gate. Some asshole ran through security and didn't stop, so now the whole flight has to get re-scanned or something. Another weekend blown to hell."

"At least you're here, and not in an airport hotel in Cleveland."

"Amen to that."

"Are you Tamara?" asked the female half of a well-dressed older couple standing tentatively by the door.

"Collectors, sorry," Tammy whispered. She spun toward them, summoning a welcoming grin learned at her part-time real estate job. "It's Ta-*mar*-a. So nice to meet you!"

Abandoned, I stuffed a crostini in my mouth and wandered to the back, where her paintings loomed over the empty booths. The largest copied a well-known Town Crier photo of Main Street after a blizzard. The tailfins on the half-buried cars dated the moment to the early '60s. The painting was black and white like the photograph, except that Tammy had rendered the red and green neon lettering of the Foley's sign in color. In other pictures, a scrum of smiling '50s teenagers downed burgers and Cokes at the counter here, and JFK made his famous visit to the Rum House. Every painting featured a single splash of bright color – the red Coca-Cola cooler behind the lunch counter, Kennedy's smiling face – like a flashlight beam peering into the black-and-white past. These flashes of pigment gave meaning to the collection's otherwise generic title, "Illuminations." They also reminded me of bad Eighties dorm-poster art. Price tags ranged from $300 to $1,200 depending on size, steep for a Foley's exhibit.

Mayor Echo and his wife moved down the line, debating the dates the original photos were taken. "Do you like them?" he asked me.

Looking at him made me feel devilish. "I think they're really, really good."

"Yes, they really are." Wine in hand, tie loosened, he looked haler than he had at the memorial service. "In fact, they're excellent."

"I definitely want to support the artist."

"Yes, yes, it's important to show that we're behind her."

"I'm thinking of buying one of the larger ones," I said.

"Yes, I'm also-" he said automatically, then blanched. "I'm sorry, what?"

"I think community leaders like us have to support the arts locally."

"Well, yes, of course, we should-"

"And that means putting our money where our mouth is, don't you agree?" I was counting on his utter ignorance of my financial situation.

His shiny pink pate creased with worry, and he glanced at his wife, who had wandered off toward the magazine aisle. "When we can, yes, I think it's important to do that. Excuse me," he said and fled.

"You're a sadist," Emmitt said. I hadn't seen him come in. He wore faded jeans, polished loafers and a thready blue dress shirt with the collar button missing. In one hand he clutched an aluminum travel mug.

"That was the most fun I've had all day."

"I'm not sure how many paintings our mayor buys. He's certainly never bought one of mine."

"Maybe you're out of his price range."

"I should hope so."

"I'm surprised to see you here," I said.

Emmitt shrugged, and I smelled the gin sloshing in his mug. "Several of the Connecticut Titwards came for the service this morning, and Elaine is serving them dinner at the manse."

"Don't like them?"

"They're Republicans," he said, as if that was all the explanation needed, and took a sip. "What do you think of Tammy's work?"

"I'm not sure about the color."

He nodded. "She ruined them with that little gimmick. But they'll all sell. People love simple-minded shit like that."

"I thought you were a fan."

"I boinked her between husbands, if that's what you mean."

"I meant the paintings."

"Oh, I told her last night that she should burn them."

"Nice."

"Life's too short to fuck around with postcard crap like this. As we've all been reminded this week."

Well, yes.

We shuffled past the remaining pictures in silence, then established a redoubt close to the buffet. Dr. Paul arrived and took the minimum viable portion of wine. He volunteered that he and Tammy's husband ran together several days a week, as if his presence required some healthful offset.

"If I was married to her, I'd run too," Emmitt said.

Dr. Paul eyed him uneasily, nostrils flaring when the gin fumes wafted his way, then turned to me. "How's your head?"

"Never better." I decided not to mention getting hit with a bottle. Just thinking about it brought a flashback to that dreamy, underwater state, and for a queasy few seconds I thought I might toss my crostini.

"I'm looking forward to tomorrow night," he said. "I already got my tickets."

"Ah yes, wish I could be there," Emmitt said, "but Elaine insists that I take the relatives for one night. I'm having a beach barbecue, in hopes that some of them will get caught in the riptide."

"Bring them to see Bax," Dr. Paul suggested.

"So he can serenade them with 'Send the Innkeeper Packing?' I think not," Emmitt said and sucked out the last drops of his drink.

"I won't be playing that one."

"Why not? It was a hit, right?"

"Have they made any headway in the investigation?" Dr. Paul asked, saving me from having to answer.

"The cops still think it's Bax," Emmitt said, "but even I know he didn't do it."

"Of course not," Dr. Paul said.

"Funny thing is," Emmitt said, "I was talking to his mother at the library this morning, and apparently my brother's murder could be just the thing to jump-start Baxter's career."

Thanks, Mom.

"I'm going to make a plate for the kid at the newsstand," I said.

SEVENTEEN

The Irie Ikes were loping through "Red Red Wine" at the Rum House when I arrived, just before ten. The band consisted of four shaggy, middle-aged white guys in Hawaiian shirts and jeans and one young black guy who wore a silk T-shirt, tight slacks and neat dreadlocks. Everyone called him Ike, although that wasn't his name. The white guys played guitar, keyboards, bass and drums. Ike sang and charmed the ladies. Over a decade of Friday nights, there had been three different Ikes, but the party never stopped.

Davey's door manager, Nicole, sat on her stool reading a paperback legal thriller. As usual, she smiled hello and let me in without paying the cover. Her total lack of interest in music of any kind made her a dependable employee, disinclined to let the band sneak ten friends in the back door, but I was a special case.

I made my way back to the Tavern Room, where I could hear the band without getting knocked down by drunken real-estate saleswomen sailors getting their groove on. Davey rattled a cocktail shaker in each hand. The only free stool was next to Capt. Bob, who sat staring gloomily into his empty pint. Maybe he was the reason the stool was open. He spent most of his free time at the Rum House lately, a sure sign of depression. The only person here more often was me.

"Yo ho ho," I said.

"Hey, Bax. Beer?"

"I wouldn't mind."

He signaled Davey, then took off his little round glasses and set them on the bar with his pipe. His skin was pale, eyes red-rimmed. He yawned and rubbed his face with both hands.

"Rough day on the high seas?"

"Rough week. I'm doing two whale cruises every day, and the darn things keep moving farther and farther off shore. I've had to schedule an extra hour for each trip. It makes for a long day."

"You must be about to start the sunset cruises."

"I don't want to think about that. I know people have a right to a good time, but they turn into animals. Binge drinking, having sex in the head. Someone always gets sick, even though we never leave the harbor. That's not what I bought the boat for."

"Why do them, then?"

"I need the money."

Davey dropped off our beers with a nod, too busy to talk. Bob put his glasses back on and drank deeply. Then he nodded, as if he'd just remembered something important.

"Are you still a murder suspect?"

"Sort of. At least until they get the test results."

"Lie detector?"

"Gunshot residue."

He nodded as if he expected this. "What about Abigail? I hear she's going to make it?"

"You know as much as I do."

His moustache twitched. "Have they said whether all this has anything to do with Jules' business?"

"Let me guess. You had money invested with him."

He gave me a startled look. "Gosh, yes. Everything I have left. Between buying the Miss Libertyport and the divorce, it's not much. But I need a new number-two engine, and sooner rather than later. If I don't get it, I'm going to start missing trips. I could lose the boat."

"And you think your money's gone."

He swallowed hard, nodded.

"You tried to pull out?"

"Tried is right. I had a hard time getting Jules on the phone. And of course I'm on the boat whenever his office is open. I was getting worried, so last Thursday, I postponed the afternoon trip an hour and went to his office. He acted happy to see me, but I don't think he was. Brought me in and printed me out a statement from his computer that said I'm up about twenty percent. Asked me did I still want to pull out. Made me feel almost guilty about it. But I said needed the money, and he said he'd get it for me."

He picked up his beer. The Ikes rolled into "One Love," as they did every week about this time. The set list didn't change much. Bob Marley wasn't writing any more songs. Capt. Bob nodded along for a minute, never remotely close to the beat.

"What happened?"

"Jules said he had to do the paperwork, could I come back first thing in the morning? I couldn't, because I had a group coming for an eight a.m. cruise, but I said I'd be back at lunchtime. He promised he'd have a cashier's check by then. Of course at lunchtime the receptionist told me he was gone for the day and wouldn't be back until Monday. I left him some pretty strong voicemails over the weekend, let me tell you. But I had the entire Seabury Junior High School on the boat Monday, and then Tuesday I had a shaft bearing go, so I never got there. And you know what happened Tuesday night. My luck's terrible, as usual."

"Jules' luck was worse."

He shrugged as if to say, *Not much.* He didn't seem like he could muster the energy for murder, but desperate people weren't predictable.

Davey took advantage of a momentary lull to stop by. "How'd it go with Greg?" he asked.

I glanced at Capt. Bob, still staring glumly into his beer. "I'll tell you about it in the morning."

"You find out anything about Shimmy Jimmy?"

"A little."

A waitress at the other end of the bar yelled, "Ordering!" Davey ignored her.

"Any connection with Jules?"

"Not so far. Maybe it was my imagination."

The waitress shouted louder.

"I gotta go."

The band swung into a reggaefied version of Van Morrison's "Brown Eyed Girl." We'd worked up the arrangement one January night when I filled in for the flu-stricken Ike, to the disappointment of his many female fans.

Capt. Bob cleared his throat. He and his decrepit boat were starting to sound alike. "What's this about Jimmy?"

I'd hoped he wasn't listening. But I'd already told half the town, and I didn't think Bob would remember in the morning, anyway. "I saw him in the parking lot on Wednesday, right before I found Jules. I thought he might have something to do with Jules getting killed. Like they had some old grudge or something."

Capt. Bob shook his head slowly, as if it was heavy, and I saw how drunk he was. "It was Emmitt."

"What was Emmitt?"

"Jules was there, but Emmitt's the one Jimmy got in the scrape with."

"Emmitt was out of town on Tuesday night."

Bob looked at me like I was an idiot. "No, no. The night Jimmy had his accident."

I felt a moment's vertigo, a dizzying gravitational pull, as if a black hole had suddenly opened under my barstool. I didn't dare speak. Ike was still singing about the brown-eyed girl.

"I feel guilty every time I see that kid pedaling around town." That kid. Suddenly there were tears in Bob's eyes. "That spring was the only time in my life I've behaved like that and I'm not proud of it." He took off his glasses and wiped them.

Ike told the band to *"take it down, take it down."* They dropped the groove to a whisper. *"Ladies and gentlemen, we have a special guest in the house tonight!"*

Uh oh. The crowd sat up and looked around the room, hoping for an actual celebrity. They were going to be disappointed.

"Bob, what happened that night? What did you do?"

"Nothing," he said, choking. "That's the problem." His gaze focused inward, replaying some awful scene in his head.

"This is a funk soul brother that you all know and love! And in fact he's playing right here at the Rum House tomorrow night, so be sure to come back and see him!"

"Damn it," Bob said through his tears.

"The brother helped us with this arrangement, so I was think-ing he oughta come up here and finish it with us! What do you say?"

Wild cheering. A hundred-odd drunken Irie Ikes fans weren't going to take no for an answer. Davey avoided my eye, so I knew this was his idea.

"Ladies and gentlemen, Baxter McLean!"

I stood up. "Bob, this will only take a couple of minutes. Don't go anywhere, all right?"

He nodded, but while I sang, he wobbled toward the door. When the number ended, I ran out to the parking lot, but he was gone. I couldn't bring myself to chase after him. I knew where his apartment was, but I didn't want to go there, maybe because I knew how lonely it would be. We were too much alike; staying faithful to our dreams had cost us our marriages and more. I stood for a moment looking across the harbor at the blinking green eye of the lighthouse on Plover Island, and then I went back to the bar.

EIGHTEEN

Someone burst through the front door and came pounding up the stairs. I must have been too hammered last night to lock up. I lay still, bludgeoned by hangover, and hoped it wasn't the killer. Although on second thought...

"Dad! Get your butt out of bed! We're supposed to be fishing!"

Now I was glad Nicole had just rolled her eyes at my last-call proposition.

"Come on," Zack moaned, fidgeting in my bedroom doorway. He had the same thick, dark hair I enjoyed at his age, but he was short and compact, and his face baby-fat soft. The McLean family growth spurt hadn't hit him yet. "Davey's waiting for us."

All the time Amy was pregnant I pretended to be thrilled, when mostly I was scared. I didn't want my life to change. I knew nothing about parenting, couldn't imagine how I would handle the responsibility. Even as I raced home from a gig in Amherst at four in the morning to attend the birth, I was looking for a loophole. And then I saw Zack and went directly from lying wuss to Hallmark Dad. Just being around him made me happy.

"I'm up, I'm up."

"You're not *moving*."

"Hypothetically I am."

"I don't know what that means."

I swung my feet down to the floor and yawned.

"Here. I brought you a coffee."

"Thanks. You're a good son." I noticed he had a cup for himself. "Hot chocolate?"

"Quad cappuccino."

He wore baggy black shorts, a black pullover and a black Kangol cap, worn backwards of course. He was cool. Maybe his high school years would be happier than mine.

"Does your mother know you drink coffee?"

He made a *duh* face. "She dropped me at Foley's."

As far as I knew, drinking coffee was just the sort of thing Amy didn't want her "little man" doing. She had been furious when I allowed him to pierce an ear for a tiny gold stud, a birthday present during February vacation. She insisted I should have consulted her before allowing him to "mutilate himself," and maybe she was right, but I stopped feeling reasonable about the fifth time she brought it up. I sipped my dark roast and pondered her change in tactics. Was she trying to compete with me now?

"You don't have to drink it all before we go, do you?"

"Sorry."

Five minutes later we were headed cross-town. Zack consented to walk without turning on the iPod that the headmaster had bought him for his birthday. Apparently the jerk was allowed to curry his favor even if I wasn't. The headphones dangled around his neck like a threat, warning me what would happen if our conversation bored him.

"So how's your mother?"

He shrugged. "She's OK."

"She stop bugging you about the earring?"

"She forgot about it after I asked her for a tattoo."

I stifled a laugh. "Even I wouldn't say yes to that."

"Mom said that if I talked you into getting me one, she'd strangle you."

"I have no doubt."

"Then she said she was sorry, because you're not supposed to joke about killing people." He looked at me sideways. "She told me not to ask you about that guy who got shot."

I realized we'd been headed here all along. "What do you want to know?"

"What happened, I guess."

"I found the body, but I didn't kill him."

"I know, of course not!" He reached for the headphones and held onto them for security. "Who did?"

"I don't know. A lot of people were mad at him."

"I read online that you were fighting with him about that hotel." *Abigail.*

"Yeah, I was, but people argue about stuff like that all the time. That's normal."

"So was it, like, a robber or something?"

"I don't think so. I think it was somebody from town, somebody who knew him. But you don't have anything to worry about, sport. It's got nothing to do with you. You're not in any danger unless you get that tattoo."

Big grin. "Can I?"

"No way."

"Come on!"

"What kind would you want to get?"

Normal father-son topics consumed the rest of our conversation. I especially liked the part about what a jerk the headmaster was, iPod or no iPod, although I tried not to let on.

Davey had renovated his family's rambling saltbox over the years in open contempt for good taste and historical accuracy. Bay windows, vinyl siding and an outmoded satellite dish rusting in the yard were among the outrages that caused members of the preservation commission to sputter and fume when they drove past. The suburban-style two-car garage had been sheathed in Tyvek insulation when it was built, years ago, and never sided. Next to the driveway, a gas grill under a tattered Bud Light parasol delivered the *coup de grace* to delicate sensibilities.

When Zack and I walked into his driveway, Davey sat frowning behind the wheel of his old green Jeep Cherokee, listening to the robotic voice of a marine weather radio forecast. Five white PVC pipes were bolted to the front bumper: Rod holders.

He brightened up when he saw us. "Hey kid, you ready to show your old man what real fishing is?"

"You know it."

"How come you're sitting out here?" I asked.

"Nora's pissed because I bumped Trouser Weasel."

"Sorry about that."

Davey had grown up in this house, when the lower end of Lime Street was the toughest block in a tough town. Slime Street, the kids called it. His wife had grown up two doors away. If I got in certain kinds of trouble and Davey wasn't around, I would have called Nora for help before most of the men I knew. Being in her doghouse was no small thing.

"Ain't your fault. It's that little prick nephew of mine. He made a big stink. The bright spot is, now I won't have to see him or Nora's sister until Christmas."

"Trouser Weasel is an excellent band," Zack said.

"They ain't exactly the Allman Brothers."

"Who?"

Davey shook his head sadly. "Who's raising this child?"

I decided not to point out that one of his three sons was in jail, and his daughter had just moved home with her three toddlers after a second divorce at age twenty-seven.

Zack did most of the talking on the way out to the island. Did we know what Trouser Weasel meant? Wasn't it *hilarious?* The ranger in the gatehouse at the nature refuge waved us through without checking Davey's pass. At the visitor center, Zack let ten pounds of air out of each tire while Davey signed the logbook. Then we headed down the island.

The refuge's terrain was low and scrubby except for the occasional soaring sandhill. The road hugged the marsh side of the island. Town was visible across the flats, with its water towers and steeples, but we were in a different world, where we could hear the surf booming just over the dunes. The deer and coyote mostly stayed out of sight when the gate was open, but migratory birds swarmed every thicket and pool. Twice Davey had to swerve to avoid carloads of birders who stopped short to eyeball an egret or a rare whimbrel with their expensive German optics.

"I can't believe they don't smash into each other," Zack said.

Song fodder! I could do it as a parody of one of those teen carcrash ballads that were popular in the '50s and '60s, like "Last Kiss" or "Teen Angel." Then I remembered what happened to Jimmy, and it didn't seem so funny. Zack would be agitating for his learner's permit soon enough.

Davey turned left through an open gate onto a rough sand track and switched to four-wheel drive. The Jeep rocked through a thicket of beach plum and bayberry, branches scraping the sides. On the other side, we rolled down a gully between sloping dunes crisscrossed with coyote tracks and the hasty prints of one scared rabbit.

Atop the next rise, a rectangle of old timbers lay half-buried in the sand, the last remnant of one of the hunting camps that used to dot this part of the island. After World War II, the feds took the land to create the refuge. That was the first time the townies had been screwed by change, long before they were priced out of their neighborhoods on the mainland. Now the elements were slowly burying the evidence. Tufts of wind-whipped compass grass etched circles in the sand.

Soon we came out onto the beach, facing the endless blue sea. It was mid-tide, with leisurely, rolling surf that glittered in the sun. The only other people in sight were fishermen sitting in ones and twos outside a string of campers parked just above the high tide line, tending their rods and staring out at the water. The soft tires floated us over the sand until we were well beyond the last camper. We got out, disturbing a handful of gulls pecking at a tangle of seaweed. They flapped into the air briefly, cawing in annoyance, then landed a few feet away and returned to their meal, one sentry posted to keep a wary eye on us.

"Welcome to paradise," said Davey. "You better enjoy it. We're shut out starting next week."

The feds closed the refuge beaches for months every summer to protect the piping plover, the tiny, endangered shorebird for which the island was named. It didn't go over very well with the locals. Drive-on fishing permits were the last vestige of the sporting culture that had once ruled the island. Back in the day, the men came to their unheated, unwired camps to fish and hunt waterfowl and deer. They came early on weekend mornings and on the sacred vacation week in the fall, living on bologna sandwiches and coffee and Seagram's Seven. There were years, especially during the Thirties, when the venison and duck and goose, the bluefish and cod and haddock, kept more than a few families fed.

To men who had fought in Italy and the Pacific and Korea, the refuge land-takings in the '40s and '50s seemed like a declaration of war from their own government. There weren't many of them still alive, but the resentment lingered among their descendants, who had never known the island as it was, only heard the stories. To them, the beach closures were the last straw. They put PIPING PLOVER TASTES LIKE CHICKEN bumperstickers on their trucks, and after a couple of beers, they'd tell you they were the real endangered species.

Davey set up the rods while Zack peeled his sneakers off and ran down to test the water. I got two lawn chairs out of the back of the Jeep and unfolded them. Davey handed me a rod rigged with a bright orange plastic plug bristling with treble hooks. We walked down to the wet sand where my son mimicked the sandpipers playing chicken with the waves.

"It's coooold," Zack said, already wet to the knees.

"When is it ever warm here?" Davey said and handed him a rod.

We spread out in a line and launched our lures over the break to the smoother water beyond. Davey's toss was long and effortless. For the first time, Zack outcast me.

"Kid's getting the hang of it," Davey said.

"I drink coffee now," Zack told him.

Davey shook his head. "I wouldn't wanna be your teacher. Half the seventh grade all hopped up on double espressos."

Zack grinned and jabbed the heel of his rod into the sand. "Mr. Keeler calls us caffeine monkeys." He lowered his chin and pursed his lips, held his arms out from his sides and hopped around the beach whooping and grunting like a chimp. More song fodder.

After a while without a nibble, Davey and I went back up to the chairs, leaving Zack to tend the rods. Davey broke out a cooler with sodas and meatball subs, a manly breakfast. I wondered if there were any beers in the bottom of that cooler. Then I thought about how many I'd put away last night and opted for a soda instead.

"So how's the Sherlocking going?"

"I don't know. Plenty of people had reasons to kill Jules."

"You think it's about the hotel?"

"No." I took a bite of my sub. Salvation. "Jules supposedly invested for a lot of people. And people who wanted to cash out were having a problem getting their money from him. I talked to Arnie and Sara McNulty, and they were trying to get fifty grand back without much luck. Capt. Bob was into him for twenty and needed it for the boat, and Jules was ducking him too. I bet they're not the only ones."

"Ponzi Scheme," Davey said.

"What?"

"Pyramid scam. Invented right here in Boston. He steals the money from the first suckers, and then recruits new suckers and uses their cash to pay off the old ones. It's the oldest trick in the book, but it always fails in the end, because you need a bottomless supply of new customers to keep it going. Sooner or later, you can't find anyone you haven't already ripped off. And then you're fucked."

"Elaine said he admitted he was having financial problems. It sounds like he was counting on a big injection of cash for the hotel to save his ass."

"It would have worked for a while. But you ruined that for him."

"*We* ruined that for him. I think it was already too late, actually. His problems had been building up for months."

"That explains why he was so pissed. Easier to blame us than to face how he fucked everything up." Davey chewed thoughtfully for a minute. "So how's your friend Guido Argento?"

"He said Jules came to him a week or two ago looking for money."

"Jules thought he was sharking, because of his old man?"

"Exactly. When Greg said no, Jules asked him for a personal loan of fifty grand."

"Ho ho ho."

"I figure that would have been enough to get people off his back until the hotel money came in. He was really feeling the pressure, though. He was shitfaced when he showed up at the Schooner."

"That must have gone over well."

"I think Greg felt sorry for Jules, actually."

"And put him down like a rabid dog?"

"I didn't get that vibe. He said he drove Jules home."

Davey looked out to sea. "I knew his father."

"Carmine? Seriously?"

"Yeah. This was a long time ago, back before I bought the bar. Me and him used to be in the shipping business. I told you about it."

So it was Carmine Argento waiting upriver when Davey brought the bales in from the mother ships at sea. What was it Wankum had said? *Interesting friends.*

"So who do you really think popped Jules?" he asked to change the subject.

"I'm leaning toward a disgruntled customer. Somebody who wanted their money and wouldn't be put off any longer. When I found him, it looked like somebody had gone through the glove compartment of the Beemer. And there was the break-in at his office. It's like they're looking for a check or something."

"Makes sense, as far as it goes. But three in the ticker? Doesn't seem like a disgruntled investor, does it?"

"Well, there is another possibility." If there was anyone in town I could trust, it was Davey. When I told him about Ashley, he made a face like he'd just hit on a skunked beer. "I don't know if he was messed up because his business was failing, or if his business was failing because he was messed up for some other reason. But doing the nasty with Ashley could have gotten him killed."

"Your friend Marcy would have torn him apart with her bare hands if she found out."

"True. But the more likely suspect is this boyfriend of Ashley's. He's a hothead and a doper – he's the one who got her the E. If he found out about Jules and Ashley, it's not hard to imagine him doing something about it."

"So it's probably this kid. In which case you should tell Wankum everything and leave it up to him."

I ate more of my sandwich and watched a platoon of sandpipers running along the shore. They scattered to go around Zack, then reformed on the other side and continued on their way.

"There's more," I said.

"Jesus, what else?"

I put the rest of my sub down on the cooler lid and wiped marinara sauce off my chin with a napkin. A couple of seagulls saw an opportunity and waddled slowly toward the cooler, greedy eyes locked on my food, until Davey leaned forward and stopped them with a look. They settled down on the sand to wait.

"It's Shimmy Jimmy. For starters, I wasn't the only one who saw him on Wednesday morning and thought something was strange. The McNultys were there that morning, and they said it looked like he was pedaling right toward Jules' body. Like he already knew that Jules was dead."

"But he's Shimmy Jimmy. What could he have to do with it?"

"Velma told me what happened to him, why he's the way he is. He was drinking out on the island when he was in high school and wrecked his car on the way home."

"I remember that. There was a picture on the front page of the Daily Crier. He tore his Trans Am in half."

"And they never found out where he was drinking or who he was with."

"Right. That was the big mystery in town for months. Everybody wanted to find out who gave him the booze and hang them."

"Last night, Capt. Bob told me that he was there the night Jimmy had his accident, and so were Jules and Emmitt."

Davey gave a slow whistle that briefly drew the gulls' attention away from my sandwich. "What happened?"

"I didn't get details. Ike called me up on stage before I could get it out of him – thanks very much for that, by the way – and then he was gone. But I'm going to get him to tell me the rest."

"Thirty years seems like a long time to stew about something."

"True. But what if Jimmy just remembered what happened that night, for some reason? Or what if somebody reminded him?"

"No way Jimmy got a gun, met up with Jules in the middle of the night and shot him."

"I know. But maybe Jimmy told someone what he found out. Has he got any family besides his mother?"

"Not that I know of. Wankum could find out for you. Sooner or later you've gotta tell him all this."

"You know what will happen if I do. They'll haul Jimmy down to the station and grill him. He'll lose his mind. You should have seen him when I tried to ask him about Jules. He looked like he wanted to jump out of his skin. I don't want to do that unless I'm sure."

Davey looked like he was about to talk some sense into me when Zack screamed, "Got one on!" We ran for our rods. The gulls moved in, their patience rewarded.

NINETEEN

Townies ran the insurance agencies, the full-service gas stations and hardware stores, the comfort-food restaurants that served breakfast all day. Artists and ex-hippies opened galleries and health food markets and import-only garages, made "unique" jewelry or "educational" toys from "sustainable" materials. Yuppies commuted to Boston or hunched over computers in their home offices, building web sites or analyzing mutual funds.

Dan Ockerbloom defied stereotypes in that he was a townie who ran an arts business. A bluegrass phenom as a teenager, Dan gave up touring at twenty-one and opened a recording studio. The low cinderblock building on River Street was too close to the sewage treatment plant to be viable for condo conversion. At least it was upwind, most of the time. I recorded "I'm Not Doing This For My Health, You Know" there when Dan had been in business only six months. Now it had become the go-to spot for successful folksingers and up-and-coming Americana bands.

Dan's black 1960s Lincoln sat by itself in the gravel parking lot, so I didn't have to worry about interrupting a session. Inside, Ockerbloom Studios was cool and deserted. The building, owned by Dan's father, had been an auto parts store for decades. A dusty cash register sat atop a high counter in front of an empty pegboard wall. The front window framed a steady stream of Saturday-afternoon traffic headed for the island.

The lounge area in back held a TV and couches. I put a bag of fish in the refrigerator, which contained a six-pack of spring water, deli leftovers and one forlorn beer. Not much in the way of decadence here, unless you counted the autographed Flatt and Scruggs album cover framed on the wall. Studio time was valuable and no one screwed around much anymore.

The control room was dark and quiet except for a galaxy of tiny red and green lights on the board and the soft music coming out of the speakers hanging from the ceiling. Out in the main studio, Dan was teaching himself to play four-string banjo. I sat in one of the big leather Capt. Kirk chairs behind the 72-channel board and listened. He'd been a prodigy, playing guitar and dobro at festivals when he was thirteen, but when he married and started a family, he began searching for a saner way of life. Amy thought he was great. I looked at him sitting there in a cone of light and saw my life as it might have been. We were friends anyway. He finished the breakdown he was playing and said, "C'mon in," his voice issuing from the speakers above my head.

Dan was lean and compact, with short reddish-blond hair and a close-trimmed beard. He radiated a kind of organized calm. Dozens of microphones and instruments were arrayed around the smallish room, including an organ, an upright piano, a rack of a dozen guitars, and a full drum kit behind clear Plexiglas. Everything was in its place and squared away. There were none of the empty bottles, tangled wires, crumpled Frito bags and cracked CD cases that littered most studios. Dan had built the place himself, with help from his brothers who were in the trades, and he'd paid off his bank loans early. I don't know what he was doing in the music business, the domain of deviants and scoundrels.

"I brought you a couple pieces of striper Zack and I caught this morning. It's in the fridge."

"Fantastic, thanks. Beach or river?"

"Beach."

"Must have been nice today."

"It was beautiful."

"I've got to get out there."

"You better hurry. Davey says they're closing it next week for the plovers."

"Check out this guitar I just bought." He lifted a fire-engine red Flying V. "Custom made by a guy down in Austin."

He set it across his knees, grabbed a glass slide and played a screaming psychedelic riff, but the guitar wasn't plugged in, so the music came out faint and tinny, like The Borrowers covering Jimi Hendrix. Dan's decision to stop touring baffled many, because he was a virtuoso on any stringed instrument he picked up. But he seemed happier than anyone I knew who had stayed on the road, myself included.

He put the guitar back in its stand. "Way more expensive than I wanted, but I saw it online and I had to have it. Now I just have to convince someone to let me play it on their album."

"Maybe I will."

"I thought you were all done with making records. I seem to recall you giving a pretty good speech about it at our Super Bowl party. Something about the deaf, ignorant, greedy motherfuckers who run the music business."

"Dormer Records reached out to me."

"I heard they were gearing up. I've got to get in touch with them, see if I can get some business before they spend all their dotcom millions."

"Well, they sent a scout out to see me the other day, at least partly because of all the publicity over Jules."

"That's right, I forgot, you're notorious. My wife said she saw your picture on the news."

Dan didn't worry too much about the twists and turns of today's headlines if they didn't immediately affect him. He was inner-directed. Maybe that was why he hadn't pursued his music: He didn't need fans and spotlights and applause to feed his ego the way most of us did.

"Hey," he said, "are you still auditioning for Old Home Days?"

"Yeah, when is that again?"

He looked at me strangely. "Tomorrow, two o'clock. You forgot, huh?"

"Busy week. You know, murder suspect and all."

"Worth it, if it got you on Dormer's radar."

"I don't know how serious they are. But she said they're looking for some established artists to put in the mix."

"She?"

"Jane Bassett."

"I've heard of her. She's smart." Dan was not the sort to leer.

"She said they'd want me to make a new album pretty quick. They might try to get my catalog together under one roof, too."

"Sounds like a good plan."

"Jane used to work for a couple of the majors, and she wants to pimp some of my songs out for soundtracks, TV shows and stuff."

"More money, no more work. That's great."

I shook my head. "I dunno, I just-"

"Fear success?"

"Maybe you're right." If anybody else had said it, I wouldn't have given them a straight answer. But Dan was ten years younger than me, and I'd been taking his advice for years. "It just seems so out of the blue, especially since it came out of the whole murder thing."

"You know that for a fact?"

"Pretty much."

"Well, I bet you were on their radar beforehand. And then they saw you on the news and decided they'd better get on it before somebody else did."

"There's not even an offer yet."

"Do you know what their time frame is?"

"Jane's coming up to see me play tonight, to hear some new material, and then we'll see."

"Say you sign sometime in the next month, they'd probably want you in the studio this summer?"

"I suppose so."

"You thinking solo or band?"

"Light band, if they'll pay for it." I hadn't thought about it consciously till now.

"I can play bass, slide, maybe a little piano. We'll get Dave M. or somebody like that to play drums. Do it as live as we can. Not too many overdubs."

"Sounds perfect," I said truthfully.

"You're pretty easy. Figure fifteen songs, maybe sixty hours to start?" He grabbed an appointment book off the top of an old analog

Fender piano and flipped ahead. "I've got Greg Brown, a couple of demo sessions."

"But you could fit me in?"

"You get a deal, we'll fit you in," he said. "Now maybe you should go home and finish some songs."

TWENTY

The sandwich board by the entrance to the Rum House advertised BAXTER MCLEAN FOLKSINGER COVER $12. Double what Davey charged the last time I'd played. Big markup for the murder suspect. I wasn't complaining; I got half the door. To be fair to the customers, though, the sign should have continued with the bad news: RAPIDLY AGING, COMMERCIALLY IGNORED, DEAD BROKE.

In the foyer, Davey was getting an earful from a stout, pop-eyed woman who waved her arms like she was going to start whaling on him any minute. She wore faded yellow stretch pants, flip-flops and a Dale Earnhardt memorial NASCAR T-shirt. Her badly dyed brown hair emitted noxious fumes from a recent perm, and a lit cigarette clung to her lower lip. She could have gone up like a torch.

"You can't do this shit to my kid and get away with it," she snarled, spittle flying, and waved a finger in Davey's face. The last guy I'd seen do that got a broken wrist, but Davey looked almost contrite.

"I didn't mean to-"

"You stabbed my boy right in the back. Your own flesh and blood. His band is going to be huge, and when they make it, they're never going to come back and play this shithole, do you hear me? I don't care how many times you say you're sorry."

So this was his sister-in-law, the mother of Trouser Weasel's lead singer. Fortunately she was too busy reaming Davey to notice me slipping past into the bar with my guitar case.

As always, the main room reeked of stale beer and sweat, cut now with the detergent tang of the floor mop. Empty, it was quiet enough to hear the AARP crowd in the upstairs dining room complaining about the size of the fried clam bellies in the early-bird special. I set up my guitar and amp, turned on the PA and strummed a few bars of "Wild Horses." I was supposed to conduct a sound check, but I'd played here hundreds of times and knew what I'd find. The room had been drunk-proofed long ago, stripped of every bit of fabric or ornament that could be torn, stained, smashed or easily set on fire. The resulting harsh acoustics highlighted every missed fingering and turned my reedy voice into a car-alarm whine.

If I drew a decent crowd, the sound would get better, warmed by all those bodies. But even with the publicity from the murder case, that was a big if. When people chose a folksinger these days, they seemed to prefer imaginatively pierced lesbians singing gender-neutral, radio-friendly love songs, or earnest, goateed boys with their whole lives in front of them who chain-smoked as they lamented their existential despair. I was a balding single father in shorts and a Plover Island Grille T-shirt, and I saw irony everywhere. This habit, rendered into song, had earned me a loyal but perilously small cult of fans.

After a few minutes of aimless strumming, I settled my guitar in its stand and walked back through the archway into the Tavern Room, where I sat at the bar and ordered a coffee. Then I pulled out my cell and called the headmaster's residence. As I hoped, Zack answered.

"Hey kiddo, it's your old man."

"Don't call me a kid."

"OK, your lordship, how was the fish?"

"It was excellent. Lawrence grilled it." No one ever called the headmaster 'Larry,' not even my ex-wife.

"I'm sure it was delicious."

"I put, like, a bunch of Insanity Sauce on it while it was cooking, and it was so wicked hot, Mom and Lawrence could hardly eat it."

"I'm sure they enjoyed that."

"Lawrence got all red in the face and I thought he was going to throw up!"

"That's too bad." I'm pretty sure I was only laughing on the inside.

"Are you getting ready to play?"

"I just finished my sound check."

"How much is Davey charging tonight?"

One of our things was that Zack kept a close watch on my career. He was building me a MySpace page; he said I was the last musician in America without one. I doubted that he would remain interested when he got older, however, or that I would have enough of a career left to require his help.

"Twelve bucks."

"No shit!"

"Language," I said, in case Amy was listening.

"I wish I could come. Davey could sneak me in."

"You don't want to get him in trouble. Summer's almost here. I'll get some outdoor gigs, and you can be my roadie."

"Cool." I heard Amy's voice in the background, and he groaned. "I've gotta go, dad. Some crap for dessert."

"Don't call your mother's cooking crap. Keep the faith. I'll talk to you later."

"Yup." And then he was gone.

I said "I love you" to the dial tone and stared morosely at the phone for a minute before tucking it away.

"I didn't know you have a son."

I hadn't noticed her come in. She sat two stools over. Tight jeans, black pointy-toed boots, Pearl Jam T-shirt under a thin black-leather jacket. No glasses. Record Company Jane had morphed into a slightly skanky rock chick, the best kind.

"That's Zack. He's twelve."

"It doesn't surprise me."

"What doesn't?"

"That you have a son."

"Why should it surprise you?"

"You have a reputation for being a little dark. I bet you're a good dad, though." She moved over to the stool next to me, carrying a large vodka on the rocks with a twist. "I think you put on all that attitude to cover up the fact that you're really a softie."

Rock'n'roll chicks in boots and leather weren't usually looking for a sensitive guy. In my experience they preferred a handlebar moustache, a sweaty Skynyrd T-shirt and an interstate criminal record.

"Maybe I have that reputation because I *am* a little dark."

She shook her head. "It's all an act. I worked with Warren Zevon a couple of jobs ago, and he was the same way. He was always writing songs about mercenaries and psycho killers, but then he'd play a ballad, and he was the sweetest, saddest guy you ever heard."

"I sing 'Carmelita' sometimes, but somebody's cell phone always rings in the middle, kinda breaks the mood."

"See, that's exactly what I mean – making a joke to distance yourself from the emotions."

"Is that what I'm doing?"

"Of course it is. Singing is when you let your inner self show. Maybe the only time."

"If you say so."

She went on as if I hadn't spoken. "The irony is that people prefer the funny stuff. Zevon's biggest hit was 'Werewolves of London.' I bet you get more requests for 'Mirror Ball Man' than anything else."

"That's because it's the only one of my songs most people have ever heard."

"People are sheep," she said, knocking back the rest of her vodka. She smiled at me as she wiped her mouth with a paper napkin, and I wondered how many she'd had.

"If that's true, why couldn't I write another gold record?"

She waved away the thought. "All the bands I promoted in my last three jobs were pretty much one-hit wonders too. That's the system now. Blow 'em up big as we can, suck all the money out of them, and then drop 'em before they get too expensive. That's why I went with Dormer. It's a chance to actually do something good, something that will last."

"And what does that have to do with me?"

Huge snort. "Oh, will you get over yourself? Jeez!"

Davey came through the swinging kitchen door just then with a plate of calamari for her. "What's so funny?"

"Your friend here."

"Yeah, he's a stitch. You want another Grey Goose?"

"How about a soda and lime?"

"Sure." Davey poured it and appeared ready to join the conversation but I gave him a look and he went away.

"Didn't like the drink?" I asked.

"I spend three or four nights a week in clubs. If I drank every night I'd be pickled in a month. Plus I have to keep a clear head. A lot of lousy bands you hear on the radio today were signed because some record company chick got sloshed and fell in love. So when I start to feel it, I switch. Sometimes later on, I switch back."

"So why did you lie to me?"

She sagged, shook her head. "I *told* them."

We sipped our non-alcoholic beverages for a moment, eyeing each other in the mirror behind the bar.

"You told who?"

"Rick and Steve. My bosses. They own Dormer. I told them you'd figure it out."

"That you came to see me because of the news stories about the murder."

"Yes."

"And lied about it."

"Fine, I lied to you, if you want to put it that way."

"How should I put it?"

"You make it sound so awful. But you've been in the music business a lot longer than I have, right?"

"Thanks for bringing that up."

"Well, was there ever somebody from a record company who didn't lie to you?"

"Point taken."

I motioned to Davey for more coffee. There were probably musicians my age who still used coke or speed to get up for shows, but I was a folksinger. I couldn't afford white powder even if I wanted any.

"You know what?" Jane said to Davey.

"You're going to have another drink after all."

"How did you know?"

"He drives women to it all the time."

"Good to know."

"Anyway," I said as Davey moved off.

"Well, Rick heard about you and the murder on the radio, and he and Steve thought you might be just what we needed to get a little publicity. So they told me to find out if you were signed anyplace, without showing our hand. I called Sol with a little cover story, and when I told Rick and Steve what he'd said, they told me to get up here."

"And all that stuff about your sisters and how much you liked 'Mirror Ball Man' and how the forty-five disappeared?"

"That, believe it or not, was the truth."

I wasn't so sure, anymore than I knew whether the business suit and the smart-girl glasses she wore on Thursday were her real workday look. I knew what I wanted to believe, though.

"Do you really think I can still sell records?"

"I think if you come through with a new album and we get a couple of critics to rediscover you, we'll do some business, yeah. Both on the new album and the back catalog."

"That would be okay."

"Besides," she said, "you're already doing better than I thought."

She made a *ta-da* gesture at the crowd that had filled the big room while we talked. The echo wasn't going to be a problem. I saw Velma and her cronies, Dr. Paul and his nervous lawyer wife. Most of the green T-shirt club had shown up. I wondered, did they each have more than one shirt, or had they done a group wash? I had a strange flash of them standing around topless in the laundromat.

I wished I'd set up a merch table in the lobby to peddle "Please Remain Seated Until My Career Comes to a Complete Stop" CDs, like I did when I was on the road. My usual Rum House crowd consisted of a few devoted fans who already owned the album and a larger contingent of wobbly drunks and horny locals who had no interest in buying anything but alcohol, so normally I didn't bother. Tonight, though, there were a lot of new faces, here to see the folksinger who might have killed a guy. It creeped me out a little bit, especially when I realized that the real killer might well be in the room. But I bet he would have bought a CD.

Davey refilled my coffee and pointed to the bar clock.

A stray nostalgic thought flitted through my mind, a snapshot of myself at nineteen, riding across Hollywood in a long black limo to play "Mirror Ball Man" on a late-night comedy show. I sipped Dom Perignon while a beautiful and famous singer I was in love with, a flame-haired "older" woman of twenty-five in a green velvet dress, sifted seeds from leaf on the "Mirror Ball Man" LP sleeve. It was as close to living an Eagles lyric as you could get without actually selling your soul to the devil. It was also a very long time ago. Nobody had seeds in their pot anymore. Or so I'd heard.

I wondered if the woman sitting next to me now could help me get some of it back, the parts that mattered, anyway.

"Is that the fan club you were telling me about?" she asked.

"The Cape Ann Folk & Blues Appreciation Society."

"Matching outfits. Cute."

President Donald started the applause as I took my coffee up to the stage. Davey turned on the two white spotlights and the PA system. As always, stepping into that full-body halo was like stepping back in time. No matter what else happened, there was always a little taste of the old magic. All those eager, upturned faces. I shrugged off my jacket and picked up the Berwyn D8.

"Hi, everybody, thanks for waiting."

I settled on the stool, strummed "Wild Horses" and asked Davey for more guitar in the monitor. Jane was right. There were a lot of murder ballads in American popular music. I'd written a couple myself. This seemed like the time to play one. I had to deal with the topic right at the start, or that was all people were going to talk about.

"Sometimes I wonder what it would be like if historical figures lived today, in the age of twenty-four-hour cable news."

I began to pick a simple rising and falling pattern, like a train rolling over the ties.

"Take Paul Revere. He drank in this bar once. I wonder what ol' Paul would have thought of Fox News."

Some smiles, even a chuckle or two. My guitar train rolled slowly along in the background.

"If we had CNN back then, we wouldn't have needed 'One if by land, two if by sea.' It would have been right on that crawl across the bottom of the screen: 'The British are coming, the British are coming, twister kills four in Indiana trailer park.' "

Supportive laughter.

"Of course, Paul Revere's not the only historical figure who would have made an interesting fit in the cable news era."

I goosed the tempo, speeding up the train and raising the volume, bending the strings slightly to insert just a hint of madness in the music, although they wouldn't know that's what it was, not yet. Then I began to sing. The melody was stolen from "The Beverly Hillbillies Theme Song," what we folksingers call "traditional."

Lizzie Borden took an ax
and gave her mother forty whacks.
And when she saw what she had done,
she gave her father forty-one.

That much was historical. I picked for a minute, let it sink in.

When the bloodshed was all done
someone called nine-one-one.
Patrolman came, said, 'Sakes alive!
Better call them CSIs!'

Nervous laughter, understandable given the circumstances. I plunged ahead anyway.

Soon reporters made the scene,
with mini-cams and the Spotlight Team.
They were rough and tough but it turned them green,
those last sixty whacks were simply mean!

Maybe this was my forensics show song. Most of the audience smiled now, a little shame-faced about it perhaps, but I had them. I was relieved to see that no one close to Jules had shown up, like Elaine or Emmitt. That would have been awkward.

Lizzie got her perp walk done,
Cameras and questions, all good fun.
Didn't even hide her head,
Just smiled and said, 'I'm glad they're dead.'

I slowed the train down, looking into the eyes of the people sitting close to the stage as it pulled into the station.

After the arraignment, her lawyer's phone rang.

The train eased up to the platform, softer and softer, until the sigh of air from the brakes as the locomotive finally stopped. I put my lips to the mike and stage-whispered:

Gerallllllldo calling.

Whoops, followed by cheers and applause. I let it go on for a few seconds, then started up the train again.

This was a long trip. "The Ballad of Lizzie Borden's Publicist and the Killing of Geraldo" ran about ten minutes. Turned out that Lizzie offed her parents because they'd tried to end her tabloid-TV addiction. I wrote the song 10 years ago, during the O.J. trial; on her trip to the TV station, Lizzie rode a white bronco, the four-legged kind. By the time she started swinging her ax in the studio, everyone in the Rum House was on the train with me.

I followed up with a mix of originals and covers. In a show of unusual restraint by the locals, no one requested "Send the Innkeeper Packing."

After the first set, I made my way back toward the bar while the applause was still fading. Dr. Paul motioned me into the chair his wife had just vacated on a beeline for the powder room.

"I'm kind of with someone." I nodded toward Jane, who waved.

"It will just take a minute. I think you want to hear this."

I sat, edge of the chair, and cracked a bottle of water.

"I hear you're still poking around in this thing with Jules," Dr.

Paul said. He had not entirely succeeded in relaxing his wardrobe for Saturday night at the bar: khakis, polished loafers with argyle socks, a button-down shirt under a V-neck sweater.

"Where did you hear that?"

"Davey told me."

"Ah."

"He thought I ought to tell you what I know about Jules."

"And what do you know?"

"A lot. Jules was my patient."

I wondered how Davey would have known that. Then I remembered that one of his ex-daughters-in-law worked reception at the medical office and had in fact collected my co-payment on Wednesday morning. "So how was Jules doing?"

"This is like the confessional, right?" he quoted me with a small smile.

"*Exactly* like it."

"Well, Jules is dead, so I guess it doesn't matter anyway. He came in for his regular checkup a couple of weeks ago, after postponing twice, and he wasn't doing very well."

"In what way?"

"Blood pressure, cholesterol, sugar, liver enzymes, you name it."

"He was drinking like a fish."

"Yes, and eating badly, not exercising, not sleeping. Jumpy as hell, more impatient than usual, and that's saying something. Sweaty at ten in the morning, eyes darting everywhere. I asked him about coke or meth and he denied it."

"What about Ecstasy?"

Dr. Paul shrugged. "That could fit. In any case, he looked like a guy under severe stress. He was supposed to come in for a follow-up next week, and I was going to come down hard on him."

"Somebody beat you to it."

"You could say that."

"Did he even hint at what was wrong?" I chugged from my water. Proper hydration was so important.

"He asked me if I had any money I wanted to invest. It seemed like a strange thing to say while I was checking his prostate."

Water up my nose.

"Did you tell Wankum all this?"

He nodded. "But he was mostly interested in whether or not I'd told the State Police. Apparently there's a territorial issue."

"And did you?"

"They didn't ask."

"Thanks, doc."

I resumed my seat next to Jane.

"You were terrific up there."

"Thanks."

"I don't understand why you're not rich."

"You remember that I'm between record deals at the moment, right?"

"We'll see about that. But you promised me if I came tonight I'd hear some new songs."

"I've been practicing them all afternoon," I said, and for once it was true. "I saved them for the second set so I could be sure you'd stick around."

She smiled into her drink. "Do you take requests?"

By the second set, most of the remaining audience was on at least their third round. Seeing their grins go crooked and their eyes unfocus made it less nerve-wracking to roll out new material. "Caffeine Monkeys" turned out to be a light, jazzy number a la Mose Allison, with scat breaks and Jane Goodall jokes. I'd knocked it out in an hour after getting home from Dan's studio. Maybe because it was about parenting and coffee, two favorite local topics, it seemed to go over well.

"Now I'd like to take it down a little bit and play something serious."

Davey, from the bar: "You mean the last one was supposed to be funny?"

I waited until the chuckling stopped before I began to sing. Truth be told, it wasn't a new song, just one I'd never played in public before.

Everyone I know hates goodbyes

You most of all
And yet I watch you leave
So often.

I wrote it almost four years ago, on my last tour before the divorce. Amy and I fought before I left. For the first time, she'd asked how long I was going to "keep doing this," meaning music. That night in my motel room, I used her words for the verses and added the refrain, thoughts she had never spoken but ones that I feared had crossed her mind:

It's all just vanity and folly
These things that keep us apart.

I never wrote anything so personal. It was much easier to dissect everyone else's foibles. I couldn't say why I'd decided to play the song now. I needed new material for Jane, sure. Maybe too the song had aged enough for me to face the feelings that came with it. Or maybe I had.

When it came time to play "Mirror Ball Man," Jane's request, I looked for my amateur beatboxer but he hadn't shown up with the rest of the green T-shirts, probably because he wasn't twenty-one. Everyone seemed happy to hear the song, though. When I was done, Jane hopped off her barstool and urged them to their feet for a standing ovation.

Davey had placed my traditional post-show beer atop the rack of tourist brochures outside the restrooms, where the cigarette machine used to be. The post-show beer is the fastest beer of any day and the best one, too, a reward and a remedy. I bet Axl Rose feels the same way about the bucket of industrial-strength tranquilizers and antidepressants the roadies push in front of him when he comes off stage.

When the audience started clapping in rhythm, I went back for my standard one-song encore, which is always a cover version. Nick Lowe's "(What's So Funny 'Bout) Peace, Love and Understanding?" allowed me to bash at the strings a little bit and wear my rock'n'roll heart on my sleeve. It was also a way of saying one more time that I was no killer.

Afterward, I bowed to the ovation and said, "Goodnight, and thank you!"

President Donald called out from the darkness: "No, thank *you!*"

The house lights came up, killing the applause. Folksingers didn't have the rock-star luxury of escaping the stage in the darkness. The audience and I faced each other like strangers in the unforgiving morning light after a drunken one-night stand. The best you could hope for was kindness and a sense of humor. Mostly we just avoided each others' eyes.

Davey announced last call and turned the jukebox back on. I quickly packed my gear and hauled it out to the car, so I could get back to the bar to see what would happen with Jane.

The Sunbird was parked in the darkness around back by the dumpster. The humming exhaust fans pumped out a greasy fog of fried-fish stench. I had just set my guitar case in the trunk when I heard two quick footsteps behind me. Before I could turn around, someone punched me in the head, and everything went all bright and sparkly.

This was getting *really* old.

He yanked my jacket up like in a hockey fight, and pushed me headfirst into the trunk, raining punches on me. I still had my hand around the neck of my guitar case. I could have swung it back and clobbered him. But I couldn't bring myself to destroy the beautiful instrument that my father had given me so long ago. I let go of the guitar and began to feel that warm, slow-motion, underwater feeling again, which made it hard to mount a counterattack. Once, he missed me and punched the bumper, yelping in pain. That brought a pause in the punching, so I stomped on his toes as hard as I could. That bent him over, and I swung around with an elbow and caught him in the eye. He staggered backward, squealing like a girl, and I turned around to finish him off.

Unfortunately, it turned out there were two of them. The other one stepped in and drilled me square in the face. All I saw was his fist. I don't remember anything after that.

I woke with a start, sitting on the ground with my back against the bumper of the Sunbird. I clutched my battered ribcage. One ear felt as if it was on fire. I tasted blood. I felt a flash of panic and struggled to my feet to look in the trunk. At least they hadn't stolen my guitar.

Dizzy and relieved, I slid back down to the ground. Something poked me in the side. My cell phone. I'd only programmed two speed-dial numbers, one for Amy, two for the Rum House. A waitress answered on the first ring and went to find Davey. I greyed out again while I waited and came back when I heard his voice.

"Where the hell are you?" he said. "The record company chick is getting antsy."

"Sorry. I just got beat up in your parking lot."

When he arrived at my side, I was still saying, "Hello? Hello?" into the phone, a little confused.

"I wish I could have seen it," Jane said a few minutes later at a table in a corner of the deserted Tavern Room. She was cleaning the blood and dirt off my face with a wet cloth napkin and a gentle touch.

"You wish you saw me get beaten up?"

"I came all this way for the show, I hate to miss the big finish."

"It wasn't all that glamorous."

"I'm sure you gave as good as you got."

"I don't know about that."

She dipped another corner of the napkin in a glass of water. I took a long swallow of the vodka martini Davey had brought me. No olives or vermouth, just about a gallon of Grey Goose shaken over ice and poured into a chilled glass. Jane was having one to keep me company.

"I really liked the new material," she said. "You've definitely got the start of an album there."

"Start?"

"Well, you only played, what, five new ones? You can fit a lot more music on a CD than you ever could on an LP. But I really liked 'Vanity and Folly.' That's definitely a hit for the Adult Album Alternative crowd. At the very least, I'm sure you'll get some major artists looking to cover it."

The minor artist absorbed that for a second, then asked Davey, "How'd we do on the door?"

"You saw the crowd." He pulled a wad of bills from his jeans and began counting out my share, as my nurse went back to work.

"Ow."

"Sorry."

Davey harrumphed. "That's what happens when you play detective."

"If you're so smart, who beat me up?"

"My money's on Guido Argento."

"Who's that?" Jane asked.

"Carmine Argento's son." At her puzzled look, he explained, "Carmine was like the Godfather, only from Danvers."

"Tough crowd," she said.

"We don't know it was him," I said.

"It has to be," Davey said. "You go see Guido yesterday, ask too many questions, and then, whammo! You even talked about the gig, so he knew where to find you."

"Greg said he hasn't been in the family business for a long time, and I believed him."

"Old habits die hard."

He had a point. I wondered about the hockey move, pulling my jacket up over my head.

"How was this Greg or Guido or whatever involved with the guy who was killed?" Jane asked.

"I'm not sure," I said. "Jules went to Greg's restaurant to try to borrow money off him a couple of weeks ago, figuring Greg either was a loan shark or knew where to find one."

"Did he get the money?"

"No. Greg insists he doesn't have it to give and isn't in the mob anymore. Jules was drunk, and Greg ended up driving him home."

"Maybe he really did give Jules the money, and he just don't want you to know," Davey said. "Could be he's running Carmine's crew now, and he had some of his boys kick your ass as a message."

"Maybe, but they didn't say 'Mind your own business!' or anything."

"Maybe you're supposed to figure it out for yourself."

"Maybe. The other possibility is these kids I mixed it up with out by the supermarket the other day."

"What kids? You didn't tell me about that."

"It was nothing. They were giving Shimmy Jimmy a hard time and I ran them off."

"Shimmy Jimmy?" Jane asked.

"Sort of the village idiot," Davey explained. "Harmless, though. He's lucky Bax was there."

"My hero," Jane said.

"It was no big deal."

"You lead an exciting life." She drained her drink and waggled the empty martini glass at Davey. "How about one more of these, and then I better get the patient home to bed."

TWENTY-ONE

The naughty rock chick outfit didn't lie. But in the morning Jane stood in front of the slider by the bed, blocking the sun so that its rays burst out all around her, like an angel. She held out a glass of water and the aspirin.

"You're going to feel worse later, you know."

"That's not possible."

"Didn't you say you had some pain pills from the other day? I'll get you one if you want."

"Thanks, but I want to be full speed the next time I find myself fending off thugs."

"So next time you're hoping to fend them off?"

"I'm an optimist. Hey, you're already dressed."

"I've got to get the train home and feed my cat."

"I would have bet anything you were a dog person."

"With all the traveling I do, and living alone, there's no way to have a dog. I've got to be ready to go at the drop of a hat, you know?"

In fact I'd been using the same argument with Zack; the headmaster's allergies made me his only hope for a canine companion.

"What are you going to do today? Assuming you can walk, that is."

"Read the papers. Maybe take a nap. For some reason I don't feel very rested."

"I meant about the murder and everything."

"I don't know," I said truthfully.

"You still don't want to tell the cops about last night?"

"They would just envy my stamina." My grin failed to dent her serious expression.

"I mean about getting beaten up."

"The last thing I need is to be in the newspapers again."

"You still think this Jimmy had something to do with the murder?"

"I don't know. What happened to him was so long ago. It could all just be coincidence."

"You should tell that detective about it."

"I already told Wankum I didn't see anyone that morning. He half thinks I killed Jules as it is. If he finds out I lied to him, I might end up in handcuffs."

"One way or another," she promised sweetly, then kissed me on the forehead. "I'm going now."

"When are you coming back?"

"I don't know. Not tonight. I have to take the shuttle down to New York and see this open mike at the Knitting Factory."

It had been years since anyone flew me in to play a gig. They paid her just to go and listen.

"Monday then."

"I'll try. Do you always leave the back door open like that?"

"Pretty much."

"I'll bring something good to eat from the city."

"Yum."

I showered and dressed, then hobbled down to Foley's. The day had dawned sunny and bright, but high, wispy clouds were moving in from the west. On weekends the coffee shop was mobbed by people who were too busy to eat breakfast with their family any other time. I intended to grab the papers and go home to bed. I didn't want to explain my battered face to half the people I knew or listen to the parents appeasing their howling, syrup-smeared offspring. Before I could make my escape, though, I was waylaid by Marcy, waving as she headed down the restaurant aisle with a handful of pink packets.

"Bax! Come join us! Amy's back here!"

Marcy was not usually eager to socialize with me, but this week I was notorious, making me a sort of prize. I should have run screaming, but I didn't. Some juvenile, pathetic part of my brain wanted to let Amy know I hadn't spent the night alone.

"Look what the cat dragged in!" Marcy announced brightly to the big round booth. All eyes turned, so it was too late to flee when I saw who else was sitting there.

Jackets and newspapers and breakfast dishes were relocated to make a place for me. Someone nudged the table and coffee sloshed out of mugs. There was just enough room if I snuggled in next to Headmaster Lawrence, my rival for my son's affection. He was tall and cleft-chinned, with wavy auburn hair, round tortoiseshell glasses and a superior smile. I suppose he was good looking, in an inbred, Ivy-League fashion. At one gallery opening, I had seen him wearing an ascot. I liked to think Amy had chosen him for contrast.

"Baxter," he said with his usual poorly concealed distaste.

"Headmaster," I said, ditto.

His sidekick Jeffrey, a beetle-browed egghead who chaired the English department, sat across from us. We exchanged a curt nod. I pitied rather than loathed him because he was married to Marcy. How had the two of them created a lovely creature like Ashley? All I could figure was that the mailman was Swedish. And not picky.

Completing the guest list from hell, Elaine Titward and Ora Buffem sat elbow to elbow in the back of the booth, their expressions hard to read. It wasn't that I didn't like them, but I wasn't eager to see either one of them at the moment.

"Well, here we all are!" Marcy said. "How *are* you, Bax?"

"Fantastic," I said.

Lawrence snorted. Jeffrey buried his face in The New York Times.

"Where's Zack?"

"He had a stomachache," Amy said.

"I think it was that fish you gave us," Lawrence added.

My son, the crafty little liar, had managed to avoid this gathering. I wished I had. Ashley arrived at my elbow right away with a mug and the coffee pot. Either her waitressing skills had improved dramatically in the last couple of days or she wanted to eavesdrop. She started to refill cups and Marcy told her, "Be careful honey," eliciting an icy glance. Everyone was in a mood. I said I wanted to order breakfast, and Ashley parked the pot on the edge of the table, directly above my lap, so she could get out her pad and pen. I took the placement of the pot as a threat; I was the only one here who knew about her and Jules, and she expected me to keep the secret. Mindful of the wobbly surface, I rushed through my order and forgot to ask for salsa.

"Some nasty bruises you've got there," Lawrence said, glancing at me only briefly, as if he wished to spare his eyes.

"Somebody tried to mug me outside the Rum House last night."

Gasps of surprise from the women. Even Jeffrey said, "My God," and lowered his paper, albeit briefly.

"Looks like they did more than try," Marcy said, recovering.

"You're having an awful week," Amy said, sounding sincerely worried. "Are you alright?"

I shrugged modestly. "You should see the other guy."

Marcy smiled. "Funny how you always seem to be around when these things happen."

"Did the police catch them?" Amy asked.

"I didn't call the police."

"Why not? How could you not report something like that?"

"He's a murder suspect," Lawrence said, as if that explained everything. "No offense."

"None taken," I said. "How's the education business?"

"I wish I dealt more with education and less with administration."

"Don't we all," Elaine said and made a face at him. He didn't notice.

Marcy took the paper away from Jeffrey and added it to a pile on the shelf behind her. Jeffrey frowned and looked around the table. "When are you going to come to school and give a reading?" he asked Ora.

"Anytime you'd like."

"How much of an honorarium do you pay?" Elaine asked, as if she was Ora's agent.

"I don't have much of a budget," Jeffrey said.

"Of course not," Elaine said. "Not with all the trouble you're having collecting tuition."

"No one has much of a budget for poetry these days," Ora said, trying to smooth things over. "I'd be happy to come and read, do a class, whatever you'd like."

"I'll call you," Jeffrey said.

An uncomfortable silence fell over the group. Ashley delivered my breakfast, then escaped as fast as she could. I grabbed the Tabasco and doctored up my eggs.

"Excuse me, I'm going to get the check," Lawrence said then, my plot working.

"How's Zack doing?" I asked Amy when he was gone.

"Other than bragging to all his friends that his dad is a murder suspect, fine."

"At least his tuition is all taken care of." Elaine said.

Amy started to say something and changed her mind.

"I love Sunday brunch," Marcy said brightly to no one in particular.

By the time I finished my eggs, it was just me and Elaine and Ora in the big booth. Ashley cleared the table, expressionless.

"What was all that about?" I asked. "Not that I mind anyone giving Lawrence a hard time."

"He had the nerve to ask how Elaine was going to pay the kids' tuition now," Ora said.

"He's such a dickhead," Elaine said. She watched Ashley closely as she lugged the bus tray away, and I wondered if there were any secrets in this crowd anymore. Other than who'd killed Jules, of course. Elaine excused herself and headed for the ladies' room.

"I've really been enjoying your CDs," Ora said when we were alone.

"Glad to hear it. I wasn't sure if they were your sort of thing."

"I liked them very much, although it's true that I don't listen to a lot of popular music."

"I'm not sure my music qualifies as popular."

"I think you're too self-deprecating. Did you have a good turnout for your concert last night?"

"Yes, I did, actually."

"Sorry I missed it."

"There will be other chances. I hope so, anyhow. How is she?" I asked, pointing in the direction of the rest rooms.

"As well as you can expect. Her husband was murdered, and now she has to put up with that pompous jerk." Meaning Lawrence. Her eyes leaped to mine. "I didn't mean to sound-"

"Don't worry, you're preaching to the choir."

She took a sip of her tea. "I feel bad for Amy. She and Elaine are such good friends. She looked horrified when Lawrence said that."

"She picked him."

"Our choices are not always entirely our own." She was never satisfied with the banalities of ordinary conversation. She had to get deep. I guess that's why she was a poet. "What happened between you two, if you don't mind me asking?"

"She thought I should be something other than a starving musician. If I'd put on a tie and gone to work in an office somewhere, we might still be together."

"You have to follow your muse."

"Sometimes it was difficult to pay the bills. Amy didn't like that."

"Well, at least Lawrence can't bother you about tuition."

"Nice one," I said.

Capt. Bob ran an early morning whale-watch cruise on Sundays, packing the decks with geriatric birders and earnest European trekkers in socks and sandals, people who never stayed out late on Saturday night. I figured I would catch him around lunchtime, restocking for the afternoon trip.

Weak sunlight filtered down through thickening clouds, and the boat bobbed at the dock uneasily. A boy with greasy black hair and a shiny, spotty complexion was swabbing the deck when I stepped aboard. His head looked too big for his body. His sullen expression suggested that this was just one unfairness among many.

"Minimum wage sucks, huh?"

"I don't get paid. This is my father's boat, and it's his weekend to have custody. This is supposed to be our visit."

"That's not so much fun."

"It's been this way ever since he got this piece of crap. It's all he thinks about, the stupid boat."

"Too bad he's not still teaching. At least you could get extra credit."

"I don't get credit for anything," he said and turned away. "He's up in the bridge."

Bob sat at the chart table, looking at spreadsheets on a laptop, which he clicked shut when he saw me climbing through the hatch. He checked his cap, then picked up his pipe.

"I see you met Carl."

"Good kid," I said, because that was what you said.

"Considering everything he's gone through in the last year, I think so. What happened to your face?"

"A little fuss outside the Rum House last night. No big deal."

"You haven't been on board since that sunset cruise last August. You gave an excellent show. I wish we'd filled the boat that night."

"I told you I wasn't going to do as well as the Ikes." I hopped up into the captain's chair. The boat faced upriver, with a view of the Rum House, Hewett's Boatyard and the Route 1 bridge. Because of the weather, it wasn't a big day for pleasure boating. Most of the activity on the docks was beginning-of-the-season prep work, scrubbing and sanding and painting. "How are things going, anyway?"

Bob stroked his moustache a few times, till it started to creep me out. "Actually, what happened to Jules has been good for business. When we got back from the cruise, a couple of the news people interviewed the passengers. After their stories aired, the phone was ringing off the hook. Filled up the voice mail."

"Get enough business to pay for that number-two engine you need?"

"It's a start."

"That's good. You didn't look so happy in the bar the other night."

"Long day."

"Have you heard anything more about your money?"

"I asked Detective Wankum. He said they're still going over the books Jules kept. Apparently there are two sets."

"Jules knew he was in trouble," I said. "He went to see Greg Argent."

"Who's that?"

"Greg owns the Schooner down in Ipswich. He used to be a mobster. Jules went to see him and asked to borrow a lot of money."

"Really." Bob looked out over the bridge.

"My guess is, he was trying to get enough to pay you and some other people. But Greg wouldn't loan it to him."

"Detective Wankum said that in 'situations of this type,' the victims are usually the ones left holding the bag."

"That's rough."

He frowned at me. "I didn't kill Jules."

"I didn't say you did."

"Then why are you here?"

"I wanted to ask you some more about the night of Jimmy Wilmot's accident."

For a second he looked confused, then his head snapped to, as if he'd just remembered our conversation at the bar. "I don't really have anything to say."

"I think you do."

"What does this have to do with what happened to Jules?"

"I won't know until I hear it."

"I don't see-"

"Jimmy was at the waterfront that morning. He knew Jules was dead. Maybe he knows who killed him."

Bob thought for a moment, weighing the situation, then nodded. "Well, see, I was a pretty good kid in high school. I ran cross-country, kept my nose clean, hardly drank, never smoked cannabis. Sometimes Jimmy and I ran together in the summer. We lived near each other. He was already a football star. You'd think he'd be a jerk, but he was a genuinely nice kid. You know what high school is like, the kids are awful to each other. I saw it all the time teaching. It's Darwinism run amok. But people noticed Jimmy was decent to me. The other football players started saying hi to me in the halls. And then when August rolled around they talked me into trying out for wide receiver, because I could run. And I made it. You see? All of a sudden, over the course of a few months, I go from being a nobody to a somebody. A starter on the football team. I got a girlfriend and everything. It was all thanks to him."

"So you and Jimmy played together."

"We had a great season." Bob nodded to himself, looking happy for a moment. "I caught six touchdown passes. We won our division. And then it was the middle of our senior year, and football was over. And damn it, it was time to have some fun before we graduated. I'd been good my whole life, an A student, never in trouble. And I guess I felt like I was making up for lost time.

"Jimmy and I drank quite a bit that winter. He did drugs with Jules, too." He looked both ways, as if to make sure his son wasn't listening. "I didn't do that. But I did see things. I tied one on with them almost every Friday and Saturday night. I've always regretted not going back for cross-country that spring, I could have had another letter. But I told myself that cross-country was the old me, and the new me wanted to get hammered." He stared out through the windshield at the harbor, lost in the memories.

"So, the night of Jimmy's accident?"

He thought before speaking, debating with himself. "That Saturday night, we all went out to the island to party with Emmitt. He was what, three or four years older. An adult, legally, but he didn't mind having us out there, usually. That night I was with this young lady, a cheerleader. The kind of girl who wouldn't have looked at me before I started hanging around with Jimmy. We'd been going out for a few weeks. Jules caught a ride out to the island with us. We were supposed to meet the rest of the crowd there. I went to the door with Jules, just to make sure it was OK if I brought the girl in. He was going to ask Emmitt. But when we got there, there was already an argument going on between Jimmy and Emmitt."

He picked up his cold pipe and fondled it. "Jules went in. I said I was going to go park around the corner and we'd walk back, but, well, the young lady suggested she and I might go someplace private." He actually blushed.

"Bob?"

He put down the pipe as if it burned his hand. "That's really all I know. We left. We parked up at the end of the island and walked on the beach. There was nobody else around. You know how quiet it can get out there at night. We had a bottle and a blanket. The lighthouse was flashing green. I took it as a signal. But it wasn't very long before we heard the crash, a loud bang like a gunshot, only worse, and then the sirens." His eyes glistened. "We walked around to the harbor side, and we could see all the flashing lights coming from town. Police, fire trucks, an ambulance. It was awful. We figured the police would stop anyone driving the causeway, so we hid out and waited. I didn't get her home until nearly dawn, so she had to sneak in.

"By the time I got home, it was on the radio what had happened. Everybody was talking about it. Jules came to my house and said I'd better forget that I'd seen Jimmy that night if I knew what was good for me, and I'd better make sure my girl did too. He said we'd all get in trouble if it got out. And so I didn't say anything, and neither did she."

I pondered his story. I was surprised he'd invested money with Jules, even all these years later, but maybe he'd been bullied into that, too.

"Are you sure you don't know what Emmitt and Jimmy were fighting about?"

"No idea. I told you, I never went in. I know Jimmy was never really too fond of Emmitt or even Jules to begin with. He had kind of a chip on his shoulder about them not being natives and having a place at the beach. His family had a cabin out there but the government took it to create the refuge. He used to make remarks about it after he'd had a couple. I think he was just looking for a reason to dislike them because they weren't from here."

"You never talked to any of the other kids about that night?"

He shook his head. "Not a word. I don't know who else was there, and I didn't ask."

"What about your girlfriend?"

He sighed. "She was sort of like me, a good kid who'd gotten a little off track. I think that night shook her up. The drinking. We were close to giving each other our virginity. And then the accident happened. I don't think she ended up with very pleasant associations with that night. Or me."

"You never talked about it?"

He shrugged. "We hardly spoke again. Graduation was a few weeks later, and I haven't seen her since. I'd had a crush on her for months. I was thrilled when we made a date. But after the accident, it was like we were total strangers. We sat in my car and didn't touch each other and watched the lighthouse blink, waiting for morning."

"What's her name?"

"I won't drag her into this. She moved away after graduation. Her father got transferred, or at least that's what her friends told me. They weren't townies or anything. As far as I know, she hasn't been here since."

"Not even for class reunions or something like that?"

He shook his head. "It was our thirtieth last year. I was so stupid. I'd just gotten divorced and I actually went hoping to see her. Can you imagine?"

"Yes, I can." I knew how divorce could turn you inside out.

"She didn't come, of course. She's probably forgotten all about Libertyport by now."

I doubted that, no matter how hard she tried.

Bob picked up the pipe again, turning it over in his hand. "I wish it never happened."

"It was a long time ago," I said.

"Not long enough."

When I climbed down from the bridge, Carl was still swabbing the deck. A few early-arriving afternoon passengers watched from the boardwalk. He looked up when I passed, and we nodded. I hoped he'd remember his high school years more fondly than his father did.

TWENTY-TWO

Sarah McNulty and three sympathizers stood on the plaza in Dock Square holding up her homemade WAR IS NOT THE ANSWER banner, which had a rainbow border and a dove in one corner. I pressed the walk button and waited, feeling moderately guilty because I'd never joined their lonely vigil. I agreed with their cause, but I couldn't share their idealism. Maybe that was the difference between a folksinger and a singer-songwriter.

Sarah saw me crossing the street and waved me over. Next to her was a small folding table with buttons and bumperstickers for sale, and a basket for donations. She studied my bruises with a combination of concern and disapproval. Clearly I hadn't been waging peace.

"Baxter, how are you?"

"Not bad, and yourself?"

"Still outraged by the atrocities our government commits in our names. But being out here makes me feel better. Would you like to join us today? You look as if you could use a little more harmony in your life."

"Not right now, thanks, but I'll buy a button."

"That'll do for a start," she said.

"My purchase is contingent on you agreeing not to mention this" – I pointed to my face – "to my mother." They were both members of a group that gathered at the library on Monday nights to knit scarves and mittens for the needy while dishing about their friends who hadn't shown up.

"I won't bring it up," she said, watching me put my two dollars in the basket. "But I won't lie to her, either."

"Fair enough."

"Have you found out any more about what happened to Jules?"

"A lot of facts but no answers."

"That's the way it often is in this world," she said. "The answers must come from within."

"How about you? Have you heard anything else about your money?"

She pursed her lips and shook her head. "Our lawyer is not optimistic. My husband is beside himself."

I tried to summon some encouraging words as I pinned the button to my shirt. The best I could do was, "Keep the faith."

"Of course," she said. "By the way, I'm sorry I missed your performance last night. Nightclubs aren't really possible for us now. I'm lucky if Arnie can stay awake through '60 Minutes.'"

"My playing wouldn't help keep him awake either."

"Hush up. I *am* looking forward to your audition this afternoon."

"Right. Where is that, again?"

She shook her head at my irresponsible nature. Ma was going to hear about this.

Wankum sat on my front step when I got home, blocking the door. I needed to get ready for the audition, but he was in no hurry. He frowned at my peace sign button.

"Doesn't look like that's doing you much good."

"What do you mean?"

He nodded at my lumpy face, with no trace of Sarah's concern. "I heard someone jumped you in the parking lot, beat the crap out of you."

"Not exactly."

"Want to tell me about it?"

"Hypothetically speaking, it was in a dark corner of the parking lot, and he pulled my jacket up over my head so I didn't see a thing. One minute I'm putting my guitar in the trunk, and the next thing I know, I'm waking up on the ground. So there isn't much I could tell you."

"He take your wallet?"

"Nope."

"He didn't take Jules' wallet, either."

"I don't think it was the same person. This guy had a partner. And they didn't shoot me, they just knocked me around a little."

"On the other hand, it's the second violent crime in the parking lot in five days. At almost the same time of night. Could be a pattern."

"I suppose it's possible."

"But you'd rather not help us out with a statement."

"I'd rather not be in the papers again."

"I understand that. But if it's connected?"

"I really don't think it is. Not directly, anyway."

He gave me a hard look, a cop look. "I also heard you had lunch with Guido Argento. Is it connected to that?"

"He calls himself Greg Argent now."

"Uh huh. So did Guido have something to do with this?"

"Which part?"

He sighed in exasperation. "With Jules getting killed. With somebody beating you up in the parking lot. With any of it."

"I don't think he had anything to do with Jules getting killed."

"Why?"

I didn't see any way around telling him. "Jules went to see Greg a few days before the murder and tried to borrow money off him. Jules thought that Greg is still, you know."

"A coke-dealing mafia scumbag."

"Something like that. But Greg says he's not anymore."

Wankum smirked. "Right."

"I knew him when he lived here," I said.

"He supplied you and all your playmates, right?"

"I knew him. So I thought I'd ask him what it was all about. What Jules was doing there."

"Great, so you're a detective now."

"He wasn't going to talk to *you* about it."

"Who said he'd have a choice?"

"You want to hear this or not?"

He held up a hand. "Go ahead."

"We had a nice lunch, couple of beers, talked about our kids, and then I asked him about Jules. And he told me Jules came down and hit him up for money, or at least an introduction to a loan shark. He seemed to feel bad for Jules, actually."

"The Argentos don't have ordinary human emotions."

I shrugged. "I believed him when he said he's out of the business. So I don't think Guido – Greg – is behind it."

Wankum made a face, spat on the sidewalk. "But you've got an idea."

"Everything seems to point to Jules' business. Have you talked to any of his clients?"

"You mean, have I found out that his business was all fucked up and he was stealing from them and that probably a dozen of them had enough at stake to think about whacking him?"

"Um, yeah."

"We're not completely incompetent, you know. I talked to his clients myself, and we're running down their alibis now. But none of them acted the least bit twitchy, and none of them owns a .22. So humor me. You say Jules went and begged Argento for cash."

"More or less. He was pretty drunk. A really embarrassing scene, the way Greg described it. He ended up driving Jules home. You can ask Elaine. She was there when he brought Jules in."

"But you think he might have something to do with smacking you around."

I shrugged. "Maybe me poking around in his business pissed him off."

"So even though he's clean, he sends a couple of goons to smack you around, to send you a message?"

"More like this big guy who tends bar for him. There were two of them, so either Greg was with him or he brought a friend."

"And yet somehow you think Guido can't be the one who shot Jules."

"I don't know about *can't*. But I don't think he did it, no."

"You're very understanding." Wankum grimaced at my naivete, then stood and brushed off the seat of his pants. "Stay away from Guido and don't go asking anybody any more questions, will you? You're messing around with the wrong people, and for once it's not just me."

As a seventh-grader, I shot endless racks of eight-ball in the Second Religious Society basement while my parents attended choir rehearsals upstairs on Thursday nights. The game was always me against Minnesota Fats, and I always won.

Now the low-ceilinged grotto of yellowed linoleum and cheap paneling had been done over with wall-to-wall carpet and recessed lighting. The crisp white walls were hung with Sunday School art projects. I missed the worn green felt of the warped youth-group pool table, where I'd learned that a straight line wasn't always the surest route to the pocket. Outside the ground-level windows, the sky had clouded over and a breeze stirred the trees. Despite the new decor I felt the old gloom of being trapped in the church basement when I wanted to be anywhere else.

Red Suspenders sat in the front row of a bank of folding chairs. Instead of his trademark apparel, he wore a glitter-trimmed white jumpsuit that stretched around his beer gut in obvious distress. His black hair had been tamed into the rough equivalent of a pompadour. Suddenly the sideburns made sense. He was the spitting image of late-period Fat Elvis. He held a boom box on his lap like a pet, and I had a creepy premonition that he was about to play "Mirror Ball Man."

His small, dark eyes lit up when he saw me, with the same simple joy that chasing me home from school had once brought him. Seeing him with a belt, even a wide white one covered in costume jewels, I finally remembered his real name: Ronald Terwey. He had grown up on a farm on the edge of town until it was taken to expand the industrial park. His family moved to an apartment in the South End, and he targeted me as a way to work out his social anxieties.

"I guess we're in the same line of work now, huh?" He stood and extended a hand. This time I took it.

"When did you become a singer?"

"Oh, I started goin' to karaoke nights up in Seabury a few years ago. People said I was good, so I got myself the outfit and started practicing. Now I got a gig at Boot Scooters up there on Wednesdays."

"Wow. Um, congratulations."

"Thanks, man," he said and clapped me on the back. "Hey, what happened to your face? Somebody smack you?"

"It was nothing."

"If you need backup, man, call me anytime. Seriously. And hey, good luck today!"

Should I have said, *You too*? I slipped into the back row with my guitar. The other hopefuls included the Blacksmith Alley busker known as Harp Girl and the lesbionic coffeehouse favorite Kit Bragg.

Kit turned around and folded her elaborately inked arms on the back of her seat. She wore black, Doc Martens, and a platinum-blond brush cut. "Hey, so they think you killed that guy, huh?"

"I didn't, though."

"Of course not. You are not that kind of guy." She was in her late twenties, sober and far removed from a teenaged cutting habit, although all the ink couldn't quite conceal the scars. "What happened to your face?"

"A little misunderstanding in the parking lot outside the Rum House."

"Oh, I've been *there*."

I had the feeling that she'd made out better than I had.

Libertyport Old Home Days started in the 1950s as a way for the natives to celebrate their heritage amid the first wave of factory closings. It had grown into a ten-day, town-wide festival that attracted hordes of tourists. A free concert series in the waterfront park was attended by a couple of thousand people on blankets and lawn chairs and dozens more partying on boats. For most of us it was our biggest audience of the year.

This year, the board of directors had decreed that all performers would be required to audition or else submit a 10-minute video of a live performance. That was fine for out-of-town bands and first-timers, but I'd been playing the event for nearly twenty years. The new hurdle rankled, and I wasn't the only one who felt that way.

"It just ain't right," said Fred "Sugarpine" Gurganus, an overweight white guy with a grey ponytail who'd been playing the same dozen blues standards in local bars for just as long. His down-home nickname was just the most obvious symptom of a wildly inaccurate self-image. "We should boycott."

"It *is* ridiculous," Kit said.

"Strike!" Harp Girl said and giggled. She wore her regular busking costume, a medieval frock displaying a perhaps anachronistic amount of cleavage.

"I haven't been a musician long enough to know what's right," said Ronald Terwey, "but it doesn't look like we got much leverage."

He nodded toward the dozen newcomers. A bunch more had sent DVDs that were piled on one end of the table in front of the committee.

A fake cough from Sarah McNulty brought us all to attention. She sat between Dan Ockerbloom and the mayor. On a shelf behind them were a hissing coffee urn and a bag of Mint Milanos.

"Welcome to the auditions for this year's Libertyport Old Home Days Concert Series," Mayor Echo said, rising from his seat with a protective glance toward the refreshments. "Nice to see so many of you here. I want to thank you all for participating."

"Why *do* we have to be here?" Sugarpine growled. "Locals never had to audition before."

"You're right, it *is* a change in policy," the mayor said. "Sarah, perhaps you can explain."

"Certainly. As you know, this is the fiftieth anniversary year of Libertyport Old Home Days," she said. "We want to ensure that this year's festival is the best we can make it. And many on the central steering committee felt that an audition process was the best way to guarantee that."

As she spoke, the mayor slid back into his seat and reached for the Milanos.

"What was wrong with the performances in previous years?" Sugarpine was a public aid social worker by day, thus experienced at hassling the system. "Were there complaints?"

"I'm not aware, specifically, of everything that went into the decision," Sarah said. "But my general sense is that there were some acts last year that just didn't quite fit the venue or the audience as comfortably as we would have liked. There was a consensus that there ought to be a little more scrutiny."

"Could you name any specific acts?" Sugarpine said. "Because I would hate to think that we were being censored based on politics, or you know, ethnic profiling."

Sarah took a deep breath and let it out slowly, summoning patience. "I believe it was more a matter of what was suitable content for families, especially during the daytime, when quite a large number of those in the audience were children."

"So after all these years, we aren't good enough for the yuppies, is that what you're saying?"

Frustrated, Sarah turned to the mayor, who froze with a cookie halfway to his mouth.

"We just want to ensure that this is truly an event for the whole family?" he ventured before taking a bite.

"Usually that means no queers." Kit said.

The mayor had a coughing fit. "Crumbs! Wrong way!" he rasped. Sarah gave him a withering look.

"I know what it was." Dan Ockerbloom leaned toward a mike. "It was when Trouser Weasel got up there at two in the afternoon and played 'Handjob on the Ferris Wheel,' and half the people packed up their kids and left. That's what it was."

Trouser Weasel again. Kit stifled a giggle. Fred sat down. Sarah colored slightly and shuffled her papers. The mayor became intensely interested in the Sunday School art hanging on the walls. Even Ronald Terwey, whose teenaged signature still adorned fading pornographic graffiti on several railroad underpasses in town, found a cuff that needed adjusting.

"So anyway," Sarah said at last, "we're going to start the auditions now, first-come, first-served. As there are quite a large number of acts, you'll each have just one song to give us an idea of what you do. Those of you whose applications have been accepted will be notified by the end of May."

Ronald Terwey's karaoke version of "Suspicious Minds" wasn't half as bad as I'd expected. His hip-swiveling dance moves were oddly delicate and girlish for a man of his frame. The overall effect was memorable.

"This still ain't right," Sugarpine said as we tuned our guitars. "Hey, did you really kill that guy? You didn't, did you?"

"Crumbs! Wrong way!" I said, grabbing my throat, although I hadn't been anywhere near the cookies.

TWENTY-THREE

By the end of the afternoon, the weather had gone downhill, with a heavy overcast and a damp, salty east wind. I drove out to Plover Island with the top up. As I crossed the marsh, curtains of mist closed around me. The *NO EVACUATION POSSIBLE* sign regained the ominous feel it had lost after two meltdown-free decades.

Emmitt didn't look surprised to see me standing on his doorstep. He made me a drink, then led me to the living room. He sat down in a leather armchair by a table that already had a glass on it, along with a dish of peanuts and a yellowed paperback. The Ross MacDonald mystery had probably been here since his father's time. A small fire hissed and crackled in the hearth, just enough to ward off the damp. I stood by it and warmed my hands, getting a close look at Alden Titward's "Plover Island Light in Winter," the painting so cold and melancholy it seemed to counteract the fire's heat.

"Somebody beat you up," Emmitt observed. He didn't sound either happy or unhappy about it.

"No big deal."

"Well, you didn't come out here for the view." He nodded out the rain-streaked windows at the roiling surf. "So to what do I owe the honor?"

I sat down. "Tell me about the night Jimmy Wilmot had his accident."

He nodded as if he expected it, but said, "I don't see what that has to do with what happened to Jules."

"Neither do I, yet."

"Well...if you think it will help." He stretched, took a drink. Outside a seagull caught an updraft where the wind came off the water and went up over the roof, out of sight.

"I dropped out of college in my junior year and moved out here," Emmitt said. "This place hadn't been built yet. It was just that little shack that my father liked so goddamn much. I'd come out here to wrestle with his ghost, I guess. To see if I was as good a painter as I hoped I was. I didn't have a girlfriend, which was unusual. I was trying to bear down. Just me and a few books and records and my paints.

"Jules was in his last year of high school, getting the crap kicked out of him on a weekly basis and hating the place. He didn't have many friends. Our dear mother was well into her long decline, out of it on booze and pills. So that winter he started coming out to see me. I was surprised at first, given the way things usually were with us. But I don't think he had anyplace else to go. I had beer and weed, and pretty soon he started bringing around a couple of townie kids he was trying to impress. They'd come out on a Friday night and we'd play cards and party. You know how the island is, or how it used to be. No one bothered us. I was trying to take care of him, in my own way. Bad judgment on my part, I suppose, but I wasn't much more than a kid myself then."

"Jimmy was one of the townies?"

Emmitt nodded. "Good kid, funny, hell of a football player. I was glad Jules was making friends like that. Someone to stick up for him, now that I wasn't around. Jimmy's only problem was that once he started drinking, he didn't want to stop. He had the Trans Am, so he usually drove when they came out here, but more than once I had to drive them home in it and hitch back. He got so bad I was about to tell Jules he couldn't bring him out here anymore."

"But you didn't."

Rueful smile. He got up and walked to the window, his voice downshifting into a slow, dreamy cadence. "One night Jimmy brought his girlfriend with him. This absolutely beautiful blonde. And as soon as I saw her, I had to have her. I didn't care if she was underage. So I did exactly the opposite of what I'd planned to do. I started inviting them all out here more. So I could see her, work on her. You know what I mean."

"You painted her, I bet."

He sat again, as if the memory had taken his legs, the chair groaning under his bulk. "You bet I did. She was bored more than anything. She was having problems with Jimmy's drinking, too. I was the handsome older guy who took an interest. She came out here on her own to pose for me. I even offered to pay her, but she wouldn't take my money. It was her adventure, you see. It was a Thursday night. She kept it secret from everyone. More exciting that way. It was easy to get her to take her clothes off. God she was beautiful. She had to sneak home before her parents got up in the morning. And Saturday…"

His voice trailed off.

I said, "Saturday was the night Jimmy had his accident."

He took a long pull on his drink and sighed. "Jules invited them all out here. Her and Jimmy, and some little mouse who had a crush on Jimmy, and another couple, they never even came in. I didn't know the other ones. Everyone was drinking a lot. All those hormones. And then Jimmy found the painting I'd started on Thursday night. I'd been working on it for, like, thirty hours straight. I guess I wasn't in my right mind, either, or I would have put it away." He chuckled, and I was certain he'd left the picture out on purpose for Jimmy to find.

"He was angry?"

"He went apeshit. Screaming at me, screaming at her. Screaming at Jules when he came in, as if it was his fault. He was already more shitfaced than the rest of us, of course. I think he'd started drinking before he got here. And I suppose finding a naked painting of your girlfriend can be traumatic. Jules wrestled him away to keep him from smashing it." Emmitt couldn't suppress the note of triumph in his voice. "Jimmy and his girl went in another room and had a huge fight. While they were in there, I took Jules aside and asked him what we were going to do, because she wasn't eighteen yet, you know, and we weren't townies. There could have been a lot of trouble. Christ, I'd defiled the vestal virgin of Old Home Days. And Jules said, just keep giving him booze, he'll pass out, and we can deal with him tomorrow.

"So I grabbed a bottle of rum, and walked into the room and took a big swig right in front of him and said we should be men about it and talk. I handed him the bottle and he guzzled like it was beer. She tried to get him to stop, and he wouldn't. Which I guess I liked, because it drove the two of them even further apart.

"Jimmy took a piss off the deck and almost fell over the railing. And when he came back in, he threw the bottle at me and missed, even though I was, like, five feet away. And then he screamed at her that she could fuck anyone she liked, he was through with her, and he called her some names. She started crying, at which point I tried to shut him up. It got pretty rough. Jimmy tried to slug me and ended up hitting Jules. We were all rolling around on the floor. Finally Jules got us separated. Jimmy pulled out the keys to the Trans Am and said he was leaving, and none of us made a move to stop him. Not even her. He peeled out of the driveway. And you know what happened next."

We considered this for a moment, with no sound but the surf crashing on the beach outside.

"Who was the girl?"

"I thought you would have figured that out by now." The strangest smile I'd ever seen spread across his face. "It was Elaine."

By the time I followed him to the master bedroom, he was banging around in the walk-in closet. I opened the slider and stepped out onto the Juliet balcony overlooking the beach, leaning on the metal railing with the chilly mist in my face. Houses made a broken line of twinkling lights that curved to the north and vanished in the gloom. To the south, the refuge was pure velvety darkness.

It was a beautiful spot, even in this weather, but I didn't think I could have lived here after what had happened. Maybe that was why he tore down the cottage and built this house. Trying to start fresh.

"Since you're so interested," he said, dragging a wooden packing crate out of the closet and depositing it on the bed with a grunt. "My juvenilia."

He unlatched the top and grabbed one of several paintings inside. He knew which one he wanted without looking. He slid it out and leaned it against the headboard, facing us. "What do you think?"

The canvas was unfinished, the background only sketched in. One corner was crumpled from the struggle. Technically the picture wasn't as accomplished as Emmitt's later work, but in a way it was more powerful. It was a portrait of the then-Elaine Gordon lying naked on an old green couch. Her legs were bent at the knee and slightly parted. One arm dangled toward the floor, and the other was folded behind her head. She was completely exposed. Her expression was the most thrilling part of the picture. It seemed to say that this was not her idea, but that she would do anything for him.

I did the math in my head. The picture was painted five or six years before Elaine and I had our little fling. When I knew her, she'd still been gorgeous – even today, she was a beautiful woman – but there was something about her expression in that picture that suggested an intensity of passion we had not discovered. I wondered if she and Jules had ever found it in their marriage.

"You can see why I thought she was special."

"It's some picture."

"It was the first piece I did that made me think I really could follow in the old bastard's footsteps." Finally he tore himself away and looked around for his cocktail. Realized he didn't have one and turned back to her for sustenance. "I had to keep it out of sight through my marriages. Jules knew about it, of course, but he never once asked what happened to it. Maybe now I should hang it up."

"What would Elaine think of that?"

That smile returned, and it told me his last secret.

"How long have you two been seeing each other again?"

"About a year, this time." No hesitation.

"This time?"

He grinned and put the picture back in the crate.

"After the accident, of course, she had to act the grieving girlfriend," he said in the kitchen, pouring Tanqueray. "Sitting by his bedside for hours, spending time with his mother, and all the time knowing the truth. We were all terrified that it would come out. There were enough people here that night that it was hard to believe we could keep the secret, but we did. We all kind of went our separate ways. I don't think any of us even talked to each other, except for Jules. He made sure everyone kept quiet.

"I didn't dare call her. Every time someone came to the door, I kept expecting it to be the police. And then one night, there was a knock, and I turned on the porch light and opened the door and there she was."

For a moment he was lost in the memory. I resisted, but the image came anyway, Elaine hurtling into his arms.

"We were together that summer, always hiding, sneaking around. She parked her car in the beach lot or at an empty house and walked here after dark. It was fantastic. The thrill of the forbidden, I suppose. And then her father sent her away to college. It gave her an excuse to finally let go of Jimmy. I visited her there a couple of times but…it was difficult. I was older. We drifted apart. I met someone else and got her pregnant. You knew Debra, my first wife, right?"

An artist herself, a smoker and drinker and wineglass hurler. "I think you were already separated when I came back to town."

"Right. Elaine and I got back together then." A flicker of remembered pleasure crossed his features. "I wanted to go public. My divorce was coming. We could have done it. But I think she was feeling delayed guilt about the accident. We drifted apart. She had other boyfriends." He reached across the counter and clinked glasses with me. "She said you were a riot, by the way. She spent more time with that goombah, but she liked you better."

Emmitt had been drinking and talking for so long now that he seemed to have no inhibitions left. I was feeling far too loose myself. It occurred to me that I hadn't eaten since lunch. I grabbed a handful of peanuts.

"How did Elaine and Jules hook up?"

"After Guido, she lived in Boston for a while, worked at the Museum of Fine Arts. I always thought it was interesting that she chose art as a career. A little while later I married Irene."

Ex-wife number two, a psychiatrist.

"Irene and I donated a couple of my father's paintings to the museum, and the deal was they were going to take one of mine too, for the permanent collection. But at the last moment they decided they didn't want mine. I wasn't enough of a name then, I guess. So I boycotted the party, and Jules went in my place. Maybe he knew Elaine was going to be there, I don't know.

"Truthfully, I think he wanted her from the beginning. He saw her first, you know, in high school. But he couldn't compete with Jimmy, much less me. I've always figured he was biding his time. By the time they ran into each other at the MFA, he was almost thirty, and cut much more of a figure than he used to. When I heard they were dating, I told myself, oh well, we were done anyway. She married him, had his kids. Made friends with my wife. Hell, she got along better with Irene than I did. The past was always there, but we had sort of a silent pact to ignore it. That went on for years."

"And then?"

He drained his glass. "A few years ago, after Irene left me, I called her one night when Jules was out of town. She hung up, but I kept calling. It took her a while to come around, but eventually she admitted she felt the same way I do. That it was never over, not since that first night. We've been seeing each other on the sly ever since. We were going to wait until her kids were off to prep school, and then she was going to divorce him. What's a couple more years, right?"

"Did Jules know?"

"I don't think so. I don't think he could have lived with it." He winced.

Something was driving Jules toward the edge. Business problems. Money problems. He was dating teenagers, taking drugs. Doing it in Emmitt's house to boot. Making a point? Finding out about Emmitt and Elaine could have set him off. But how did it connect to his murder?

"I didn't kill my brother," Emmitt said, as if he'd read my mind. "But I didn't do him any favors, either."

He turned to fill his own glass again and hide his sudden tears. When he turned back and reached toward me with the big green bottle, I pulled my glass away.

"I better get going."

"But we're having so much fun," he said, cheeks still wet.

"I've got to drive, and if I stay any longer..."

"Sleep in the guest room."

"I don't think that's a good idea."

He shrugged, frowned. "Your call."

I was afraid he would try to swear me to secrecy, ask me for promises I wouldn't keep. But instead he yawned and said, "It is what it is." And then he waved as if across a great distance. I showed myself out.

I'd been letting him out-drink me two or three to one. Even so, I knew I shouldn't get behind the wheel. But I couldn't stay here. Too many bad vibes. As I pulled out of the driveway, I rolled down my window to let the cold air wash over me, hoping it would help me stay alert.

Even the lighthouse couldn't penetrate the murk. All the way back to town, misty phantoms separated themselves from the thick fog on the marsh, twirling and dancing across the pavement in the headlights. I kept my eye on the telephone poles as they flashed past, wondering which one marked the spot where Jimmy had finally lost control.

The one thing Emmitt hadn't said was that he was sorry.

TWENTY-FOUR

I skipped breakfast at Foley's on Monday morning and went straight to the Rum House. Rain came and went, splattering the windows in wind-driven squalls. Run-down fishing boats and sleek yachts alike rode uneasily on the chop. Even the gulls kept their heads down, hunched in a line on the deck railing, as evenly spaced as if they'd measured wingtip-to-wingtip.

Davey stood behind the bar, tallying the weekend's receipts. He pointed in the direction of the coffee without looking up. I poured gratefully, headachy from Emmitt's gin and twitchy from too-vague memories of the drive home.

"What you been up to?"

"I talked to Capt. Bob yesterday, and he finally told me what happened to Shimmy Jimmy."

"No shit?" Looking at me now.

"Then I went out to see Emmitt, asked him a few questions."

"You're a regular Columbo," he said, betraying how long it had been since he watched prime-time television on a regular basis. "I don't know if you're cut out to be a private eye, though, liberal folksinger like you. You don't even own a gun. What are they gonna call you, the Blue State Detective?" He hardy-harred while topping up his coffee.

I was in a blue state, all right. If there was a song in my heart now, it was a saxophone solo as bleak as the weather.

"So, detective, what happened to Jimmy?"

I told him what Emmitt and Jules had done to Jimmy. And what Emmitt and Elaine had done to Jules. Old crimes and recent misdemeanors. A long trail of shitty behavior starting in adolescence and loop-de-looping right to the present day, when everyone was old enough to know better.

"I've turned it around and around in my mind, but I still can't figure out who killed Jules, or why," I said. "Emmitt and Elaine are possibilities, alone or together. But they were driving him over the edge already. Why take the risk of actually killing him?"

"Unlikely," he agreed, running a pencil down a column of figures.

"It could have been any one of the clients Jules was stealing from, but Wankum has talked to most of them and doesn't think any of them did it. Capt. Bob is a possibility, I suppose, but it's kind of hard to believe he could do it."

"What else you got?"

"The other ones with an obvious motive are Jimmy and his mother, but how would they find out what Emmitt and Jules did all those years ago, if Jimmy didn't remember?"

"I don't see either one of them committing murder, anyway, do you?"

"No, and even if they did, I'd think it would be Emmitt they'd go after."

"It's a puzzler."

Neither one of us said anything for a while. Davey worked his numbers and I stared out at the rain. Normally on a morning like this, I might have returned to bed with a book, ready to wallow in my blue state. I had a feeling, though, that if I didn't find out who had murdered Jules, no one would. And in a few years all anyone would remember was "Send The Innkeeper Packing" and the fact that I didn't have an alibi.

I said, "I'm going to go see Greg Argent again."

Davey looked up, frowning. "That don't sound like the greatest idea. You really think he's going to tell you anything?"

"He's not a bad guy. I think if he sees my face, he'll feel bad about it. Maybe I can convince him to tell me the truth."

"Good plan, Lucy. You want Ethel to come along for backup?"

"No, I'll be fine. He's probably at the restaurant, doing exactly what you're doing. Even if he is a bad guy, he won't do anything to me there."

"Be careful," Davey said. He never said that.

The strip mall parking lot was nearly empty. Nobody was spending money in the twee little shops this morning. A sign hanging inside the glass door of the Schooner said CLOSED MONDAYS. But there was one car parked close to the entrance, a black Mercedes coupe with the license plate GRGSBNZ.

No one answered my knock. I tried the door. Unlocked.

"Hello?" The chairs were up on the tables, just a few lights on. I heard music down the side hall and followed the sound, passing the restrooms and a door to the kitchen. A windbreaker hung by itself on a row of pegs. The music came from a door at the end of the hall. Led Zeppelin, "Immigrant Song." Thudding guitar, crashing drums, wailing vocals. Greg was Classic Rock all the way.

I took a deep breath, willed away the butterflies in my stomach and knocked. No answer. Led Zep drowning me out? I knocked again, louder.

"Greg? It's Bax."

I pictured him pulling a gun from a desk drawer or slipping on some brass knuckles. I felt a strong urge to turn around and run. But I put my hand on the doorknob and turned.

"Greg?"

Robert Plant's shrieks leaped in volume as I pushed the door open to reveal a small, windowless office, with fake pine paneling and fluorescent lights. Greg slumped in the black leather chair behind his desk, three or four bullet holes in his chest, a surprisingly small amount of blood on the front of his long-sleeved Life is Great T-shirt. The little cartoon guy on the front of the shirt was playing hockey. Greg's chin rested on his chest, and his face was a greyish blue that almost matched the shirt. His eyes were open, but he hadn't seen this coming.

Bullet holes in a Life Is Great shirt. It was the kind of cheap irony I would have written a song about, normally. But it wasn't so funny when it happened to someone I knew.

My heart pounded and my hands and feet tingled. The office suddenly seemed very small. Robert Plant kept screaming. I wondered if the killer was hiding behind the closet door, about to leap out and nail me, too.

I was backing out of the room when I thought of my finger-prints on the doorknob. My worries immediately switched from the killer hiding in the closet to what would happen if I was identified at a second murder scene, again with motive. Was someone setting me up? I had a napkin from the Rum House in my pocket, and I used it to wipe the knob. I'd just get out of here and hope no one saw the guy with the red convertible. But that wasn't a good bet. The shopkeepers next door had nothing to do this morning but look out the window. The police would find out I'd been here, so I might as well call them myself. Again. But this time I would look harder for clues first.

On the radio, Led Zep was replaced by Steve Miller, the one where Billy Joe and Bobbie Sue offed a guy while robbing his castle. That wasn't what happened here, to judge by the neat piles of cash on the desktop. Mostly small bills, stacked by denomination. A night de-posit bag sat next to them, unzipped and empty. A cylindrical wall safe hung open, a few documents visible inside. The screen of Greg's PC was blank, but when I touched the space bar with my napkin, a spread-sheet popped up. He was doing the books, preparing to deposit the weekend's receipts. But whoever killed him hadn't cared about money.

Framed family snapshots stood on a corner of the desk, includ-ing one of Carmine, the murderous old lizard looking mellow in the good seats at Fenway Park. Why couldn't I get seats like that?

Amid the stacks of money was a small wineglass with a puddle of purplish liquid drying in the bottom. I sniffed sweet, grapey port. It didn't do anything good for my stomach.

Two armchairs sat in front of the desk. A manila envelope rested on the seat of one, flap open, papers sticking out. A handwritten inscription in black felt-tip marker ran along one edge of the envelope.

Pictures of You and Jimmy.

I used the napkin to peek at the envelope's contents: a thin stack of blank paper, probably right out of the printer tray on the sideboard. Someone had needed to make the envelope look like it was full.

Was the envelope what the killer had been looking for? Was "*You*" the killer? And who was "*You*" anyway? I was trying to conjure an idea of what it all might mean when I heard the front door open.

"Ipswich police! Anybody home?"

"Just me," I called back, stuffing the napkin into my pocket.

I heard footsteps in the hall, something scraping along the wall, an urgent whisper.

"Are you Mr. Argento? Argent, whatever the fuck it is." Of course the local cops knew all about Greg and his father. "You were supposed to take the kids to school. Your ex-wife reported you missing." More than Elaine had done for Jules.

Deep breath. "I'm not Greg. I'm a friend of his from Libertyport. He's here, though, and I think he's dead."

More whispers. "Are you armed?"

"No, I'm a folksinger."

Long pause.

"Put your hands behind your head and step over where we can see you."

I did what they said, feeling a scrotal quiver when I saw the two big, square, black guns pointed at me through the open doorway. Both cops were young, blond, gym-rat types in crisp new uniforms. The taller one had a neck as wide as his head. The other one had no neck at all. They pressed their bodies against opposite sides of the hall, aiming with both hands. No Neck was in front, and he lost his determined scowl when he saw my face.

"Hey, I know you," he said. "You played for my high-school music class."

"I did?"

"You were really funny. You brought your guitar and-"

The other cop said, "*Dude.*"

"Oh, right. Would you turn around and put your hands against that back wall, please, Mr. McLean? Sorry about this."

I did what he said. They came into the room fast, one of them bumping the door. No Neck swore softly when he saw Greg, then started talking on his radio. The other one cuffed me behind my back, and not gently. Maybe he was pissed that I hadn't come to *his* high school.

They took me back to the station and sat me at a table in another small conference room. No Neck stood in the open doorway and stared into space, determined not to slip up and act friendly again. My mind raced, trying to fit it all together. Jules. Greg Argent. *Pictures of You and Jimmy.* The accident. Emmitt and Elaine. The telephone poles flickering past in the fog.

Two State Police detectives arrived half an hour later, wearing identical trenchcoats. They made a show of it, walking in on either side of me, scowling. The big one with the round face and the red nose said his name was O'Hurley. The thin one didn't give his name. He had a face like an arrowhead, with taut features and hooded, dead eyes. He looked like Vladimir Putin. His expression said, *I've done things you don't even want to think about, and I'll do them to you if I have to.* One glance from him and No Neck beat it out of there, closing the door behind him.

O'Hurley took a small digital recorder out of the inside pocket of his suit coat, turned it on and set it on the table in front of me. Putin took out a reporter's notebook and an expensive silver pen. O'Hurley identified the three of us, the time and location, and then read me the Miranda warning.

"I don't need an attorney. I didn't kill anyone."

"Really?" O'Hurley said. "We kind of think you did." Putin remained silent.

"I took a gunshot residue test when Jules Titward was murdered. I'll take another one now. You'll see I didn't shoot anybody."

"What's your relationship with Greg Argent?"

He sold me weed didn't seem like the right answer. "Acquaintances. We saw each other around town. Bars. We dated some of the same women." Come to think of it, that probably wasn't the right answer either. "It was a long time ago."

"Are you dating the same woman now?"

"Not that I know of."

"Not that you know of?"

"I have no idea who he's dating. Until last week, I hadn't even thought about him in fifteen years."

"Why did you come to see him this morning?" Putin asked, his first words.

"We had lunch last week." Surprise flickered on their faces. "We kicked around the idea of me playing in the lounge some night. He wanted me to come back and talk more seriously about it, see how we might set things up."

"That was the reason for this lunch?"

"No, I wanted to ask him about a mutual friend of ours."

"Who?"

"Jules Titward. This is part of the same case, isn't it?"

"You tell us," O'Hurley said.

My theories were as vague and murky as they'd ever been. So I stuck to the topic. "Word was going that Jules had financial problems. And then I heard he had gone down to see Greg and made a scene. I guess I was curious about what happened, and it gave me a chance to catch up with Greg."

"Why would you watch to catch up with a Mafiosi puke like Guido Argento?"

"Greg said he's been out of the business a long time. I believed him."

"Guys like that never get out of the business. It's in their blood."

"Were you also anxious to find out about Jules Titward's financial problems?" Putin asked. "Because of the dispute over the Harbor Hotel?"

So they knew all about that. I wondered if they had a tape recording of "Send The Innkeeper Packing."

"Jules was dead. I don't think the hotel matters anymore."

"Did you argue with Argento at lunch?" O'Hurley again.

"No, we got along pretty well, actually. Ask that big guy who tends bar, he waited on us. We showed each other pictures of our kids. And like I said, he asked me if I wanted to play in the bar. I'm not the type of act they usually book, but he said he wanted to give it a try. I don't know if he meant it."

"What happened to your face?"

"Some asshole jumped me after I played the Rum House Saturday night."

"Music critic?" O'Hurley asked with the faintest hint of a smile.

"I don't know. I never got a look at him. He ambushed me in the parking lot and pulled my jacket up over my head."

"Like a hockey player?"

"I guess so."

"He didn't say anything?"

"Not a word."

"That's strange, isn't it?" Putin.

"I don't know, people don't punch me very often."

He found that hard to believe, to judge by his expression.

"Where were you last night?" O'Hurley.

"I had a few drinks with Jules' brother, Emmitt. But I was home by nine-ish."

"Where did you have these drinks?"

"At his house on Plover Island."

"What did you talk about?

"Nothing special. Jules, the funeral, that sort of thing."

"You were catching up with him too?"

"I guess so."

"Did anyone see you this morning before you came here to the restaurant?"

"I had coffee at the Rum House. Ask the owner, Davey Gillis."

"We're aware of Mr. Gillis," Putin said, and they both let the remark hang there for a minute.

"Do you own a gun?" O'Hurley asked.

"No. I'm a folksinger."

"What did you have against Guido Argento?" Putin leaned forward into my face. "What do you get if he's dead?"

"Not a thing, I told you. He wanted to give me a gig. I guess that won't happen now."

They kept it up for a while, covering the same ground from different directions. They still seemed convinced that I had a part in Greg's death, but they were running out of questions.

"Can I ask something?" They didn't answer, so I looked at O'Hurley, who seemed marginally more sympathetic. "What happened to Wankum?"

"This isn't his case anymore." He looked at Putin, then said to me, "You're free to go, for the moment."

I got up. Putin made the stop sign.

"You know Greg Argent's real name," he said. "So you know his roots."

"Yes."

"And if we think you killed him, then so does Carmine's old crew."

"So?"

"Put it this way," O'Hurley said. "Until we figure this out, you might want to have someone else start your car for you."

"Someone you don't like," Putin said.

Wankum stood fidgeting, a visitor in the squad room. When he saw me, he tried to put on a casual face, as if he just happened to be there when I was released.

"They're letting you go?"

"Yes, with a warning that the mob might try to kill me at any moment."

"That's possible."

"Then would you please hurry up and find who did it?"

"Those two are pretty convinced it was you. But they said you can pick up your car from the scene. You need a ride over there?"

"Sure. When we get there, will you start it for me?"

Wankum didn't smile.

"You *are* going to get yourself killed if you keep up this amateur detective shit," he said as we drove out of the station parking lot.

"You're supposed to be off the case too, aren't you? Hand over all your files to the Staties and go back to busting shoplifters in Dock Square?"

His sour expression told me I had hit a nerve.

"I can see from my office where Jules was shot," he said after a moment, looking straight ahead. "And Abigail may be a nasty old biddy who treats the department like shit, but what happened to her pisses me off on general principles. I'm not letting this go."

"What about Greg?"

"Guido Argento was a goombah dirtbag and the world is better off without him. He's not my issue here."

"He showed me pictures of his kids."

Wankum shrugged, not caring. "So what is it you're not telling me?"

"What do you mean?"

"You've been holding something back. I knew when we were sitting at Foley's. I just figured after a day or so of being a 'person of interest' you'd be shitting bricks and come in and volunteer it. I guess I underestimated you. But now I want to know what it is."

"Seriously, I don't know what you're talking about." I couldn't meet his eye, though.

He slammed a hand on the dashboard and the cruiser swerved on the wet pavement. "Damn it, tell me, you idiot."

"I can't."

"Somebody got you by the balls? They threatening you? I can help."

"It's nothing like that."

"Jesus Christ, Bax, I've got two murders here, almost three. You're not making sense."

I could only shrug.

"I know about you and Elaine," Wankum said.

"What about us?" Lame.

"You and her used to be a couple."

"It was a long time ago."

"And then Guido stole her from you."

"That didn't have anything to-"

He held up a hand. "I know. Probably got nothing to do with the murders. But you can see my problem here, right? First her husband gets whacked, and then the guy who took her from you. And you're first on the scene both times. That's enough for the Staties to lock you up."

Neither of us said anything for a moment while he waited for traffic, then turned into the strip mall parking lot. There were still several cruisers on hand, and a State Police crime scene van, but only one TV truck, and no reporters in sight.

"I'd like to solve this thing myself, before those two assholes," he said. "I haven't told them about you and Elaine yet. But I'll have to, if you won't cooperate."

He stopped behind my car. An Ipswich patrolman guarding the door of the restaurant eyed us warily. Behind him, evidence technicians in paper booties and jumpsuits moved around inside. Wankum put it in park, then turned to face me. "So?"

I wasn't a cop or a detective. I wasn't thrilled to be playing truth or dare with a murder case. But I knew what my gut was telling me.

"Sorry," I said and got out of the car.

He gunned the engine and drove away without worrying too much if he ran over my feet. The patrolman at the door smiled when I jumped back.

I got in the Sunbird and headed home. For a while I thought I was being followed by a black SUV with tinted windows, but it turned in at a Rowley antique store. The rain had stopped, but the roads were still wet, and the fields and woods had that dark, saturated look they got after a storm. I was crossing the marsh when gaps suddenly appeared in the clouds, and shafts of sun prowled the landscape. It was pretty, but it didn't solve anything.

As soon as I walked in my front door, I heard footsteps in the kitchen and smelled a rich marinara. Didn't mobsters like to make sauce? Or was that only in the movies? I almost ran back out of the house and called Wankum, until I heard Jane humming along with the radio.

She had sausage meat browning, red sauce simmering, and my big lobster kettle coming to a boil for the box of lasagna noodles on the counter. Also on the counter were two bottles of good Chianti and a baguette. One of the bottles was open. She was dressed like the Italian grandmother in every pasta commercial, with an apron wrapped around her midsection, her hair tucked up in a kerchief, sweat beading her forehead. She let me kiss her, then pulled away. She had work to do. She wore a CBGB T-shirt under the apron, though, so there was some hope that naughty rock chick might reappear after dinner.

"When you said you'd bring something for dinner, I thought you meant takeout."

"Davey said you eat at the bar most nights when Zack's not here. I thought a home-cooked meal might be a nice change."

"Isn't that kind of retro? Trying to hook a man with food?"

She scoffed. "Martha Stewart I am not. When my mom was teaching my sisters to cook, I was sneaking out to clubs. This is the only thing I make, and you won't have it often enough to get sick of it."

"I'm sure it's delicious."

And it was.

I waited till we were finished eating to tell her where I'd been, and when she heard, she threw a piece of bread at me.

TWENTY-FIVE

I had been threatened a few times by club owners who claimed mob connections, usually when they were trying to stiff me. One night a guy said he was going to have me stomped if I didn't play "Mirror Ball Man." I ignored him and nothing happened. But now I woke up thinking that while Carmine Argento was dead, someone else might want to avenge his son. And even if I survived that, I could find myself in jail by the end of the day, charged with murder.

I rolled over and nibbled on Jane until she woke up.

I woke up again an hour later to the sound of the trash truck in the next block. I got dressed, found the stinking barrel under the back porch and wheeled it out to the curb. *I bet Sting doesn't have to do this.* The nice weather had returned. Blue sky and bright sun, that clean smell of the first sunny morning after a couple of days of rain. Jane adamantly resisted a second wake-up, so I headed out for my morning walk.

Around the neighborhood, puddled rainwater splattered to the ground as workers tugged tarps off half-finished additions and un-sheathed roofs. Freshly showered and suited yuppies poured out of the Fitness Fortress and jumped into their Audis and BMWs for the daily Libertyport-to-Boston German-auto rally. A knot of small boats around the base of the Route 1 bridge announced that the stripers had come in with the tide.

A banana-yellow super-deluxe tour bus had pulled up in the parking lot near the boardwalk. AMERICAN FREEDOM TOURS, it said in English, next to a scribble that was either supposed to be Paul Revere atop his galloping steed or a tornado in a tricorn hat. An entire retirement home's worth of grumbling oldsters trickled out of the bus and walked toward the Miss Libertyport. Most of them wore red, white and blue track suits stamped with the logo of the Scranton Senior Travel Club, along with souvenir sun visors from the Foxwoods Indian casino in Connecticut. They shuffled toward the dock warily, stretching their brittle bones, a few of them pushing walkers.

Captain Bob stood ready at the top of the gangplank, Greek fisherman's cap tilted just so, holding his clipboard and megaphone. His pipe peeked out of his shirt pocket. He watched his passengers' achingly slow progress with a long-suffering, oddly defiant look on his face. *I know you're doing this to torture me,* the look said, *but you'll have to try harder.* It was the expression of a veteran high-school teacher.

He startled when he saw me and set down his clipboard with a nervous giggle. "Hello, Bax. In the mood for a cruise?"

"Jesus, Bob, are you afraid of me?"

"I don't know what you mean."

Besides the seniors, the only other people on the boardwalk were a couple of middle-aged guys sitting two benches apart, one napping behind shades with his mouth open and his iPod on, the other sipping a coffee and reading the sports page with a sour expression under his Red Sox cap. The bird lady moved slowly across the empty parking lot with a jumbo bag of popcorn, trailed by a chattering, fluttering swarm.

"I didn't kill anybody." I was getting so tired of saying it.

"I know that."

"So why do you look so weirded out?"

He stroked his little moustache. He still held the megaphone, perhaps thinking he would use it to call for help.

"You didn't have to go running right to Emmitt with what I told you," he said. "He called me last night and read me the riot act."

"Sorry about that. But the State Police think I killed Jules now, so I'm not really worried about whether you and Emmitt are still best buddies."

His shoulders slumped. "I know. But I've got enough on my mind without that."

"Still no word on your money, huh?"

"No, not at all," he said in a strangled voice. Glancing around at the milling tourists, he looked as if he might cry. "If that engine goes, I'm really in trouble."

"What did Emmitt say, exactly?"

"He said I should mind my own business. He said I should have listened to what Jules always told me, which was to keep my mouth shut."

A few of the seniors were close enough now to overhear. The guy in the Red Sox cap dug for something in his ear. A policeman on a mountain bike rode toward us along the boardwalk. The bird lady spotted him and headed for her car, avoiding a $300 ticket.

"What time did Emmitt call you?"

Capt. Bob shrugged. "I was on the couch watching television. Maybe around ten. He said you'd just left."

I thought about it. Emmitt had time to drive down to the Schooner and kill Greg, but he had been drunk enough that I didn't think he would have made it there and back. And I couldn't see any reason for him to do it. Greg didn't know anything about that night at the beach. I was no closer to solving Jules' murder than I was three days ago.

"I used to think teaching high school was boring," Capt. Bob said with a sigh. "I'd give anything to be bored again."

"I know what you mean."

I tried to think of something else to ask him. The bicycle cop pedaled slowly closer, looking fit and imposing in his shorts and dark blue golf shirt, with his equipment belt and mirrored shades and bike helmet. He rang the bell on his handlebars to get the Scranton seniors to step aside. They smiled and elbowed each other. *Did you see that, Ray? A policeman on a bicycle. What will they think of next?* He stood up on the pedals to scoot through them. Probably I imagined him staring at me from behind his shades. The bird lady backed out of her parking space.

"Well, time to get to work," Capt. Bob said and raised his megaphone. "Folks, could I have your attention, please?"

They turned to him politely.

"Now," the guy in the Red Sox cap said loudly, and his voice also came out of the walkie talkie on the bicycle cop's belt.

They moved fast. The bicycle cop jumped off his ride and let it drop in one smooth, practiced motion. In two strides he was close enough to grab Capt. Bob's arm. Capt. Bob dropped his megaphone and watched, horrified, as it went sailing over the railing. It splashed into the water ten feet below as the bicycle cop jerked Bob's arms behind his back and took out a pair of handcuffs. The seniors shrank back. The guy in the Red Sox cap and the sleeping iPod guy brushed past me, brandishing badges and guns, and grabbed other parts of Bob.

"Robert Norment, you're wanted for questioning in the murders of Jules Titward and Guido, uh, Greg Argent," the guy in the Red Sox hat said. "You have the right to remain silent..."

A siren whooped once as an unmarked cruiser skidded to a stop by the elk made of rusting rebar. O'Hurley and Putin jumped out and came running, accompanied by two uniformed troopers, with Wankum bringing up the rear. The two college-age crewmen of the Miss Libertyport stepped to the rail to see what was going on. *Bro, what the hell?*

"Why are they doing this?" Capt. Bob asked me as they led him toward the cruiser. "I didn't do anything!"

All I could do was shrug. The Scranton seniors all talked at once, mostly about refunds. One remarked that the event was not as exciting as the Boston Tea Party reenactment they'd seen yesterday. Wankum wove through them until he was at my side.

"Sorry about this, but it was a state operation."

"You couldn't have picked him up at home?"

"They just got the warrant half an hour ago, and he was already down here getting ready to go out," Wankum said. "They wanted to grab him before he got out on the water with fifty passengers."

"What have they got for evidence?"

He looked around to make sure he wasn't overheard. "Jules' secretary told us Capt. Bob made a couple of threatening calls to Jules' office before he was killed. Jules had ripped him off for a bunch of money. So we already liked him for that. And several witnesses said he was seen down at the Schooner on Sunday night, near closing time."

I had told Bob about Jules trying to borrow money from Greg Argent. He must have thought Greg could solve his problem with the number-two engine.

"That's all they've got?"

Putin put his hand on top of Capt. Bob's head and pushed him down into the back of the cruiser.

"That's all I know about. They don't tell me everything. They must have more, though, because I know they were *really* hoping it was you."

"You don't think Bob did it?"

I shook my head. Davey and I stood on opposite sides of the bar, with the sliding glass doors open to let in the afternoon breeze. Fluttering on the bar between us was the second Town Crier EXTRA in just over a week: LOCAL SKIPPER ARRESTED IN MURDERS. I couldn't stop looking at the picture of Capt. Bob in handcuffs, being perp-walked out of the station to a State Police cruiser, surrounded by photographers. "Deer in the headlights" hardly described how panicked he looked.

"Twenty grand seems like motive enough," Davey said.

"I just can't see it."

"One, he's upset about Jules ripping him off. Two, he's worried about losing that tub of a boat, which already cost him his marriage. It's a sad story. Bob's told it to me about five times in the last week, sitting right where you are now."

"Say he killed Jules over the money. Do you really see him taking a gun down to Ipswich on a Sunday night to hit up Greg Argent?"

"You told him that story about Jules trying to borrow money off the guy. He tried to do the same thing to save his business."

"But I told him Jules didn't get anywhere. He knew the answer would be no."

"Guy's desperate, he don't listen so good."

"But even if he did kill Greg, why wouldn't he take the money that was lying around on the desk? It wasn't twenty grand, but it was probably enough to make a difference, keep him afloat for a few more weeks."

"*Afloat*, funny," Davey said. "Maybe the sight of blood bothers him, maybe he turned and ran."

"Then do you really see him hitting Abigail in the head three times? He taught with her for twenty years."

"Truthfully, I can understand wanting to hit her in the head after a lot less time than that."

I shook my head and slid my empty mug across the bar. "I don't see it. I mean, who kicked my ass on Saturday night? The cops are missing something."

"Maybe that's because *somebody* didn't tell them everything."

"I know. But if I try to tell them now, I don't think it's Jimmy they'll be looking at."

Davey slid the fresh beer across the bar to me. "The sad thing is, I actually find myself wondering what Abigail would say about all this."

The Sox took a big lead early. Rum House regulars kept coming over to say, "We knew you were innocent all along." They all wanted to buy me beers, but I kept picturing Capt. Bob sitting in jail, and I headed home just after nine.

The air was cool and dry, fall-like. I took the scenic route along the boardwalk to remind myself that this was still a beautiful place, despite everything that had happened in the last few days. The boardwalk was deserted. I walked briskly, because of the temperature and because I didn't want anyone gaining on me. Sailboats bobbed at anchor, dark and unmanned. A few running lights near the mouth of the river told me where the fish were. The green eye of Plover Island Light flashed on and off.

I followed a brick path up to the square. The little white lights in the trees turned it into a magical retail fairyland, just waiting for the summer tourist crowds. For now it was deserted, except for a couple of smokers leaning outside the Thirsty Lobster. I crossed River Street and followed the bricks up Blacksmith Alley. More lights in the trees. No one there either, except a handful of skateboard kids standing around a bench in the shadows, near the passage to Main Street. I caught the faint, sweet scent of weed. Miscreants.

As I passed, one of them separated from the group. He circled around the abstract stone fountain that only ran in the daytime and got behind me. Remembering Saturday night in the parking lot, my heart started to beat faster. I kept walking, past the barber shop and across Parker Street into a cobblestone alley that was supposed to be the oldest original street in town. A shortcut home.

My pursuer waited for a pizza delivery driver to pass, then crossed the street after me. The hood of his sweatshirt was pulled tight around his head and his hands stuffed deep in its pockets. He kept to the shadows so I couldn't see his face. There was no one around, and the only light was from a condo three stories up in the old factory building. If he wanted to catch me, he could do it before I got to the other end of the alley, by the library. Maybe he and some of his buddies were the ones who jumped me on Saturday night. He was only a boy, and I could take him, but I didn't need another fight. Plus I hoped he didn't have a gun inside that sweatshirt.

"Hey," he said. "Hey, *wait.*"

I turned to face him, trying to look as tall and as angry as possible. "Yes?"

"What's up?" The voice was familiar, and a sliver of light showed me his face. It was Carl, Captain Bob's son. I'd never even factored him into the equation. Did he know Gareth?

"Not much." I tried to sound casual, but my heart was racing.

"They busted my dad this morning."

"I know, I was there."

"He didn't do nothing." His voice broke on the last word. Another victim. Which didn't mean he was harmless.

"I think you're right."

"Then how can they arrest him?"

"It's complicated." I hoped it didn't sound as lame to him as it did to me.

"They won't give him bail," he said, tearing up. "It's not fair."

"They'll figure it out eventually."

"We already lost two whole cruises today, and we had to give all their money back," he said, irate. His feelings about the family business had changed under pressure. He needed something to hold onto.

"That's rough."

"It's all your fault," he said, stepping forward, and my heart sped up again.

"My fault? How's that?"

He looked around us in all directions, as if making sure we weren't overheard. Back across Parker Street, his friends horsed around and cursed each other, paying us no attention.

"Because *you* fucking did it," he said, his voice a wounded snarl. He was seconds from violence. "You killed those people and you're letting my dad take the rap."

"I didn't do anything," I said. "I'm in the same situation your dad is. It looks like I did it, but I didn't."

"I don't believe you," he said. "That's exactly what you'd say if you did it."

"Of course," I said, and he blinked in surprise or confusion. "If I was the killer, I wouldn't admit it."

"That's right, you wouldn't."

"But I wouldn't be too happy with you right now, either."

He heard the threat and took a step back, and I knew then he didn't have a weapon. "You better not do anything. My friends are watching us." He said it loud enough so that a couple of them turned our way.

"I'm not the one you're looking for, Carl. And you shouldn't go around accusing people."

"I have to do *something*." Frustration and fear replaced the anger in his voice, and he suddenly sounded younger, more like Zack. They were only a few years apart.

"Go home. Hanging out here isn't doing anything. You're not helping your dad."

"If you didn't do it, why don't you help him? Aren't you supposed to be his friend?"

It was a good question. I pictured Capt. Bob learning the ecology of prison.

"Just go home, Carl," I said. "Please."

He shook his head, then suddenly bent forward at the waist, as if he was about to vomit. "Fucking useless," he said, his voice a toxic mix of fury and despair. Then he spun away and walked back to his friends. There was nothing else to say. I headed for home.

TWENTY-SIX

The next morning, Davey called and asked if I wanted to go for a ride, without saying where. I looked at Jane making coffee in her plaid boxers and one of my old Rum House T-shirts. I told him I'd be ready in an hour or maybe two.

He said, "I'm out front now."

He took the ramp onto the Route 1 drawbridge. As we neared the top, a siren sounded and then a horn. Lights flashed and a bell clanged. Davey swore and braked to a stop. A gate came down across our lane. The center section of the bridge split in two and began to rise, open-the-doors-and-see-all-the-people style. Grumbling, Davey jumped out and walked around to the bridge railing. I followed, as the line of cars stopped behind us began to grow.

The river glittered in the sun, and the harbor was busy with fishing boats and skiffs and cabin cruisers and kayaks. The boat that requested the bridge opening emerged below us, heading seaward: A fifty-foot motorsailer pulling an inflatable dinghy that bounced in its wake like a yippy little dog on a leash. At the wheel in the stern was a shirtless middle-aged guy with the leathery tan of a year-round boater, a guy who probably spent the winter in Florida or the Caribbean. He looked up at us and waved. Davey chose that moment to spit over the railing. Nowhere near the boat, but the guy stopped waving.

"I don't think you're supposed to do that," I told Davey.

"Really."

I told him about my conversation with Carl Norment in Blacksmith Alley.

"You feel bad for the kid, huh?"

The sun glittered on the windows of the distant cottages on Plover Island. Beyond the island was a low, deep blue horizon line that could have been the Atlantic or an optical illusion.

"Bob's in a tough position. I should do what I can to help him."

The bridge started to lower. It seemed to come down twice as fast as it went up. Davey just stood there in the breeze, watching the tanned guy navigating through traffic toward the ocean. "I made a couple of calls and figured out who jumped you on Saturday night."

"Who?"

"You'll see."

"Was it Greg?"

"It had nothing to do with Guido."

"So, who?"

Davey shook his head and turned away from the bridge rail as the roadway settled into place. "You'll see."

We jumped back in the Jeep just as the bell stopped ringing and led an impatient procession racing down the Seabury side. Davey took the first right after the bridge, passing a motel and marina favored by weekend fisherman. The road forked at a sign that said, WELCOME TO KING'S ISLAND. The island was a small granite outcropping in the middle of the marsh. In Colonial times, it was a landing point for ferries coming across from Libertyport.

Davey took the left fork, away from the river. We passed a handful of homes built among the trees. One had stacks of lobster pots in the yard, another two large red channel buoys. Then we were past the island, on a narrow, potholed marsh road, between ten-foot walls of pale, brittle reeds. Visible above the reeds on the right was a widely spaced row of telephone poles, each with a wooden platform on top intended to lure nesting osprey. None had taken up residence this year, as far as I could see.

Soon the road entered a wet, scrubby woods level with the marsh. Here and there were small houses, mostly well-kept, their foundations built above ground. Davey turned into the dirt driveway of a rusty white trailer home set flat in the middle of a shabby lawn. Sharing the small clearing were a rusty swing set with no swings and a clothesline stretched to a small, dead pine tree. Hanging on the line were an assortment of granny panties and bras, beer company giveaway T-shirts and stretch pants in Fruit Loops colors, all in heartstoppingly large sizes. At the back of the yard, a mint green Ford Pinto rested on four flat tires, half-buried in the unmown grass. Davey stopped the Jeep abruptly by the front door, then jumped out and ran up the steps and went in. I started after him. Banging and shouting emanated from inside.

I was at the door when I heard breaking glass. Davey yelled, "Around back!" I ran back down the steps, swung around the end of the railing and headed toward the rear. My foot smashed into a car battery hidden in the tall grass, and I stumbled forward, headed for a face-plant.

Asshole Gareth came running full-tilt around the corner of the trailer. He was barefoot in camouflage pants and a white T-shirt, brandishing a gun, a small automatic. He looked almost as surprised to see me as I was to see the gun. Instead of shooting me point blank, he spun like a halfback as I careened past, then kept running. I caught myself against the hood of the Pinto, which groaned, then pushed off and ran after him. It wasn't until then that I had time to wonder if the gun had killed two men.

"Stupid fucking kid," Davey yelled, bursting out the trailer door. "Get back here!"

Gareth kept running, but he caught one foot in a length of coaxial cable that snaked through the grass, probably a souvenir of a previous attempt to pirate cable. He hopped on one foot for a second, trying to untangle himself, the gun pointing to the sky. It gave me just enough time to cross the distance between us in three long strides, like I was going for the long jump. I tackled him at the ankles and he went down. When his elbow hit the ground, the gun went off. There was a second's pause while we both checked ourselves for wounds – Davey had dived behind the Jeep – and then Gareth got up and ran for the marshy woods.

It might have taken me longer to get to my feet but for the enormous adrenalin rush. *The stupid fucking kid almost shot me!*

Gareth was young, but he smoked, and I was taller and insane with rage. I was only a stride behind when he reached the tree line. He hit standing water and slipped on the leaves underneath. It slowed him down just enough for me to plant a hand in the middle of his back. The shove sent him face-first into the narrow trunk of a swamp maple. He went limp instantly, bounced off the tree and landed on his back, out cold. It was funny in a Three Stooges kind of way, except the wet *thock* his head made when it hit the tree was no sound effect. Rage immediately turned to worry. I hoped I hadn't killed him. Davey ran up, tried to stop short of us and fell on his ass in the water.

Five minutes later we were inside the trailer, the two of us standing over Gareth, who hunched defensively in a grimy green recliner. In this light, he didn't look much older than Carl Norment. He pressed an orange Popsicle, still in the wrapper, to the swelling knot on his forehead. He had a black eye too, although that was at least a couple of days old, already healing. Davey and I had helped ourselves from the fridge: Bud kingers. It was early, but gunfire rewrote the rules. The gun, now tucked in a pocket of Davey's windbreaker, was a .25 and therefore not the murder weapon.

"Can I have a beer?" the kid said.

"Shut the fuck up," Davey said, tugging at the wet seat of his jeans.

"What did I ever do to you?"

"What didn't you do?"

They glared at each other. I was kind of impressed that the kid didn't look more frightened. I hadn't seen Davey so enraged since Grady Little left Pedro Martinez on the mound against the Yankees in Game Seven of the 2003 American League Championship Series.

I said, "Gareth is one of the little shits who was going to take Shimmy Jimmy's bike."

"You don't say."

"So how do you know him?"

Davey sighed and looked out the window instead of answering.

"He's my fucking uncle," the kid said.

"Wait a minute. You're Trouser Weasel?"

The kid nodded eagerly, forgetting why we were here. "I play guitar and sing."

"Sing?" Davey said with a snort. "You scream like somebody's got your nuts in a vise."

"Fuck you."

Davey slapped the Popsicle out of his hand and it flew across the room.

"Jesus!" the kid said, cowering.

Davey leaned over him with a hand on each arm of the chair. "What fucking moron let you have a gun?"

"One of mom's douchebag boyfriends left it here when he got hauled in for a parole violation. It was in the kitchen drawer. You can ask her!"

Davey stood up and massaged his temples. Family.

"You're the one who bushwhacked Bax in my parking lot, ain't you?"

"I don't know what you're talking about!"

"Bullshit. I talked to your buddy Boyle, and he ratted you out in about three seconds."

"That cunt! It was his idea."

Davey turned to me and smiled. "I made up the Boyle part."

The kid moaned. "Fuck. *Fuck!*"

Davey turned back. "So why'd you do it, nitwit? Because I canceled your gig?"

Gareth shook his head.

"Was it because I stopped you from hassling Jimmy, so you couldn't steal his bike?" I asked.

"We didn't want his stupid bike. We were just messing with him."

"Then why?"

"Because you're fucking Ashley," he blurted out, face suddenly hot with outrage.

Davey looked at me, slightly wide-eyed. "Didn't see that coming."

"I wasn't f- I wasn't doing anything with Ashley."

"I saw you," Gareth insisted. "At the party at that dead guy's house."

"You mean the wake?"

"Whatever. I walked away because she was being a bitch, and then I came back and saw you with her."

Davey turned to me and folded his arms across his chest, trying to suppress a smile. "Do tell."

"We were just talking."

"Bullshit, something was going on," the kid said. "She's been breaking dates and won't tell me where she's going. And Boyle told me he saw her get out of some fucking yuppie's car and kiss him goodbye. Tongue and everything."

"That wasn't me, Gareth."

"Then who was it?"

"Yeah," Davey said cheerfully, "who was it?"

"That was Jules, the guy who got murdered."

Gareth looked confused. "The guy - what?"

Davey whistled and turned back to the chair. "What that means, lad, is I have to ask, did you kill Jules Titward?"

"What? No way! I don't even know who you're talking about. That guy who got whacked down the boardwalk?"

"Yeah, him. And if you knew he was boning your girlfriend, you might have killed him. That's what the police will think, anyway."

Gareth's eyes got big and round. "But I told you, I thought this douche was the one doing Ashley."

"Well, this douche and I might believe you, but I wouldn't count on everyone else. So keep this to yourself until I tell you different, all right?"

"Sure, whatever. Shit. What about the gun?"

Davey looked at me. We could let the kid off the hook and tell him it was the wrong caliber. But where was the fun in that?

"I'm taking it and throwing it in the goddamn river. You can figure out how to explain it to your mom."

Gareth groaned.

"And from now on," Davey said, "spend your free time learning to play guitar. Don't go around jumping people in my parking lot."

"OK, fine!"

"And you better figure out what to tell your sweet mother to get me out of her dog house."

The kid sagged, chin on his chest. "Can I have my popsicle back?"

"What I don't get," I said to Davey as he backed out of the driveway, "is how this helps us solve Jules' murder."

"I guess it don't," he said, shifting uneasily in his wet jeans.

TWENTY-SEVEN

Like so much else in town, the public library was a marriage of convenience between the old and the new. For more than a century, the library had occupied an imposing brick mansion built for one of the city's merchant princes; George Washington slept there, presumably in comfort. A few years ago, the town built a brick and glass addition with a three-story atrium and high-speed Internet access. The library was a short walk from my house. I was barely employed, lived alone and in normal times tried not to drink before five, so I was a steady customer.

At the front desk, I returned unfinished a fat thriller that I hadn't picked up since life in Libertyport had gotten so much more dangerous. I asked the librarian on duty if they had Libertyport High School yearbooks. Without looking up from the pile of cards she was date-stamping, she directed me to the local-history archive in the basement.

Two white marble busts of local patriots guarded the staircase down. The archive had its own glass door and a more determined hush than the rest of the library. When I entered, the only sound was the wheezing breath of an old man in a blazer and tie sitting at the microfilm machine. He scanned an old Town Crier through the bottom half of his bifocals. I signed in and told the woman behind the desk what I wanted.

"Those are some of our most popular items," she said and reached to a shelf next to the desk.

"Good that you keep them handy, then."

"They tend to walk away otherwise." She eyed me for a second as if mulling my character, then gave me the yearbook.

I sat down at a worktable. A sign said USE PENCIL ONLY. The old man chuckled at a microfilm discovery, perhaps the key evidence for his next broadside against City Hall on the letters-to-the-editor page. I hoped I'd be as lucky.

Living through them as a boy, the Seventies had seemed dramatic and tumultuous. But the high-schoolers on the pages of the yearbook looked happy and carefree. Boys wore plaid shirts and jeans and wide leather belts. The main signs of rebellion were bushy hair and the occasional moustache. No ponytails or peace signs or pot-leaf belt buckles that I could see, although a few squinty smiles hinted at a morning bong hit. The girls looked even more well-behaved, in makeup and polite sweaters. In the warm-weather shots there were no exposed navels or tattoos, not even much cleavage.

The teachers were mostly crewcut old-timers and kindly-looking women, except for a couple of disco rebels with plaid sport-coats and porn-star moustaches. Abigail had seemed old to me when I arrived as a student, a couple of years later, and it was a shock to see her leaning on a podium, still in her late thirties, gazing into the camera with a saucy smile, wearing the shortest skirt among the faculty. She seemed alive on the page, something vibrant and strange in her eyes even then.

I flipped through to the individual portraits of the graduates, starting at the back. Jimmy Wilmot's photo showed him handsome and bright-eyed and confident, just like you'd expect a popular high school quarterback to look, with bangs that predicted his present bowl cut and a Vince Lombardi quote under his picture. One of the nicknames listed was "Mr. Gordon," a mocking reference to his relationship with Elaine. The yearbook must have been on the way to the printer when he had his accident, because there was no mention of the tragedy.

Jules Titward was smaller and blonder, smirky. There was hardly anything written under his name, no wisecracks or nicknames suggested by friends, just a short list of extracurricular activities. Bob Norment, "our surprise gridiron star," looked eager to please behind aviator-framed eyeglasses and a scant moustache. There was no mention of a girlfriend.

When I got to the Gs, I must have made a noise, and the guy in the blazer looked over and frowned disapprovingly. I couldn't help it. Elaine Gordon's portrait had been scribbled over with a blue ballpoint pen, completely blotted out, the point pressed down so hard it almost tore through the paper. The ink was faded, though, as if it had happened years ago. Somebody sure didn't like her. I could see why they didn't want us to use pen in here.

I flipped through the pages of candid photos and found Jimmy smiling in front of an open locker with a Jack Daniel's label taped inside the door. Another picture showed him slow-dancing with Elaine under streamers in the gym, the two of them staring into each other's eyes in unconcealed lust. There was only a single picture of Jules, manning a spotlight for the student theater troupe. Bob turned up here and there, mostly in the background; he wore his snorkel coat to a meeting of the nerdy Radio Weather Club, his face almost hidden inside the furry hood.

Jimmy appeared in more than half the pictures devoted to the football team, in game action and posing at practice, acknowledging the cheers at a big pep rally. One showed him and Bob celebrating in the end zone after a touchdown pass. Still no clue to the immediate mystery I was trying to solve.

Finally I found a two-page spread devoted to couples. Jimmy and Elaine's picture occupied the center, of course. Whoever had put the collage together must have discovered they didn't have photos of all of the pairings they wanted to immortalize, a problem solved in those pre-computer days by cutting out individual heads from other pictures and pasting them next to each other. Around each duo was a hand-drawn heart pierced by a cupid's arrow. Bob appeared inside a heart with one of the cheerleaders, a blonde with a wry look. I thumbed back and found her portrait. Her amused expression gave me little hope she held the key to solving the murders. But I wrote her name in pencil on a piece of scrap, then took the yearbook back to the desk. On impulse, I asked for my own, dated five years later.

I had no interest in seeing my Picture Day portrait, with the bad suit and the impossibly naïve expression. But I flipped through the candids until I found what I was looking for, a shot of me sitting on the wide front steps of the school, strumming my guitar with a soulful expression for a rapt audience of exactly no one. The more things change, et cetera. Despite the lack of an audience, I had been happy with the picture. It made me look like a romantic loner. I'd expected that later, when I was famous, the girls would sigh over it and wonder how they'd let me get away. I stared at the picture for a few minutes, thinking of all the dreams I had when it was taken, how many of them I'd achieved and how many had been lost. When I started really wanting a drink, I closed the yearbook and left.

"Oh my god," Margaret Doyle said good-humoredly when I introduced myself and told her where I was calling from. "I haven't set foot in that town in, what, twenty-five years? More."

"You went away to college?"

"My father worked for Polaroid, and they sent him to Europe. We decided I would take a year abroad before starting college."

"You're in California now?"

"Last time I checked. This is a tiny little town in the Sierras, two hundred people, and I'm the postmaster. I also run a massage therapy business."

"Married? Kids?"

"Divorced, two grown, and I think that's all the questions I'm going to answer until you tell me why you're calling. Why does a big rock star want to talk to little old me?"

I imagined her from her voice and how easily she had slipped into the conversation. The same blond hair and freckles, still an attractive woman, upbeat most of the time, but with lines of experience in her face, a little grey in the hair, something sad in her eyes.

"I'm not exactly a big rock star anymore. Never was, really."

"I remember hearing your song on the radio a few years after I graduated. Kasey Kasem said you were from Libertyport, and I was like, holy cow, I wonder if I ever dated him?"

"I'm a few years younger than you."

"Too bad then. How did you find me? The Internet, I suppose. Well, what can I do for you?"

"I'm trying to find out about the night of Jimmy Wilmot's accident."

She didn't say anything for a long moment, and then she said, "Well, shit."

"Bad memories."

She puffed air through her lips. "Not as bad for me as for him. I thought someone would come around asking about that a long time ago. But you're not a cop or anything, so why are you asking? Don't tell me you're going to write a song about it."

"You knew Jules Titward, I take it."

"Sure, smug little prick."

"He was shot to death last week."

She groaned. "Wow, thanks for the ambush."

"Sorry."

"I'm glad I had my coffee. So what happened?"

I gave her a brief rundown of events, including my collision with Jimmy and finding Jules' body. I explained to her my suspicions that his murder had something to do with the night of Jimmy's accident. And I repeated what Bob and Emmitt had told me about that night, skipping the carnal details.

"Sorry, there's not much I can add," she said. "I never went inside the cottage. I don't think I even saw who else was there that night, just Bob and Jules. I guess I got a glimpse of the older brother when he answered the door. But what you told me is pretty much what happened, as far as I know. At least that's the version Jules told me when he cornered me at my locker on Monday morning and told me to keep my mouth shut. I wish I could be more help."

"To be honest, I don't know what I expected. I'm just trying to talk to everyone who was there."

"No bother. How is Jimmy these days?"

I told her.

"That's so awful. He was a special boy. I'm so sorry for what happened."

At least somebody was.

"By the way," she asked, "what did Bob say about me?"

"He said he really liked you, and that he was sorry that night ruined things for the two of you."

"Did he say I wouldn't put out?"

"Actually, he did."

She chuckled. "I'm glad he told you, instead of lying like most guys do. I always felt kind of bad we never did it, actually. I liked him. But what happened was so awful. That was one of those before-and-after nights, you know? I grew up in this nice quiet town, and I guess all the boarded-up buildings and economic problems didn't really make much impact on me. That was for grownups. I was just worried about cheerleading and dances and things like that. But then that night happened. And suddenly everything just seemed darker and scarier. I kept waiting for the police to come to the door. I think I would have told them the truth. But they never came. And a couple of weeks later I was packing for Paris. I was relieved to get out of there. It was a relief when Libertyport kind of slipped into the rearview mirror."

"I understand."

"You stayed, though, after your big success."

"By the time I got packed to leave, my big success was already over," I said.

"What's it like there now?" she asked. "Did they ever finish redoing the waterfront and all that?"

"It's pretty nice," I said. "I couldn't afford to buy a house here now."

"It's the same here," Margaret Doyle said. "Dotcom kids from San Francisco buying up little shacks and turning them into weekend places.

"Sounds annoying."

"Yeah, but it's good for my business."

Neither of us spoke for a moment, and then she said, "Have you talked to Elaine about all this?"

"A little. I don't want to bother the widow too much."

"It's funny she ended up married to Jules, because at the time, she was really in love with the older brother, the painter."

"Still is, maybe."

"No kidding? Well, there you go. Ask her what happened that night. If I remember, she's a hard one to rattle. But ask her. Because take my word for it, if anybody knows what happened, it's her."

TWENTY-EIGHT

Elaine didn't look overjoyed to see my convertible coming up her driveway. She knelt at a garden bed by the side door, cutting down white tulips that had gone by. Her faded jeans, pale blue turtleneck and blue-and-white silk scarf all seemed designed to complement her eyes. She sat back on the grass and wiped her brow, the chopped-up remains of the flowers scattered around her, beautiful debris. The wisteria wound around the portico over her head was in full bloom.

"Isn't it kind of early to be chasing after the widow?"

"I'm just trying to figure out a couple of things."

"Still playing detective, hmmm? I suppose you didn't kill Greg, either."

"You know I didn't."

She nodded with what looked like contrition, peeling off her gardening gloves. "That was a pity. He was a decent guy, despite his father."

"He and Jules must have been killed by the same person."

"I'm not sure the police will ever find out who shot my husband. It appears there are a number of suspects, all disgruntled clients. Apparently all these years I was married to a swindler and never knew it."

"Never knew it?"

She frowned down at the cars passing on High Street. Deciding how much to tell me. So much was calculated with her now. "I knew Jules was having troubles. He sold that painting to Emmitt a couple of months ago for twenty thousand, which was highway robbery – it's worth three or four times that, maybe more. But Jules said it was just a cash flow issue."

"Why didn't you tell me that the other night?"

"I didn't think it was any of your business."

"Was that the only 'cash flow issue' he'd had in the last year or two?"

"Not exactly."

"But he had a new Beemer and you got a new kitchen. And is that your Range Rover in the driveway?"

She nodded.

"I don't know much about jewelry, but I bet that's a real diamond you're wearing. That's a lot of expensive stuff for a guy who was short of cash."

She fingered the necklace. "Jules liked to buy me nice things, especially lately."

"He was trying to compete."

"With who?" Trying to sound baffled.

"You were seeing Emmitt again."

The last thing I expected was the smile that spread across her face then, not unlike the one on Emmitt's face the other night. A smile that said she was happy, regardless of the consequences or what everyone would think.

"Jules found out almost a year ago, I think. Suddenly he was willing to do that kitchen renovation I'd been asking for years. Bought me the Rover to replace my old Volvo. Bought me jewelry and dresses and took me to New York. It took me a while to figure out what was going on. Like any of that was going to change my mind about Emmitt."

Jules had been an arrogant prick, but he was still the frustrated little brother, too, on the outside looking in at Emmitt and his own wife. Selling his father's art and ripping off his customers to try to keep up. Growing up an only child suddenly looked pretty good, if this was the alternative.

"Did you and Jules ever talk about it?"

"Not at first, but eventually it came out. We had some terrible fights. He was drinking heavily. I wasn't surprised when he didn't come home after the meeting at City Hall. It wasn't the first time lately. To tell you the truth, when the police car came up the driveway the next morning, I thought maybe he had killed himself." She said it without any apparent emotion, picking a white petal off the knee of her jeans. "It was almost a relief."

I wanted to shatter her calm. "Jules was having an affair too."

She snorted. "You mean with Marcy's little slut of a daughter? *Please*. I was glad. It would keep him from making trouble for me and Emmitt."

Touching sentiment. No wonder she hadn't reported him missing.

She picked up her trowel and poked at the dirt for a moment before meeting my eyes. "Have you told the police about me and Emmitt?"

"I didn't tell them anything about you."

"Good," she said. "Some secrets are better kept, don't you think? Especially since they have nothing to do with what happened to Jules."

"Wankum already remembered about you and me. He's probably telling the State Police right now. He also remembered about you and Greg."

She looked surprised but unruffled. The history implicated me, not her. It looked as if I was eliminating my rivals, after all these years.

"I'm sure they'll find out eventually that you didn't kill anyone," she said, not sounding as if she much cared.

I wondered if she had been this self-centered when we were together and I just never noticed. Or had all these years sneaking around with Emmitt changed her? It didn't matter, in the end.

"The murders have to have something to do with the night Jimmy Wilmot crashed his car."

"I don't understand."

"Jimmy keeps popping up in this. Greg had an envelope on his desk marked *Pictures of You and Jimmy*. I thought maybe you were the other person in the pictures."

She looked genuinely confused. "I suppose there are some pictures of us in our old high school yearbooks."

"I just looked at them. Nothing more recent? Or more revealing?"

She shook her head.

"Who else was at the cottage on the night of the crash? Emmitt claimed not to know everyone's name."

She stabbed the trowel into the soil and brushed off her hands. "He probably didn't. We were all younger."

"But you knew them. You were all friends."

She ticked them off on her fingers. "It was me and Emmitt, Jules, Jimmy. That Bob person and his date, who didn't even come in. She was a cheerleader too. Cathy something. Ginny? I'll think of it in a minute. But you can forget about her. She moved away right after graduation, and I haven't thought about her, much less talked to her, in twenty years."

"There was one more person there. 'Some little mouse,' Emmitt said."

"Well, Ora was there."

"The poet?"

"Yes. You met her Sunday morning at breakfast."

I met her Thursday night at the wake, actually. And she had slipped away early. In time to walk down to Jules' office and clobber Abigail?

I remembered something else: "Emmitt said she had a crush on Jimmy."

Elaine laughed unkindly. "Maybe, I don't remember. She's famous now, as famous as a poet can be anyway, but back then she was a real nobody. A flat-chested goody-goody with glasses. She was a grade below us, but she was in the A.P. program, so we had some of the same classes. She had no social life whatsoever. She didn't have a chance with a jock like Jimmy."

"What was she doing at the party, then?"

She smiled and shrugged. "She was a straight A student. She helped me with my homework sometimes. Did it for me, actually, and as a reward I let her come along that night. I imagine she got more than she bargained for. I never really talked to her again until she moved back to town a couple of years ago. She's quite a different person now, well-traveled, interesting."

Elaine was also a different person now, and it made me sad for the carefree young woman who'd shared my bed for a few weeks.

"How do you feel when you see him?" I asked.

"When I see who?"

"Jimmy. How do you feel when you're driving down the street in your Range Rover and you see him riding his bike? Do you honk? If he waves, do you wave back?"

She had lost her smile, but she looked more irritated than sad or upset, as if I was simply being tasteless. She shook her head and turned to gather the remains of her tulips. "I'll see you later, Bax."

I watched her for a moment, then got back in the convertible. I'd see if Ora Buffem could explain the connection between Jimmy Wilmot and the murders. Then I would go to the police station and tell Wankum everything. Dump it all on his desk and let him sort it out. Go back to writing songs and worrying about my career or lack thereof.

I drove down to the river and headed west. The bright sun filtering down through the new green leaves seemed unreal. It couldn't be such a nice day, could it, given the secrets I had learned? I'd just passed the old silver factory when I saw Shimmy Jimmy ahead of me, pedaling his bike in the same direction.

It wasn't the first time I'd seen him on this road lately.

I slowed down and followed.

TWENTY-NINE

Jimmy seemed happy, looking around at the sky and trees as he rode. Content. Having been a small-town high-school football star could be a heavy burden if you never became anything more, but Jimmy didn't know he was living in the shadow of his youthful promise.

Maybe I could learn from him.

I was a hundred yards behind him when a flagman in an orange safety vest stepped into the road in front of me and stopped traffic. A flatbed truck waddled out of the driveway of one of the marinas carrying a big cabin cruiser that blocked my view. By the time it negotiated the tight turn toward town, there were a dozen cars backed up in each direction and Jimmy was out of sight over the next hill.

I zoomed ahead, fearing that if I lost him I would lose the thread of the whole tangled tale. I hoped this wasn't the day the cops set up their regular speed trap by the ballfields. But not to worry. I spotted him again just past the park, pedaling along like he had all the time in the world, blissfully unaware he was being pursued.

When he turned toward the river, I caught up and passed him on the Chain Bridge. He was too preoccupied to notice me.

On the island, I turned into the dirt parking lot and stopped next to a Volvo station wagon plastered with piping plover stickers. Just across the road was Ora Buffem's little house, with lilac bushes at the corners and her old Camry in the driveway.

I had a clear view as Jimmy passed the parking lot, crossed the street and pedaled across the lawn of the poet's house. He leaned his bike against the house behind one of the lilac bushes and walked to the door, looking around to see if anyone was watching, as obvious as a child. He didn't see me. He knocked, then licked his lips and ran his hand over his hair. The gentleman caller.

When Ora Buffem opened the door, he slipped inside quickly and closed it behind him, but not before I saw them fall into each others' arms.

I sat there for two hours, turning the radio on and off half a dozen times without finding a song I wanted to hear. I made small talk with the owner of the station wagon when she came out of the woods, an elderly woman toting an expensive spotting scope. She said the osprey had not yet returned from their winter home down south. I agreed with her about how lucky we were to live in such a beautiful place.

A little later, a Libertyport patrol car came over the Chain Bridge and swung into the parking lot. The cop at the wheel saw me and glared. I thought I was busted, that Wankum or the Staties had decided to bring me in at last. It was almost a relief. But he just turned around, having reached the end of his jurisdiction. I thought of flagging him down and asking him to radio Wankum. But what would I tell him? Before I could figure it out, he peeled out onto the pavement and disappeared back over the Chain Bridge.

The embrace had been so quick. Could I have been wrong? I wasn't sure until the door opened again, and I watched them kiss goodbye. Not so hurried or furtive this time. Lingering carelessly, smiling. There was no mistaking them for anything but lovers. Finally Jimmy retrieved his bike and pedaled off toward town, happy as a puppy.

She watched until he was out of sight, then bent over and began to deadhead a pot of purple and white pansies by the front steps. Everyone was gardening today. Spring was in the air, but I wasn't feeling its promise. I got out of my car and crossed the road. When I cleared my throat, she turned. Her lips seemed fuller, her cheeks flushed. Afterglow. Then she recognized me, and her smile blinked out.

"Nice to see you again," she said finally, but her tone said it was anything but. "Would you like a cup of tea?"

"Sure."

She held the door open for me, forcing a smile back onto her face. I wondered if it was smart to go with her. She must be desperate. But I needed answers.

In the sunny kitchen, she filled a kettle with water and set it on a burner, then got down two mugs, a canister of English Breakfast and two little strainers. She turned and stood with her back against the counter, eyes darting behind those big, round glasses. Cornered. Finally her gaze settled on my CDs, which sat on the counter next to the Bose radio.

"I listened to more of your songs," she said, too brightly. "They're quite melodic, witty too, although you do sometimes strain for the punch line."

Couldn't argue with that. I let the silence hang.

"I think I've got most of it figured out," I said finally.

The smile returned, tinged with acid. "Really? What do you think you know?"

"You had a crush on Jimmy in high school. You were at the beach the night of his accident, but you couldn't stop what happened. Maybe you didn't try. Maybe you hoped that if Elaine and Jimmy broke up, he'd end up with you."

"That's not true," she said without conviction.

"You didn't start the fight, that was Emmitt's doing. But you were no better than the rest of them. You didn't stop him from driving. You didn't tell the police what happened. And you've been carrying the secret around with you ever since. How am I doing so far?"

She just stared back at me.

"I understand being angry at them. I can see how the guilt would eat you up. I just don't know why you killed Jules, after all these years. Why him and not the others?"

She shook her head as if to say I was missing the point. Sighed like it was her last breath.

"It wasn't the type of party I was normally invited to," she said. "I tagged along with Elaine. I was jealous of her and Jimmy, but I was also excited to be there, with the glamorous kids. I wanted to be more like them. I got drunk for the first time, or I felt drunk, anyway. Elaine had told me her secret, about her and Emmitt, so I thought I might have a chance with Jimmy. But when he saw that painting, he forgot every-thing else. I didn't have a chance with him, it was all Elaine. And then I was angry, too. You're right, I didn't do anything to stop him from driving. But as soon as he left, I was beside myself. I knew something bad was going to happen, everyone did."

Tears began to well in those big, dark eyes.

"After just a moment we heard the crash. Emmitt ran around shutting off the lights and shushing everyone, in case the police came to the house. But I was screaming and crying, because I knew something horrible had happened to Jimmy. And they couldn't get me to stop. So Jules took me away down the beach, past the last house, into the nature refuge.

"I was a terribly lonely girl with no real friends. I was sixteen, and I'd never even been kissed, and I was sure the one boy I loved had just been killed. Jules was handsome and rich and worldly, and he took me out on the beach under the stars and put his arms around me and whispered comforting words in my ear. You can imagine the rest. I suppose today we'd call it rape, because I was underage and I'd been drinking. But it wasn't. Nature took its course, that's all."

She shook her head, bit her lip. Her voice dropped almost to a whisper. "The worst thing was, we could hear the sirens the whole time, police, fire trucks, the ambulance. But it didn't stop us."

The kettle whistled us back to the present. She turned to the stove and dabbed her eyes on a dish towel before pouring the water into our mugs. She set one in front of me and sat down across the table.

"What about afterward?"

"This is how naïve I was: I woke up the next morning expecting I was going to be Jules' girlfriend. We all went back to school and tried to pretend nothing had happened. And he acted like we'd never met. I thought I was in love with him anyway, but that didn't last the week. By then it seemed too late to go to the police and tell them what really happened." A bitter smile passed across her features. "I spent even more time by myself, and my interest in poetry increased *exponentially*. I convinced my aunt to send me to Governor Willey for my senior year, just to get me out of that high school. I told her it would look good on my transcript, and it did get me into Smith. So I guess all's well that ends well, right?"

"It didn't end so well for Jules."

"I didn't really think about him that much in all these years, if you can believe it. That night was just something I had to live with. I graduated and went away to college and became a famous poet." She said "famous poet" with terrible self-mockery.

"When did you and Jimmy, um, reconnect?"

"My aunt died three years ago, and I inherited this house. At first I wasn't sure how I would feel coming back, but I love it here. I even made friends with Elaine again. She always liked having someone to tell her troubles to. Someone who wasn't a threat, I guess.

"Then one day I was driving into town, and I saw Jimmy riding his bike by the baseball fields, and I almost crashed myself, literally. I went off the road and had to slam on my brakes to avoid a tree. Frankly, I'd always assumed he was in an institution somewhere, disfigured, a vegetable. And there he was, looking pretty much the same as he did when we were in high school.

"I gathered my wits after a moment, then turned around. He was scared at first when I approached him, but then he remembered me. Nothing about that night, of course. But he still remembers things from … before. Time is frozen for him. He knew me as a girl from school, a girl who liked him. I didn't even think he knew. I was so happy I cried right there on the side of the road. He was so sweet – he thought that I was unhappy and it was his fault, and he started to cry too, and I had to comfort him. I invited him to come home with me for a glass of iced tea, but he said his mother had taught him to be careful of strangers. And I told him I wasn't a stranger and I would cry again if an old friend like him wouldn't come visit me. So he did. We ended up laughing together. And I invited him back. And soon after..." She shrugged.

I sipped my tea, trying to decide how to feel about this. Was it a tragic romance or just perverse? Or both?

"I think I was the first woman he'd been with since the accident, the only one, and he was so happy and so grateful. Even he realized we had to keep it a secret. I was afraid he would forget about me between our visits, so I gave him a copy of one of my books, with my picture on the back. And it worked. Usually he didn't remember the details of our visits, or the things we talked about, but he remembered me. Everyone in town was used to seeing him on his bike, they didn't pay much attention to where he went, he was just part of the scenery. So he was free to come and go whenever he wanted, as long as he was home by supper. We've been going on like this for a while now. I suppose you think it's terrible."

"You each found some happiness."

"Yes, we did. He'd had nothing but misery since the accident. He knows that he isn't right, and when he thinks about it, he gets terribly sad. But with me, well, you should see his face ... it's pure joy. As for myself, I was quite lonely before I found him again. And now I'm not."

"I can understand that."

"Maybe you can," she said as if she doubted it very much. "But how do you think it will be received when it hits the newspaper? Television?" Her voice took on the tones of a tabloid TV announcer, and her face twisted into a grotesque mask, the secret face of the guilt and craziness she'd kept inside all these years. I felt a chill, and the hair stood up on my arms. *"The poet and the brain-damaged man-child! Their secret affair exposed!* It would destroy Jimmy. That's why ..."

She clapped her hand over her mouth.

"That's why you shot Jules? He found out about you and Jimmy?"

She nodded. "When Elaine came here, Jules always found some excuse to stay away. I suppose he knew that it would be too much. But he needed money desperately, and he had the idea that I have some, because of my writing and because of this house. I think he was coming over here to beg, actually. I might have enjoyed that. But he parked across the road, like you did, perhaps to gather his courage, and he saw me and Jimmy kissing goodbye. A few seconds either way and none of it would have happened. But he said he had pictures of Jimmy and me together, and he wanted fifty thousand dollars to keep our secret. Like I have that much." She laughed at the ridiculousness of the sum. "I was supposed to deliver it to him the other night, outside the Rum House."

"You shot him instead."

She took a sip of tea to cover a grimly satisfied smile.

"I couldn't stop thinking about what they did to Jimmy, and now Jules was threatening to hurt him again."

"When the truth about the accident came out, he and Emmitt would have been in more trouble than you."

"I said that. And he laughed and said the statute of limitations had expired, and it was an old scandal anyway. No one would care, it wouldn't be nearly as big a story as me and Jimmy. He said I could lose my teaching career."

I wasn't sure their relationship would have gotten that much attention. It seemed pretty mild as tabloid scandals go these days. A one-day story at most.

"The worst was when he said that he'd tell Jimmy's mother everything, and she would never let me see Jimmy again. I couldn't bear that. To find him again after all these years, I couldn't lose him a second time. That was when I decided what I had to do."

"What about Abigail?"

"Jules said he was going to bring the pictures with him that night, but they weren't in the car. So I took the keys to his office and went there the first chance I got, to look for them. I thought I would be alone, because of the wake. She surprised me. I just reacted. It was an accident."

Two or three hard blows to the skull wasn't my idea of an accident, but I didn't say anything.

"And Greg Argent?"

A deep breath. "After Jules was dead, he tried to blackmail me too. Apparently Jules had told him everything one night when he was drunk. His restaurant is going down the drain, and he was afraid that his father would think he's a failure. He couldn't stand that, even though his father is dead."

"He told you all that?"

She nodded. "Funny, isn't it? He seemed to want to explain himself. He was apologetic. He said he had the pictures. He showed me an envelope."

"This was Sunday night?"

She nodded. "He thought I was going into my purse for the money. He was so surprised when he saw the gun. Afterward, when I opened the envelope..." Tears returned.

"I'm not sure it matters now."

She blinked at that. "I know you care about Jimmy," she said, her voice rising. "He told me that someone saw him that morning, in the parking lot. After reading the stories in the papers, I knew it had to be you. And you didn't tell anyone."

"I didn't think there was any point. I knew he didn't kill Jules. But he knew who did, right?"

She nodded, her face contorted with shame. "He came here early that morning. I hadn't slept all night. He asked me what was wrong. I was weak, and I told him, though I should have known it was too much for him to deal with. He ran to his bicycle and pedaled away. I thought he was going to turn me in, and I would have accepted that. But of course that never entered his mind. He went to see Jules for himself. And then he came back here, and we cried together. That's the one thing I feel guilty about, that it scared him so much. That made me get hold of myself. I calmed him down and told him not to worry. I think by now he's forgotten what happened. He hasn't mentioned it to me since."

"That's good."

I wasn't at all sure that Jimmy had escaped feeling guilty. *Shimmy Jimmy killed the shimmy man.* Maybe I'd misunderstood him entirely.

And if I'd told the cops about Jimmy in the first place, they might have caught Ora Buffem before she hit Abigail or shot Greg Argent.

"You're going to turn me in, aren't you?"

"I guess I am."

She sighed. I didn't see where the gun came from, maybe a drawer under the tabletop. Suddenly it was in her hand, a shiny little automatic with a mother-of-pearl handle. We both stood up. She pointed it vaguely in my direction.

"Poet with a gun?" Now my voice sounded too bright and cheery by half.

The corners of her mouth turned up for a second. "Absurd, isn't it?" She looked down at the weapon, which she'd already used to kill two men. "It was my father's. When I was a little girl, they paid the workers at Gordon Electrical in cash. There was a robbery. I guess he got it for security after that. He taught me how to shoot it when I was a teenager."

"What are you going to do with it now?"

She looked at me, calculating. "They'll find your car in the parking lot, with your wallet and keys on the front seat. In a few days, your body will wash up somewhere downstream. They'll think that you killed them all and you couldn't handle the guilt. People will start to remember that you've been acting oddly. It won't matter that they never find the gun."

My son would remember me as a murderer and a suicide.

"How many more people are you willing to kill?" I asked her. "What if Jimmy starts to get loose lips?"

She gasped. "I wouldn't-"

"Turn yourself in today, and I'll help you keep him out of it. We'll come up with a story."

She thought about it. For a moment she looked off into some other life, one where terrible things didn't happen. Then she grimaced and raised her gun hand. I wasn't sure if she was going to shoot me or herself, but I didn't wait to find out. I lunged for the gun.

There was a loud crack and a tinkling of glass. I thought she'd fired, but she hadn't. Blood sprayed the stove behind her. I looked toward the sound, and saw the hole in the window over the sink. Wankum stood in the middle of the yard, feet spread, aiming a big black automatic with both hands.

I looked back at Ora Buffem as a bloodstain bloomed on her chest, darkening and growing. Her eyes widened with surprise, and her knees gave way. I caught her before she fell to the floor, but the medical examiner told me later that she was dead by then anyway.

THIRTY

What happened was this: Wankum finally got the results of the gunshot residue tests, which supported my claim that I hadn't shot Jules. He wanted to tell me the good news in person. He called my cell, but I'd forgotten it that morning. He got on the radio and asked if anyone had seen me. The cop who turned around in the parking lot reported my location. Wankum drove to the island just in time to see me go inside with Ora, which made him suspicious, especially since my car was parked across the street. Sneaking up to look through the kitchen window, he saw her pull out the gun. He thought she was about to kill me, so he shot her.

I wondered what it was like for him, working so hard to revive her afterward. The EMTs came with siren screaming, but there was nothing any of them could do for Ora Buffem. I stood with my back against the kitchen counter, trying to stay out of the way. Soon there were cops everywhere, people yelling. I was frisked three times, not gently, then driven to the station and put in an interrogation room.

The patrolman assigned to guard me said that the Staties were grilling Wankum in another room down the hall. I wondered what he was telling them. If he had seen Jimmy while on the way to the island, he hadn't mentioned it to me. Maybe I could still keep Jimmy out of it.

The scene in the kitchen played over and over in my head, the poet falling in slow motion. I still had her blood on my shirt.

By the time O'Hurley and Putin came into the room, I had figured out a story. I told them that Ora and Jules were having an affair, but Jules broke it off, so she killed him. I figured it wouldn't bother Elaine, and if it did, I didn't care. As soon as the lies came out of my mouth, the two detectives relaxed. Neither one had a problem believing the woman-scorned scenario. I said Greg knew what she did and tried to blackmail her, so she killed him too.

There was no telling what Abigail would remember, so I said I didn't know anything about what happened to her. They didn't care. I'd closed the case for them. No one asked me about the envelope marked *Pictures of You and Jimmy*.

They left me alone to use a phone. I called Amy and asked her to let Zack and my mother know I was all right. Then I called Jimmy's mother, so she could prepare him for the bad news about the death of his "friend." She thanked me without asking any questions, so I think she knew or had at least guessed about their relationship. Then I called Jane.

It was dark when I was formally released. Wankum let me out a back door of the station so I could avoid the TV crews camped around the main entrance on Green Street. He said he was going to "come out OK on the shoot." I said that was good. I walked straight down to the Rum House and ordered one of Davey's special vodka martinis. I ordered another as soon as that one arrived. I blamed myself for Greg Argent's death, and Ora's too. If I hadn't started snooping, if I had told Wankum the truth from the beginning ...

Eventually Jane came and took me home.

Captain Bob met me at the Rum House on Friday afternoon. He thanked me for finding the real killer, but he was still jumpy and mostly talked about how much his lawyers were going to charge him. He left after half an hour in hopes his wife would let him see Carl, even though it wasn't their weekend.

"Poor guy," Jane said.

"Guys at the bank said they're going to try to keep him from losing his boat," Davey said. "But I'm not sure he's cut out to be a captain."

"Give him a chance," I said, and they both looked at me funny.

Jane left town Saturday morning, just before Amy dropped Zack off. He and I went surfcasting with Davey again, and no one talked about anything but stripers and bluefish and the Red Sox, and then we went home and grilled what we'd caught.

After a week, I drove out to Plover Island to see Emmitt. If he doubted the story about Jules and Ora Buffem and their affair, he didn't mention it. I told him he was going to make amends to Jimmy for what had happened so many years ago, and he agreed to my plan without much argument. A buyer paid a hundred and fifty thousand for Alden Titward's "Plover Island Light In Winter" at auction in New York. Emmitt's Boston lawyer set up a blind trust and told Jimmy's mother about an anonymous benefactor. She didn't ask any questions. I hope it gave her some peace, knowing that she could afford care for Jimmy when she was gone. We've never spoken again.

Jimmy doesn't wave to me anymore, so he must remember who I am. I never told anyone about him and Ora Buffem. Well, except Davey. I had to tell someone.

Elaine had to put the High Street mansion on the market to re-pay Jules' clients a fraction of the money he stole. Her future became a subject of much speculation. The day after Abigail was released from the hospital, LibertyportGossip.com broke the news that Elaine was moving in with Emmitt. Generally this was considered a good move for both parties, if a little soon.

Abigail turned up at Foley's a few days later, in what looked like a bullfighter's brocade jacket and a red beret. There was something not quite right about her face, and she walked slowly and unsteadily. She seemed happy, though. The difficulty of her recovery was alleviated by the number of people who had to be nice to her now. The scar hidden under the beret was a badge of her seriousness as a journalist. She said the worst part was that she was unable to remember what happened in Jules' office. The best story she'd ever had, face to face with a killer, and it was all lost to her. "Awful," she said, shaking her head.

To make peace with his wife and sister-in-law, Davey hired Trouser Weasel to play an all-ages show at the Rum House one Saturday afternoon in June, and I volunteered to help chaperone. Asshole Gareth nodded at me as if we were friends, but kept a safe distance. The music was a dismal, unmelodic howl, but fast and furious enough to keep Zack and the rest of the caffeine monkeys thrashing around the dance floor. The girls stood and watched.

I got a form letter saying I had passed the Old Home Days audition. Not exactly a career milestone, but when I play the gig, it will be my largest audience since, well, last year's festival.

Jane comes back to town when she can, between trips to New York and Los Angeles, Austin and Seattle. I would not be surprised if there is someone else in one of those cities. She always takes her toothbrush when she leaves my house, and neither one of us mentions the long term. But she says that with all the publicity, Dormer Records wants my album more than ever. Now I just have to stop procrastinating and book studio time. Dan Ockerbloom suggests "Vanity and Folly" as a working title.

I saw Emmitt and Elaine a few days ago, crossing Main Street near Foley's in front of my car, smiling and holding hands, oblivious, like a couple of teenagers. How many lives had been destroyed over the years so they could be together? I felt an urge to step on the gas, but instead I stopped well short of the crosswalk and, like any good Libertyporter, waited for them to get safely to the other side before driving on.#

Author's thanks

To Rob, Frank, Bill and Ben for early reads. To Greg for art direction and encouragement. To everyone else who helped. And to my parents for books, newspapers, paper and pens.

Made in the USA
Charleston, SC
17 October 2010